Valor

Beyond

Measure

A Novel About the European Air War
During World War II

Robert E. Randall Jr.

Zander Publications
2351 Sunset Blvd., Suite 170-433
Rocklin, CA 95765

First Edition 2009

Printed in the United States of America

ISBN 978-0-578-01907-9

ZANDER

PUBLICATIONS

Dedication

This novel is dedicated to all who served during World War II, whether overseas or on the home front. In particular, this book is especially dedicated to my father, U.S. Army Air Force Corporal Robert E. Randall, who, although he never fought a battle, nonetheless, did his part to fight the war against the Axis powers. As an aircraft mechanic specializing in electrical systems stationed in England, and later in France, he and many others serviced the fighters and bombers so they could set about their appointed task to destroy Hitler's Luftwaffe and war machine. Without the devoted mechanics who often worked throughout the night in appalling conditions, the pilots who won the glory would not have succeeded in their missions.

Second, it is also dedicated to my father's good friend, the best man at his wedding, and my Godfather, U.S. Army Sergeant Richard Fisher. Dick is a recipient of a bronze star and received five battle stars. The battle stars represent action in some of the best known campaigns on continental Europe, including the second wave invasion of Utah Beach during D-Day, the Hürtgen Forest, and the Battle of the Bulge. This is an impressive resume for a man I have come to know as one of those quiet heroes of World War II.

I also acknowledge members on my wife's side of the family. Her father, Major George Wellington Putman, served as a medical doctor in the states caring for wounded soldiers returning with battle trauma. I heard from one soldier who related to me that Dr. Putman saved his life. One of Dr. Putman's greatest contributions, working with several other medical doctors, followed the war with his creation of the innovative Konstant Kare Room, which was the precursor to today's Intensive Care Unit.

Additionally, two uncles also served during the war. Staff Sergeant William Kauffman had the unique experience of serving in both the European and Pacific Theaters of operation in the U.S. Army, 3rd Infantry. Reverend Kenneth Kauffman served as a Signalman in the U.S. Navy aboard the destroyer escort U.S.S. Barr. It was struck by a German U-boat torpedo while trying to protect the aircraft carrier U.S.S. Block Island. The U.S.S. Barr managed to return to Casablanca, Morocco for repairs.

Service during World War II was not limited to just the male members of the family, nor was it limited to military service. My mother, Nancy (*nee* Habelt) Randall, was engaged in clerical work with the U.S. Navy Department in Washington, D.C. Later, she joined the United States Cadet Nurse Corps where she remained for the war's duration.

It was the everyday foot soldier, sailor, airman, marine, and worker on the home front who broke the back of Nazi Germany and her allies. To them I extend my personal profound thanks and respect.

Finally, I want to thank the efforts of my wife, Susan. She not only provided moral support but also meticulously used her intellectual experience during the editorial review of this book.

Table of Contents

Chapter 1: A Boy's Dilemma 1

Chapter 2: Distant Memories...11

Chapter 3: Building a Fire in His Heart................................27

Chapter 4: A New Chapter in Life.......................................41

Chapter 5: Preparing for War...51

Chapter 6: Overseas...67

Chapter 7: Losses...83

Chapter 8: The Big Day..91

Chapter 9: Between the Action..101

Chapter 10: D-Day..111

Chapter 11: Operation Market Garden 121

Chapter 12: Mundane Missions 129

Chapter 13: The Pseudo-Hero...135

Chapter 14: Battle of the Bulge 145

Chapter 15: Dangerous Ground Missions............................157

Chapter 16: Evasive Action 167

Chapter 17: Turmoil on the Home Front 181

Chapter 18: Combating New Technology 191

Chapter 19: Honors...199

Chapter 20: The End at Last 205

Chapter 21: The Homecoming...211

Chapter 22: A Quiet Hero...223

Characters in order of appearance

Brandon Sherman
Mr. Evans – Brandon's history teacher
Brandon's Mom
Brandon's Dad
Jason Sherman – Brandon's older brother
Jeff – Brandon's cousin
Mikey – Brandon's cousin
Frank Johnson (aka Grandpa)
Dottie (nee Stoddard) Johnson (aka Grandma)
Brandon's uncle
Brandon's aunt
Jerry Talbot – a neighbor
Tom Jamison – a neighbor
Jack Habelt – Frank's childhood friend
David Billings – Frank's childhood friend
Amelia Earhart* – Aviatrix
Eddie Rickenbacher* – World War I Pilot
Sam Bullock – Frank's flight instructor
Eddie Stoddard – Dottie's father
Harry James* – Musician / Band Leader
Glenn Miller* – Musician / Band Leader
Spike Jones* – Comedic Musician / Band Leader
Ann Stoddard – Dottie's mother
Danny Johnson – Frank's middle brother
Billy Johnson – Frank's youngest brother
Franklin D. Roosevelt* – U.S. President
Captain Scotty Winslow – fellow squadron pilot
Lt. Col. William Cummings* – Commander of 355th FG
Major Henry Corcoran – Frank's first lead pilot
Master Sergeant Bud Riley – Frank's crew chief
Major Daniels – a prior squadron commander
General Ira Eaker* – U.S. Army Air Force
Bob Hope* – Entertainer
Lieutenant Jack Leslie – pilot at Steeple Morden
Earl Dennis Balfour – A friendly English nobleman
Field Marshall Erwin Rommel* – German Army
Reichsmarschall Hermann Göring* – Leader in Nazi Party
Winston Churchill* – British Prime Minister
Josef Stalin* – Soviet Leader

Field Marshall Bernard Montgomery* – British Army
General Dwight D. Eisenhower* – U.S. Army
General Omar Bradley* – U.S. Army
General George S. Patton* – U.S. Army
Lieutenant Ted Holenski – pilot at Steeple Morden
Lieutenant Paul Marston – pilot at Steeple Morden
Reich Chancellor Adolf Hitler* – German Leader
John Wayne* – Actor
Humphrey Bogart* – Actor
General James "Jimmy" Doolittle* – U.S. Army Air Force
George W. Putman M.D.* – Developed Konstant Kare Unit
General Harwell – Base Commander at Andrews
General Henry "Hap" Arnold* – U.S. Army Air Force
Nettie Johnson – Frank's mother
Harry Johnson – Frank's father

All characters are fictitious except those indicated with an asterisk.

This is an entirely fictional account. There is no intent to suggest that interactions between fictitious characters and living or dead characters actually happened, nor did any of their dialogue. They are related here for the purpose of placing this novel in a historical context. Furthermore, there is no factual basis to the fighter groups mentioned having participated in any or all of the engagements cited. This book is not intended to be used as a historical reference; it is written solely for the purpose of entertainment and to honor those who served during this righteous war.

Valor Beyond Measure

Chapter 1

A Boy's Dilemma

As the school year approached its end students everywhere were contemplating everything except school work. The summer would provide a temporary reprieve from their academic prison until it began anew in the Fall.

Thus, what would you think of a pre-teenager who dislikes homework and school especially during the final month of the school year? Well, you would probably think he is normal. And he is as normal as they come.

Being twelve years old is both a special and difficult time in one's life. Add puberty and girls to the equation and anything else thrown into the mix for good measure can well become a catastrophe. This was just such a day for young Brandon Sherman. Brandon seeks his independence from his family, not unlike ninety percent of pre-teens. If there is a choice between school and antics, you can well imagine which one he would pick.

With summer break approaching his mind has been on anything but school work. From the time Brandon arrives at school he starts counting the minutes until it will end. As soon as the school bell sounds, he is usually one of the first to bolt out the door.

He rides his bicycle to school because the bus makes too many stops on the way home. He has no time for that. It's time to change into his play clothes, grab his baseball mitt, and prepare for his friends to meet him at the park for a pick up game of hardball. They try to emulate their favorite Red Sox players, like Manny Ramirez, David Ortiz, Mike Lowell, Jason Varitek, and Josh Beckett.

You cannot live in New England without total devotion to its teams like the Red Sox, Patriots, Celtics, and Bruins. Brandon plays all the sports depending on the season. He is not great at them; he just enjoys them and he enjoys fooling around with his friends.

Brandon has been a good student, not a great student. He does enough to get by. He likes science and history to a degree. He can take or leave math. And he absolutely abhors English, especially the study of poetry. At that age, what normal boy doesn't? Of course his favorite class is physical education.

He is a normal kid as kids his age go, a little gangly as his body is going through a growth spurt. His coordination is a little off as he tries to match the signals in his brain to his physical development. At this stage he has not yet realized any great attraction to the opposite sex, but it will come as sure as the seasons. There is plenty of time for that.

As Brandon counts down the days until the end of the school year, he keeps a running total of how many assignments are due between now and then. He has one more math exam, a science exam, one two-page essay and a poem for English, plus he has a project in lieu of a final exam in history.

Since the beginning of the spring term his history class has been studying key events of the twentieth century. For the last two weeks they were concentrating on World War II. Brandon found the period interesting and exciting, and the movies they watched in class like *Patton, Tora! Tora! Tora!, Midway*, and the original *Memphis Belle* brought this ancient history to life.

Now, the entertainment factor was about to end. They were going to have to do some real work. The teacher, Mr. Evans, felt it was time for the students to play a more personal part in interpreting events of this era. The "crisis" that Brandon was about to face involved homework. He hated homework. He knew it was coming because the syllabus said it was, but he just could not come to terms with the fact that the daylight hours were growing longer and that it was baseball season. Being a diehard Red Sox fan, like every other New Englander, and who played the game himself, he could not understand how Mr. Evans could hit them with such a big assignment at this crucial time.

Mr. Evans was a fair and well-respected teacher. He did his best to keep his students' attention, many times by acting out historical characters. Yet, he knew that each student had his strengths and weaknesses when it came to the type of assignment given to them. Therefore, usually he gave them several options in an attempt to extract them from their shell.

The first option he offers allows them to read a pre-approved non-fiction book about the period and to do a written book report and make an oral presentation to the class. The second option is writing a research paper. The students can choose to research a specific event or historical figure from the period. Again, they have to prepare a written report and make an oral presentation. Or, third, they can conduct an interview with someone who served his or her country in active service, worked in the war factories, or supported the war effort in any other reasonable fashion. The finished product is to be an eight to ten page essay and oral report to the class. The assignment would be due in two weeks and contribute to thirty percent of their grade.

Brandon thought to himself—two weeks? Is he nuts? Brandon could tell by the glances from other students that they felt the same way as he did. Nonetheless, there were a couple of students who openly welcomed the assignment. You know—the over-achievers.

What bothered him most about this assignment was the oral report. The mere suggestion of presenting something orally struck fear into the boy. Previous experience with oral reports left him with nausea and sleepless nights. Those symptoms also left him ill-prepared to make an acceptable presentation. His reaction to oral reports ran contrary to his normally gregarious nature. There was just something insidious and scary about speaking about something of which he knew very little.

Brandon detested reading. So, he quickly dismissed the book report. Strike one. He also knew that the very word *research* scared him. Strike two. This left him with the interview. That sounded like the least of all the evils. But, who could he interview? As a teenager he and his friends typically did not hang out with the World War II set.

Brandon despised anything cutting into his leisure time. The weather was nice now that winter was long gone. It was time to ride bicycles, play baseball, just hang out with his friends and, perhaps, catch some turtles or frogs at the local pond. Furthermore, he was going to visit his grandparents this Saturday where he would meet up with his cousins and let loose some steam. But, he now had this lousy homework assignment hanging over his head. Besides, there were less than four weeks left before school would let out for the summer.

When Brandon arrived home after school he angrily threw his books onto the kitchen counter. His mother could see that he was agitated.

"What's wrong, hon?"

"Oh, lousy Evans hit us with a huge homework assignment."

"It's Mr. Evans; be respectful. So, what do you have to do?"

"He gave us some choices, but I don't like any of them."

"It's not that you don't like any of them; it's that you just don't like homework in general," his mother countered.

Mom continued to gently nudge Brandon for more information. "Tell me about your assignment."

"Well, I can read a book, do a research paper, or interview someone about World War II."

"That sounds interesting," she said with a supportive tone. "What did you pick?"

"First of all, it sounds interesting because YOU don't have to do it and, second, I'm going to do the interview but I have no idea what to ask or who to interview. I have to interview someone from the period, but who?"

"Hey, mom, did dad fight in World War II?"

"Come on, Brandon. He's not that old. Your dad was born five years after the war ended."

"Crap!"

"Language, young man!"

"Why don't you ask Grandma and Grandpa Johnson? They were around at that time for sure. I just don't know if they played an active part. They never talked to me about it and I guess I never showed any interest in it anyway. In any event, they may know someone who participated in the war. After all, they belong to a group of seniors who do all kinds of activities together. And you'll be seeing them this weekend."

With a glimmer of hope of finding an easy way out, Brandon quickly asked, "Did Grandpa Johnson fight in the war?"

"Like I said before, Brandon, I don't know. At least I've never heard Grandpa and Grandma talk about it. You should ask your dad if his parents did anything during the war. Of course, the big problem is that your Grandpa Sherman died ten years ago."

"Well, I'm going to the field to play ball with the guys. I guess I'll talk to the dad later."

"Okay. Make sure you are home by five."

A filthy Brandon burst through the door as the clock chimed five o'clock.

"How long before dad gets home?" he asked anxiously.

"About twenty minutes. But before you do anything else go upstairs and take a shower. I don't want you sitting on any of this furniture until you wash that dirt off."

Even with the distraction of the shower those twenty minutes seemed to take forever. Finally, Brandon heard the garage door open and the car door slam closed. No sooner had his dad walked into the house and Brandon was all over him.

"Dad, I have a big homework assignment where I have to interview someone who served during World War II. What did Grandpa and Grandma Sherman do during the war?"

"Gee, Brandon, I honestly don't know too many details. All I know is that Grandma Sherman was a nurse who worked in the Washington, D.C. area and Grandpa Sherman served in Italy and southern France. Unfortunately, that does you no good because you can't interview him. Grandma Sherman has all his military mementos in a trunk in the attic, but I'm not sure what is in it."

"Aw, that's no help," he said disappointedly.

"Why don't you ask Grandpa and Grandma Johnson when we visit tomorrow? I'm willing to bet that they did something during the war or know someone who you can interview."

"Well, Mom doesn't know if they did anything during the war and I was planning on hanging out with Jeff and Mikey."

"Well, Brandon, if you want to get some information for your report, then your cousins will have to wait and you're going to have to get cracking. Besides, it shouldn't take too long. At least ask them about what they did. You may find that they can provide you with enough information for your report."

All that Brandon could think about was the fact that his weekend was doomed. He had been waiting to raise a ruckus with his cousins. Now, this assignment was really going to cut into his plans. He made up his mind that this assignment was not going to be a pleasant experience; he was purposely turning it into catastrophic disaster.

Brandon thought about his dilemma for a moment. Then an idea came into his head. *If I don't get much information from Grandpa, perhaps I can embellish it a little bit. If they have some friends who served in the war, too, maybe I can combine their stories into one. Besides, Evans won't know anyway. Heck, I can make up anything I want. I just have to be careful dad and mom don't read my paper.* Then he thought, *well I might as well wait to see what they have to say.*

It was 9:00 a.m. Saturday morning and a forty-minute drive to Grandma's and Grandpa's Dennisport home along the Cape Cod coast. They had a nice little seasonal cottage facing Cape Cod Bay that they turned into a year-round home when they retired. The whole family had fond memories of the many summers at the beach while they were growing up.

Brandon and his older brother, Jason, always looked forward to those times when they could raise a little heck with their cousins on the beach. Their ages were close enough such that they had many common interests. They would go wading, search for critters, dig in the sand and, when the water was warm enough, they would go swimming. However, just as their car pulled into the driveway Brandon's dad reminded him of priorities. There would be plenty of time to play once he fulfilled the commitment to his assignment.

"Oh, dad. Can I play just a little while?"

"Get your work done first, then play later."

Grandma and Grandpa Johnson were waiting on the front steps along with two very anxious cousins. After the usual welcome of hugs and kisses, the adults settled in to catch up on the goings on since the last time they talked. The kids, *sans* Brandon, headed for the beach. Brandon pouted about his situation, but his understanding Grandma had a solution.

She had baked some brownies, Brandon's favorite treat. So, this would not be a total loss. The family gathered on the deck overlooking the Bay to enjoy their refreshments in the warmth of the spring day while imbibing the beauty of the ocean, watching the sailboats cruise with the steady breeze, and inhaling the fragrance of salt air.

Grandpa, a medium-framed gentleman in his mid-eighties with light brown hair with streaks of gray, sat quietly at the deck table sipping on hot tea and snacking on his brownie while Brandon's dad and uncle talked about what kind of year the Sox were having and their chances for a pennant. He had piercing blue eyes and wore glasses only for reading. The ladies were engrossed in a separate conversation about the spring fashions and home decorating ideas.

As he was wolfing down his brownie, followed with gulps of ice-cold milk, Brandon turned to his Grandma and asked almost hesitatingly said, "Grandma, I have to do a homework assignment. Do you know anyone who fought in World War II?"

"As a matter of fact, dear, I do—your Grandpa."

Brandon's mom piped in, "Gee, Mom, I had a feeling that he did, but I just didn't know for certain."

"Your dad never liked to talk about it. It would bring back some bad memories."

"I never heard a word about it."

"Well, dear, during the early years as you were growing up, that's when you and your friends were busy pretending to be playing house and dressing as princesses. War was hardly a topic for a little girl. Besides, he rarely talks about it, even to me."

"Do you think he'll talk about it now? I think it would be interesting for Brandon to learn a bit about family history and, quite frankly, I would like to know a bit more, too."

"Let's ask him."

"Frank."

"Yes, dear."

"Brandon needs to do a homework assignment about World War II. Can you help?"

"Well, I don't know. Brandon, my boy, exactly what do you need?"

"I need to interview someone who participated some way in the war."

"Which one?" Frank kidded. He had a refreshingly enjoyable sense of humor.

"World War II, Grandpa."

Dottie prodded, "Frank, you need to tell Brandon and the rest of our family everything about your service during the War. Why don't you go up to the spare room and get the scrap books, albums, and storage boxes?"

"Dottie, you know I don't like to bring up the past. Besides, it was a long time ago and he'd probably be more interested interviewing Jerry Talbot. He hit Utah Beach during the first wave of the D-Day invasion and went on to fight in some other big battles, including the Battle of the Bulge. Or, how about Tom Jamison; he was a submarine captain who led a number of dangerous missions in Japanese waters? Both are brave men with exciting war stories."

"No, Frank. This is important. You are not getting any younger and your family needs to know," Dottie coaxed gently.

"Oh, okay. Maybe I can get a few of these strong, young men to help me bring down the boxes. Brandon, you can help, too."

So, Brandon, his father, and uncle followed Grandpa upstairs to a spare bedroom and opened the closet. Grandpa Johnson directed them to pull out a large steamer trunk. He unlocked the latch, opened the trunk, and pointed to the items he wanted them to carry downstairs.

There was a large box. It was carefully labeled by much younger hands many years ago. What long-lost secrets could they hold?

Brandon began to get excited about the possibilities, but could he possibly prepare for what was to come? Or for that matter, could any of them?

Grandpa sat in his easy chair and pulled the coffee table closer. He asked Brandon to carefully place one of the boxes on it and the remainder on the floor next to him. They were tied with twine. Grandpa tried to untie it but the knot was too tight. The box had not been opened since it was stored away more than sixty years before.

"Brandon, could you go to the kitchen drawer and grab the scissors?"

"Okay, Grandpa."

Brandon returned with the scissors and Grandpa directed him to cut the twine. Grandpa carefully lifted the lid off the box and set it aside.

"Hmm. Let's see; what do we have here? I haven't opened these things in ages."

"Grandpa, open the big box now!" Brandon said excitedly.

"No, Brandon. The contents of the box were carefully packed chronologically. If you're going to tell a story, you have to organize it in such a way that it makes sense for your audience and holds their interest. You see, each box has dates on it. This first one is dated 1925 to 1940.

This covers the time from when I was seven until I was twenty-two when I finished college."

"Grandpa, can't we just go straight to the war?"

"We could, but we won't because you need to have some background and understand how I wound up where I did," Grandpa gently retorted. "Do you have a notepad, or do you plan to memorize everything," Grandpa said jokingly.

"Grandma, may I have some paper and a pencil?"

Brandon's dad chided him, "Son, you should have been better prepared."

Grandma scurried to the roll-top desk in the adjacent room and returned with a legal pad and pencil. She handed Brandon the writing implements and he settled into the couch next to his grandfather's easy chair.

"Okay. Let's begin —"

Chapter 2

Distant Memories

Brandon opened the box. In it were photo albums, personal journal, scrap book, and a beautifully polished walnut box. Here was his Grandpa's early history. It seemed so long ago to Brandon, but like yesterday to his Grandpa as he paged through the first album.

"We'll get to the journal later if we have time. Let's start with this photo album first."

As Grandpa turned to the first page in the photo album, he said, "Okay, let me start when I was a boy."

"Oh, Grandpa, do we have to start so far back?"

"This won't take long."

Grandpa's memories carried him back in time to the days long ago when he was full of "spit and vinegar." He began to recollect past events as vividly as though they were yesterday. As he wove the tapestry of his biography, everyone who listened was transported more than three-quarters of a century back in time. They were there.

Ever since he was a young boy growing up in the small, suburban town of South Weymouth on the outskirts of Boston during the 1920s and 30s, Frankie Johnson loved his surroundings and his lifestyle. His neighborhood was bounded by expansive wooded tracts, gurgling brooks, and he lived close to Whitman's Pond.

Although he had his wild periods as a youth, it did not diminish the fact that he was brought up in a God-fearing home and was expected to maintain reasonable moral standards. He was a good boy who just enjoyed pushing the boundaries for excitement from time to time. What normal boy didn't? After all, his generation would be growing up, living, and dying during the most exciting and demanding period of the twentieth century.

There was always something to do for a thrill-seeker like Frankie regardless the time of year. He enjoyed exploring the woods, trailblazing just as the Indians had done in this area centuries ago. It did not matter if it was wintertime or summertime; the woods were a place he and his friends could go to escape from the rigors of school and pretend they were engaged in some far-flung adventure.

During the Fall season, he and his buddies played football. It was none of this touch football stuff either. It was full knock down, drag out, tackle football. And they got hurt ... cuts, bruises, contusions, concussions, sprains, dislocations, and fractures. But it was still a heck of a lot of fun.

During the winter Frankie played a little hockey. But he liked to skate into some of the feeder streams of a local swamp to explore all the nooks and crannies. They created team games with a detailed set of rules that became the accepted norm for their special creation. And it was fun. Who needed another game with rules according to Hoyle?

Spring and summer were baseball season. Frankie could be found in any number of vacant lots, parks, or school playgrounds. It just depended upon wherever they wanted to play a pick up game of ball. Frank would spend much of his time hiking winding trails in the woods. During the hot, humid days of summer, the canopy of trees provided respite from the searing sun. There it was cool and comfortable and fun.

Occasionally, he and his friends would ride their bicycles to Whitman's Pond to go swimming and, if his parents would drive, go to nearby Nantasket Beach. He especially liked it during low tide because of the long, expansive beach. There was plenty of room to run and play and dig in the soft sand. During high tide, there was no beach as the surf broke directly against the seawall.

And there was more—Paragon Park, where he would test his bravery on the "Comet" roller coaster. At the top of the coaster, it seemed like he could see for miles. Reaching the pinnacle of each section of the undulating roller coaster, he could feel the sensation of zero gravity. Upon reaching each nadir or steep turn, he could feel himself being pushed into the seat from the centrifugal force. Paragon

Park was like a miniature version of Coney Island. It was situated on the Hull peninsula, ten miles southeast of Boston as the crow flies, and surrounded by water on two sides. At the highest point of the roller coaster ride, Frankie could survey the entire beach.

He loved the exciting life of the boardwalk, the arcade, and the hawkers on the midway. When he had a few extra nickels he would try his luck at winning one of the many games of "skill," or shall I say "chance." This was because most of the games were obviously rigged in favor of the fast-talking hawkers. The best anyone could hope for was some worthless trinket like a cheap, plastic Kewpie doll or a pencil or some other "prize." It was also a great place to get some mouthwatering junk food—hot dogs, cotton candy, and salt water taffy. Frankie loved the chewy, sweet confection, but it sure did not taste like it was made from salt water, as he once thought.

Paragon Park was particularly fun at night with all the bright, flashing lights beckoning young and old alike to partake all it had to offer. Nothing was better than the spell cast by this combination of sparkling, clanking machinery, aromatic treats, and the sound of waves crashing on the beach. It held all who came in a trance-like state—at least that is how Frankie was affected.

His other ideas of fun consisted of activities like climbing high into a tree until the strength of the limbs could no longer support his weight, going hand-over-hand out on a limb, then seeing if he had the strength remaining in his young, developing muscles to make it back without falling. Sometimes he didn't, resulting in innumerable bumps, bruises, scratches, and contusions. To him, this was just another battle scar, but it did not prevent him from trying again, and it wasn't anything so serious that wouldn't heal. He was always a risk taker in his early years.

In his youthful exuberance, or stupidity, depending on your point of view, he and his incorrigible friends would lie in wait after dark among the bushes for an old Model-A's approaching headlights. Then, they would dart out narrowly being missed by the panicked, irate driver. Normally, the driver would swerve to avoid them. Sometimes motorist would be so shaken that they would mistakenly turn towards Frankie or his pals. This only served to make the game that much more exhilarating. Most of the time, however, they hit their horn and screamed curses at them. Some drivers stopped and tried to chase them.

But Frankie and his buddies knew the neighborhood far too well to be cornered.

Once, when word got back to his father about his daring exploits from an irate neighbor, he was introduced to what his father called the "34-inch, leather persuader." Yet, no matter how often he got caught and disciplined, the flame that burned within him for excitement and derring-do could not be extinguished. Thankfully, for many who came to know him, Frankie's foolhardy exploits would eventually turn into more distinguished acts of courage.

Frankie was not only daring; he was a born prankster. He saw this as all part of creating an exciting world for himself. It did not matter the circumstances either—at home, in the car, at school, in church. Any time the urge struck him Frankie would pull some stunt that was so finely crafted that he rarely got caught. Often, it would be one of his two younger brothers or a friend who would reap the whirlwind of punishment as a result of his antics. He never did anything maliciously. It was all in good fun but, of course, it was at somebody else's expense.

Like the time he had a substitute teacher in the fourth grade. The poor gentleman was trying to do his best to teach an already unruly class. It wasn't as though Frankie had anything against the teacher personally. He was just seeking relief from the tedium of the classroom. As the teacher stood at the front of the room and attempted to teach the class something useful to do with math, Frankie began to craft one of his patented, sleek, paper airplanes. And naturally, as any red-blooded boy would do, he awaited his opportunity to launch them skyward. Little did Frankie, or anyone else know it at the time, these events would be prophetic indicators of his life to come.

At first the "flights" remained relatively low-key. While the teacher worked word problems on the blackboard, Frankie launched one of his finely-tuned creations in the direction of his best friend, Jack Habelt, across the classroom. BOING! Right off the side of his head. Startled, Jack let out a muffled "Hey!" There were a few laughs that followed. The teacher turned briefly to see what was causing the commotion. All was quiet, so he returned to his task. The teacher's inaction only served to stoke the fire in Frankie's heart. It was almost like the teacher's inaction was endorsing his behavior. Now that he had tested the waters, it was time for some more extensive airborne attacks. He nonchalantly began to create a production line of paper aircraft with different shapes, each carefully designed with a specific mission in mind. Some were designed for speed, some for duration, some for load-carrying capacity, and some for missions that no one had ever conceived before this time.

With his "squadron" ready, he waited for his opportunity. It wasn't long. The airplanes that he had kept carefully folded and stored between the pages of his notebook were ready for their attack.

The teacher, fully unaware of what was about to happen, asked the class if anyone knew how to solve one of the homework problems. There was silence. Just like in the military ... the class took the stance to never volunteer. So, the teacher said, "Okay, I'll show you how to do it."

Big mistake. As soon as he turned his back on the class, Frankie began his blitz. It started slowly at first. A couple of quick flicks of the wrist and Frankie had two sleek fighters aloft. The teacher continued to work at the blackboard as the class struggled to contain their laughter. Then, two more slower-moving aircraft took flight. They just seemed to hang in the air forever. Some classmates were getting nervous that the teacher would turn around before they returned to earth.

Then, as they typically do once one brave person takes the first step, all hell broke loose. Counterattacks of paper airplanes were launched from the other side of the room. This did not deter Frankie. He just stepped up his attack, and he was relentless in his pursuit of victory at any cost. Whoosh! Whoosh! Whoosh! Three more planes aloft. This was the bombing mission.

Frankie's devious little mind had concocted an interesting attack strategy. He had found some small pieces of chalk. Into the folds of each of the three bombers he had placed a piece of chalk. When the bombers reached the apex of their flight they literally fired their piece of chalk as they began their downward glide. Two of the pieces of chalk fell harmlessly to the floor. But, the third exceeded everyone's expectations for effectiveness. As it flew out of the paper airplane, seemingly in slow motion, it headed straight for the metal casing of a ceiling light fixture. DONG! The sound resonated throughout the classroom like a high-pitched carillon. The teacher spun around quickly only to find everyone sitting quietly. Fortunately, he did not notice the twisted wreckage of paper airplanes on the floor between the rows of desks.

Now, Frankie's mission and class time were coming to an end. Time for one more attack. His secret weapon—a parasite plane, which was way ahead of its time. With the teacher again diligently writing at the blackboard, Frankie let it fly. As the plane reached the pinnacle of its flight, it suddenly released its surprise, a second smaller aircraft that was hidden inside the larger one. Just as luck would have it, the small one struck the teacher in the back. He turned around to see the remaining airplane gliding back to earth, as if in a carefully choreographed dance. It was also Jack's misfortune to be caught with an airplane in mid-throw. The teacher looked at Jack. Jack looked back sheepishly. "I'll see you after class, young man." As usual, Jack refused to tattle on his friend, so Frankie had escaped unscathed.

A little more about Jack—he and Frankie had been neighbors as long as they could remember. Their parents lived in the same neighborhood before any of their kids were born. Frankie and Jack always played on the same baseball team at the local park. They caught frogs and turtles at the pond. And they rode their bikes everywhere together, like school and the five-and-dime store. Jack had an interesting trait.

When he was seven years old he and Frankie were building a poor excuse for a racing cart. It was constructed from an old wooden crate, scrap two-by-fours, and the wheels from a discarded baby carriage that they found at the town dump. As they worked diligently crafting their masterpiece, a shard of metal flew off a nail that Jack was hammering. It became lodged in his eye. Although the doctors did the best they could to save it, infection set in prompting it to be enucleated. In its place he was fitted with a glass eye. But this didn't stop Jack. Sometimes he would remove it just to gross out the girls, exclaiming with glee, "I've got my eye on you!" as he pretended that he would put it on them. The girls did not appreciate his humor.

It was a cool, crisp autumn evening. The moon was full and the neighborhood children were engaging in one of their most memorable activities, Halloween. As soon as the first of October arrived, Frankie and Jack made their plans for Halloween night. This was serious business. They mapped the route that they would take around the neighborhood, and which houses would give them the most return for their effort? They knew from experience what houses to avoid and the ones that were the most lucrative. The Wilsons, at the end of the street, always gave out Baby Ruth candy bars. This was the jackpot. On the other hand, the MacDonalds gave out lollipops. That's okay if you're a five-year old. But, Frankie and Jack were ten, much too sophisticated for such childish treats. Now, Baby Ruths were something you could sink your teeth into and, quite frankly, felt you were leaving some of those teeth behind in the candy bar sometimes.

This was only part of their plan, however. Their real plan hinged on a somewhat clandestine operation involving what Halloween was known for best, costumes. Once they made the rounds, which was essentially for reconnaissance to locate the best treats, they would hurry home and throw on a different costume. There was no sense in wasting time at houses that didn't have much to offer. Instead, they would go straight to those homes that offered the greatest prizes.

But, even the best plans go awry and, when they do, you have to adapt to the changes. This was just how Jack and Frankie handled such situations. As the boys were running from house to house on their second round of the neighborhood, Jack stopped abruptly. A piece of grit had blown into his eye and was irritating the lower lid. Frankie returned to see what was wrong. As Jack massaged his eyelid, out popped the glass eye unexpectedly. It hit the ground and smashed into a thousand tiny pieces. Jack was devastated. His parents would kill him. Yet, there was nothing he could do about it now. What was done was done. Besides, there was more candy to be had. Worry about discipline later.

So, a new plan was devised to make the best of the circumstances. The boys ran back to Frankie's house, found some scrap fabric, and quickly cut out an eye patch. Then they grabbed a handful of cat's-eye marbles. Jack donned the patch, and the two boys scurried off to greet their first victims—two sweet little girls, one dressed as a fairy and the other as a princess. The boys stopped the girls to innocently ask how they had done in their pursuit of sweets.

"Oh! Let's see what you have!," exclaimed Frankie as he set up the scam. "Not bad. That's quite haul. Look at this, Jack."

Jack bent over the bag of goodies, and lifted his eye patch as if to get a better look. As he did so, he dropped a marble that was hidden in the palm of his hand. "Oh, no! My eye fell out," as there was a "kerplop" in the bag. Then Jack showed the girls his eyeless socket.

The girls were so horrified they let out the most terrified, blood-curdling scream and the girl with the bag containing the "eye" threw it to the ground and ran away screaming into the night.

"Gee, Jack, that worked great. I figured that we could scare some kids, but I never thought we'd wind up with all this extra candy."

So went the rest of the night, though not necessarily with the same results. The boys needed to be sure they did not try the stunt on kids who knew of Jack's missing eye in the first place. Nonetheless, they turned a disaster into a memorable evening of fun—at least for themselves.

As it turned out, although Jack's parents were angry and upset about the broken eyeball at first, they understood it was just an accident and quickly suppressed their anger. Unexpectedly, sometimes parents can be compassionate, forgiving, and reasonable.

It was the Fall of 1929 and Frankie was eleven years old. The Great Depression had struck. Financial institutions crumbled, businesses closed, people lost their jobs and their homes. It was a national disaster. What would this mean for Frankie, who up to this time had been carefree, and his family?

Eleven year-olds generally don't care too much about financial matters. Their days are wrapped up in school, fun, and leisure. Frankie's days largely went on as normal.

His father was an executive who worked for Edison Power & Electric in North Weymouth. People and businesses still needed electricity throughout the Depression; so, his job was secure. Their home had also been inherited from Frankie's grandfather. Therefore, there was no mortgage on it. And Frankie's father had not invested in the stock market where so many lost their life's savings. Rather, he had invested in real estate and managed a number of multi-family homes in North Weymouth. As people were forced out of their homes for defaulting on their mortgage payments, they naturally had to move into a rental property. It turned out to be a boon for Frankie's father. They continued to survive relatively comfortably throughout the Depression years.

Frankie's father had been an avid hunter, fisherman, and camper. Although he tried to instill these same interests in his son, Frankie just didn't care for the discomforts of camping. Fishing was something that he pursued with fervor from time to time. Hunting didn't appeal to him either. He didn't care for killing, unless they were vermin, like rats—it was just the Christian tenets of "thou shall not kill" that his mother and Sunday school teachers had instilled in him. On the other hand, he liked to shoot at tin cans or other inanimate objects.

On his twelfth birthday, his parents gave him a .22-caliber bolt-action rifle. It was his greatest childhood gift ever. Frankie and Jack, who also had a .22-caliber rifle, would escape to a secluded section of the town dump so that they could shoot in peace, and also not murder any of the neighbors. This was an ideal location. There was a never-ending supply of bottles, tin cans, derelict jalopies, and rats—so many rats.

Each time Frankie and Jack went shooting, it turned into a contest. Even with one eye, Jack was still an accomplished marksman. They would keep a running total of their hits and misses. They would create new and exciting games, each one more challenging than the previous one. One such game involved shooting a tin can on the ground. Each time the can was hit, it would move further and further away. They would keep shooting until one of them missed their can. Normally, Frankie won. He was a deadeye shot. After all, Jack had only one good eye anyway.

Another game was an even more challenging test of their marksmanship. They would place Coke bottles on their side with the open neck facing them. Stepping back twenty paces, they would attempt to shoot through the open neck and blow out the bottom of the bottle. This took a keen eye and a steady hand. In their own minds, the boys just never seemed to miss. They also hung *Coca Cola* bottles from twine tied to a limb. Then they would start them swinging and try to break them before they stopped swinging.

Of course, the plethora of rats meant moving targets. As far as the boys were concerned, they were performing a public service. In their opinion, these were nothing more than filthy, disease-ridden, disgusting pests that had no business being alive.

Not everything in Frankie's young life developed into pleasant memories. Another of Frankie's closest friends, David Billings, lived on the other side of town. When he wasn't with Jack Habelt he was with David, or they were all together. If Frankie was wild, then David was downright nuts.

David was extremely athletic. He could walk on his hands. He could walk balanced on fence rails without falling. If an activity required physical prowess or strength, then David was your man. However, David's use of his physical attributes was often foolhardy.

He would try any number of dangerous stunts. Frankie admired him because of his derring-do. For example, he would ride his bicycle down the biggest hill in the neighborhood—without holding the handle bars or while standing on the seat and holding the handle bars. Or, it was he who concocted the game of darting in front of cars at night, which would get Frankie into so much trouble.

Often, he would dare Frankie to participate in his dangerous games and, more often than not, Frankie would comply. If Frankie's parents had any idea of his antics, he surely would have been grounded for life.

It was a frigid Saturday in January 1933. Frankie and Jack decided to spend the day with David. They had big plans. Frankie lived near Great Pond. They would spend the day ice skating. They had all received new ice skates for Christmas. This would be a great day to explore the reaches of the pond. So, Frankie and Jack slung their skates over their shoulder and off they went for a day of fun and bliss.

The day went pretty much as planned. They spent much of the morning skating into a strong wind. It took tremendous effort to make any headway. If they stayed close to shore, they found that they could avoid the force of some of the gale. When they reached the other side David decided to try something. He started to skate towards the middle of the pond. This time the wind was directly behind him. Making progress was so much easier now. Then he had an idea. His adventurous mind surmised that there was a way to go faster and with little effort. He hollered to Frankie and Jack to watch him. David unzipped his jacket and held it open creating a large sail. The next thing he knew was he was accelerating—faster and faster and faster. The other two boys did the same.

Before they knew it they were whipping across the surface of the ice. They must have been doing fifty miles per hour, at least that is what it felt like to them. David decided that it was time to slow down so he lowered his jacket. But his jacket was so bulky that it still created a pretty efficient sail, and he had so much momentum that he was out of control. Finally, the only way he could stop was to bend his knees and do a controlled slide along the ice with his body.

Poor Jack was not quite so adept. He tried to make a standard ice skating stop by turning sideways and digging in the blades of his skates. It did not work as intended. His skates dug into the ice a little too much and over he went. He must have tumble a hundred feet. He wasn't hurt, just shaken up a little.

Frankie used a bit more common sense. All he did was to make a gentle turn back into the wind until he slowed to a stop.

After their morning of skating, the boys returned to David's home. His mother prepared some grilled cheese sandwiches, tomato soup, and hot chocolate for them. It really warmed their insides. Then they spent the rest of the day just exploring the surrounding woods.

It was three in the afternoon when Frankie and Jack started to make their way home. They had to be home by dark, and with the short winter days of New England they needed to get going as it was about an hour-long walk. David decided to go with them part way. Sometimes, to save time, the boys would take a shortcut through the rail yard. There was a two-inch packed snow layer on the ground. On this day a locomotive was switching some box cars. David came up with the idea that they could jump on a box car and steal a ride up the line and closer to home. After all, they could not make much progress because they could not get any traction by walking on the icy ground.

As the train approached, Frankie, Jack, and David tried not to give the engineer an inkling of their intentions. Once the locomotive started to disappear from sight as it took a bend in the tracks the boys began to run towards a box car as best they could over the slippery ground. David led the way. As he approached a box car he lunged to grab a rung on a ladder. The train was moving faster than he anticipated and he was swept off his feet while still clinging to the rung. He had a grip with only one hand which was beginning to slip. He tried to grab hold of a rung with his free arm but could not muster the strength. Frankie and Jack ran along side trying to catch up but their feet kept slipping out from under them. David's strength was being rapidly sapped from his young arms. He couldn't hold on any longer.

Then Frankie and Jack heard the most horrendous scream they had ever heard in their young lives. The next thing they saw was David lying next to the railroad tracks. His right arm was missing above the elbow and the forearm was lying a few yards away. The snow was stained red.

Then all was silent. David had passed out from shock as a result of the loss of blood from the excruciating pain. A couple of rail yard brakemen heard the commotion and ran to investigate. They were shocked by what they found. One of the men stayed with David and covered him with his jacket and applied a tourniquet to the stub of his arm with his belt while the other man ran for help. Jack was sick to his stomach and Frankie just stood there trembling.

It seemed to Frankie like hours passed before help arrived but it was only a few minutes. Fortunately, David was still unconscious when they took him away in the ambulance to the Weymouth (now South Shore) Hospital.

When Frankie arrived back home his mother could see on his face that something was wrong. He had an ashen appearance and he was uncommonly quiet. When his mother asked him what was wrong, Frankie broke down in tears as he related the story. When he finished, his mother expressed her sorrow, but then railed into Frankie saying that it could have just as easily been him. His foolhardy behavior could have put him in this same predicament. This instilled even more terror into Frankie's heart as he thought about the possible consequences. For weeks after the incident Frankie mood was subdued and sullen, and he continued to mull in his mind that, yes, it could have been him. Thoughts of the event would haunt him for many years to come.

As for David, he recovered after months of rehabilitation *sans* his right arm. He would never be able to play baseball again or walk on his hand again. But after some bouts with depression, David started to engage himself in regular childhood activities. He would have great difficulty performing some of the most mundane tasks, but he never gave up. Frankie visited him from time to time. However, because of his long recovery from such a severe injury, David found himself a year behind his classmates. After a while, David and his friends started to drift apart. In the end, things would never be the same again, nor would Frankie.

After that, some of Frankie's *joie de vivre* went out of him. He no longer had the flame for taking unnecessary risks and, more importantly, anything that involved some element of risk tended to raise a specter of almost uncontrollable fear in his being. It would haunt him throughout his life during some of the most critical periods.

Following the David Billings incident, Frankie had a change in personality and started to be averse to taking any risk. Frankie met anything that he perceived as remotely adventurous or risky with an excuse that he had something else to do, like an errand for his mother or a chore for his father. He could not admit to himself or others that he was terrified of taking chances, regardless how innocuous they might seem to those around him.

So, he needed to divert his attention from the accident somehow, and to divorce himself from his companions who continued to engage in such activities. Everyone around him saw the change in his behavior, but no one seemed to understand the connection with the accident and how it affected Frankie. For some reason he felt embarrassed to discuss his feelings with friends or family. It was much simpler to bury those feelings lest he be viewed as suffering from some sort of mental disorder. As a result, he began to focus on his school work and apply more effort to his assignments. He became driven to concentrate on his studies and cut back on some of his extracurricular activities. Perhaps he felt safer by being cloaked in academics as opposed to putting himself in a possible risky situation or subjecting himself to questions from others.

In the past, Frankie was never more than a normal, grade-C student. However, this newfound concentration on his academics transformed him into a stellar student. Whenever he received a homework assignment, he had most of it done before he got home. If there was a project, he threw every ounce of his energy into it and got it done well before it was due. He realized early on that if he used his time effectively, then he would have less pressure placed on himself and not be in a rush to complete his assignments. He loved science, especially physics. He spent a great deal of his spare time reading and devouring anything to do with scientific topics.

Throughout junior and senior high he developed into a first rate student. His teachers enjoyed his presence in the classroom and the way that he applied himself to his studies. Nonetheless, his classmates started to view him as a loner. To them, it was as though he was an entirely different person whom they no longer knew.

Frankie wanted to go to college. This might be the opportunity he needed to start over with new friends who did not know him for his previously gregarious nature. Or, it would be a chance to just focus on his studies and not suffer the consequences of developing friendships with anyone who might subsequently be injured or die. He felt that it was enough to live through that scenario once during his life and no more.

He had no idea what his major would be, but he knew that if he was going to go anywhere in life he would need a college sheepskin. As he approached his final year in high school, he was anxious by what lay ahead. He began to investigate various careers and was getting nowhere. He knew he liked science but was not sure he wanted it for a career. Nothing seemed to build a fire in his deadened heart.

Then, as it happened, his parents read in the newspaper that the famous aviatrix, Amelia Earhart, was going to be at the Naval Air Station in Squantum. So, they decided to drive over and see if they could spot her. Frankie happened to be working on a science report and initially begged to be left behind. After all, he could care less about visiting an airport. But his parents urged him to get out of the house because he needed to take a break. So, he reluctantly agreed to join them.

As they drove to the airport, they cruised along Wollaston Beach and could see Boston in the distance. Frankie noticed that he could see something else, too. There were some specks in the distant sky. What were they? He finally realized they were airplanes. They were coming and going, climbing and descending, and turning each and every way. He was fascinated by their movement in all three dimensions. He got more excited about the prospects of seeing an airplane up close as they neared the airport.

When they arrived at the air field, Frankie noticed that it was situated right on the bay. The backdrop of Boston, the deep blue water, and the blue sky created an awesome panorama.

Then he saw the mixture of warbirds rumbling on the ramp. They made a racket, but they sounded great. The cacophony sounded melodious to him and only served to excite him all the more. A crowd had gathered about twenty yards away, so Frankie and his family went to see what the attraction was. It was Amelia Earhart. She was greeting the visitors and shaking hands. As she passed down the line, Frankie stuck out his hand and Amelia grasped it firmly and smiled at him. Then she continued moving down the line of admiring fans. Frankie had his brush with fame.

This had a profound effect on him. His excitement of being close to the airplanes, hearing them, smelling them, and meeting Amelia Earhart helped push him to make a decision about his future. He would design airplanes. After all, he had already created some pretty unique designs, out of paper. He set about working towards that goal. He never considered flying himself as that would be too risky. There was no way he could overcome the innate fear that continued to seize his *joie de vie*.

As a result of his academic efforts, his hard work paid off. He earned a full scholarship to the Massachusetts Institute of Technology with a major in aeronautical engineering. It was a relatively new field of study that he saw with a potential for growth. Besides, he liked to study about and disassemble and assemble complex mechanical things. Furthermore, his early paper airplane designs took a novel approach to aeronautical design that could only be improved upon with a proper education.

Upon starting college that Fall, Frankie decided to focus on his studies as opposed to nurturing friendships. No one could seem to get close to him. He, in turn, would not let them into his life. His hours would be spent in the laboratory and at the library where he devoured every book in the stacks related to aviation. It was as if he had no life outside his self-imposed imprisonment.

As he approached the end of his junior year, that was all about to change. It was then that he met the love of his life, Dottie, at a baseball game. She was stunningly beautiful in Frankie's eyes. Her hair was auburn and her eyes dark, but they sparkled. She had a captivating smile and she was equally lovely inside as well. She was the one person he finally allowed into his deepest, darkest pit of personal despair and depression.

One thing that sealed the deal for Frankie was the fact that she, too, was a Red Sox fan. Finally, he was getting out to the games and enjoying some of the wonders of life with her as his close companion.

She was a sophomore at Boston College where she studied nursing. She also worked part-time at Boston City Hospital assisting the nurses with basic patient care. Often she spent her time reading to the patients. It worked out well because she enjoyed reading, and also had a minor in English literature. So, she could actually complete her reading assignments while bringing some diversion to the patients' discomforts.

Frankie and Dottie just seemed to be made for one another. They made a lovely couple and they mutually respected and supported each other's goals. Frankie did not realize it at the early stage just how good she would be for him and his future. He was perfect for her, too. This relationship would not be one where there is a giver and a taker. They shared everything—their aspirations, loves, hates, and Frankie shared his fears, his deep-seated, tormenting fears.

Chapter 3

Building a Fire in His Heart

As a result of their busy, conflicting schedules, Dottie and Frank managed to go on dates only two or three times a month initially. They saw each other more frequently than that; it's just that they could not find time to have "real" dates. They particularly enjoyed drives to the Cape in Frank's father's 1936 Ford coupe. They loved to walk the beach, especially when they had it to themselves. They became so enrapt in their conversations that they failed to notice how far they had walked or that the tide had come in. Sometimes they had to wait until the tide turned so that they could make their way back to the car. That wasn't so bad because they used the time to delve into their innermost feelings for each other while just soaking up nature.

With every meeting, they continued to grow closer and closer. They were destined to spend their lives together.

It was on just such an outing that events were set in motion for another stage in Frank's life to change forever. During one of their typical Saturday morning drives, they decided to visit the coastal town of Plymouth. After a brief walk along the waterfront, Frank heard the deep rumble of an engine. Skimming over the beach was a bright red biplane. As he had recollections about the airplanes he had seen at Squantum, he blurted, "Wow! What a great view that pilot must have, and what a sense of freedom."

After they finished walking the beach, Frank and Dottie decided to take a drive and do a little exploring. After about twenty minutes Frank noticed a sign that said "Plymouth Airport." He turned to Dottie and asked almost apologetically, "Hey, would you mind if we checked out the airport? I hear it's only been open a couple of years."

"Why?" she said in a most quizzical way.

"You know that I plan to be an aeronautical engineer. I just want to check out the airplanes up close. There is not better way to learn than by seeing the theories applied to real-life situations. That airplane we saw flying over the beach kind of stirred something in me. The best way to design airplanes is to understand exactly how they work."

"Well, if you must," she conceded reluctantly.

So, they followed the winding road several miles before it opened upon a grass field with airplanes scattered about. They pulled the car into a small, dirt lot and walked to the edge of the field. Frank watched as an airplane taxied to the end of the runway and immediately began its takeoff roll. It seemed to quickly leap into the air and break the bonds of earth. He felt heart palpitations. By the way, the term runway is used loosely here as there were no well-defined runways. Airplanes tended to line up for takeoff and landing on the wide open field based on the direction of the wind.

The couple walked around the airport looking at and in airplanes of all types. They ranged from small, fabric-covered airplanes like the Waco and Stearman up to and including an all-metal, twin-engine DC-3. As they walked, Frank felt himself drawn to these miraculous machines. He wanted to get close to them and touch them. He had to remind himself that they were real and that they could actually fly.

Coincidently, the bright, red biplane had just landed and taxied to the front of the airport operations shack. A crusty looking man about fifty years old climbed out of the cockpit. His face and goggles were blackened from the airplane's exhaust. You could see streaks where he had tried to wipe some of the grime from his goggles so that he could see where he was going.

"Hey, son, are you or your girl interested in an airplane ride over Plymouth? It'll cost you only five dollars for thirty minutes."

Frank looked at Dottie and responded, "No thanks."

The grizzled pilot pressed a little more. "C'mon. It's fun and perfectly safe. I'll even let you try the controls."

"Naw. I don't think so. I'm not really interested."

"Frank, why don't you go? I think it would be good for you. You've been working so hard, and how will you really know how to design a proper airplane if you've never been up in one?"

"I'll go if you go too."

"No. It's really a guy thing. I want you to go but I'm keeping my feet firmly planted on good old *terra firma*."

Reluctantly, Frank acquiesced and decided to take a rare chance. He had to prove to Dottie that he was not a coward. After all, the pilot seemed to be seasoned and appeared to know what he was doing.

The risks of flying quickly raced through Frank's mind. He thought about everything that could go wrong. Perhaps the airplane would run out of fuel, or the engine would seize, or a wing would fall off. His wild imagination created numerous disaster scenarios.

However, the pilot prodded a little more, "C'mon son, it's perfectly safe. You've got to live a little."

Yes, Frank needed to live a little.

With that he was able to convince himself that logically such events as had run through his mind were statistically highly unlikely. Much to Dottie's surprise, and his own, Frank did not hesitate to accept the offer. He peeled off a five-dollar bill and was promptly fitted with flying goggles and helmet.

"Son, have you ever been in an airplane before?"

"No, sir."

"I have only one rule. If you have to puke, do it in the helmet, not in the plane."

"Yes, sir. But I thought you said it was safe?"

"It is. Sometimes people get a little nervous and lose their lunch. Don't worry, you'll do just fine."

Frank felt somewhat reassured, but still his stomach was churning.

The pilot directed Frank onto the wing and into the front cockpit. There he helped Frank get situated by strapping him into the seat and plugging in the radio jack. After a brief explanation of the controls and scant instruments, they were ready to go aloft. Except for one thing —

"Where's the parachute?"

"There ain't no parachute, sonny. I ain't plannin' on crashin'; so, you shouldn't either."

Perhaps it was a stupid question but this was all new to Frank, and he was scared. He was so scared, in fact, that he almost called it quits.

The pilot signaled for a lineman to come over. The pilot shouted "switch off" and the lineman pulled the prop through a few times. Then he hollered "contact" in a loud, clear voice. With that, the lineman pulled hard on the prop as he kicked his leg back. This was to prevent him from falling into a spinning propeller. Then, with a deafening roar the old Lycoming radial engine came to life. Frank was engulfed in oil and exhaust fumes. It smelled great. There is something different about airplane engine exhaust that is unlike anything else. It is like a living entity, giving off its very own aura. The Stearman vibrated and roared and bounced as the pilot taxied it over the closely mown grass.

The next thing he knew they were rumbling down the taxiway. In no time, the pilot lined up the old biplane into the wind. He pushed the throttle forward for full power and, before he could swallow the last remnant of saliva, they were off. All of a sudden trepidation turned into exhilaration. The wind was blowing in his face. He was flying! He harkened back to his school days when he flew paper airplanes in the classroom. Yet, instead of throwing them, now he was flying in one. He was both excited and terrified.

They cruised towards the coast at about five hundred feet, low enough to see details on the ground, and high enough to see most of the hooked arm of Cape Cod. Frank was amazed at how much undeveloped land lay within his view. It was beautiful. Soon his fear started to wane as he became engulfed in the sights and sounds of flight.

Before he knew it, the biplane was gently swooping towards Plymouth Harbor. He could see variations in the color of the water differentiating shallow flats from deeper channels. They went so low that he felt he was looking up at some of the sailboats they passed. People on the ground were waving, and the pilot and Frank waved back. Frank was entranced by all the natural grandeur, but he couldn't help thinking of Dottie and wanting to share his experience with her. For now, though, this was real living. This was a whole new dimension for him and, at that moment, he was hooked on flying and airplanes, not just designing them.

The thirty minutes seemed to pass in an instant. It was now time to head back to the airport. As the plane climbed up to one thousand feet the pilot called over the intercom, "You want to give it a try?"

Frank couldn't believe his ears. "Oh! I don't know, sir."

"Go on; give it a try. Put your feet on the rudder pedals and take hold of the stick. Hold the stick gently. Don't try to strangle it. It's all done with feel and pressure."

Frank slid his feet onto the rudder pedals and grasped the control stick. The pilot raised his hands over his head and said, "It's your airplane."

Frank couldn't believe his good fortune. He was in control of a sophisticated piece of machinery.

The pilot said, "Try making a turn to the right by applying pressure to the right rudder while moving the stick to the right."

Frank complied with the direction; however, the pilot failed to mention that once the plane attained the desired orientation that Frank had to neutralize the controls. The bank continued steeper and steeper and Frank felt the g-force begin to increase. He felt himself being pushed into the seat. He couldn't lift his feet due to the force—what an unusual, helpless sensation. The seasoned pilot quickly corrected the airplane back to its normal attitude.

"Whatcha doin', son? Think you're a fighter pilot?"

"Sorry."

Frank started to get a sour taste in his mouth. He thought he was going to be sick, but the pilot's words calmed him.

"No big deal."

"Let's try it again."

Frank couldn't believe he would be given a second chance. They continued making gentle S-turns all the way back to the airport. Frank felt as though he was starting to get the hang of it, just as the pilot signaled he was taking control again. The pilot snapped the biplane into a hard left turn, chopped the power, and softly set the airplane onto the runway without so much as a bump.

After they taxied the plane back to the ramp, Frank unhooked his seatbelt but forgot about the headset. As he tried to climb out of the cockpit, his head was snapped back. He thought to himself, *I guess that is why pilots use checklists—to keep from doing stupid things like this.*

"Well, what do you think son?"

"Oh. It was great."

"No. I mean, what do you think about taking flying lessons?"

"This was just a one-time flight. I think I've had enough."

"That would be a real shame. I think you've got a good touch on the controls."

"You're kidding. I almost rolled us upside down."

"Naw. That was nothin'. That's how I spent most of my time flyin' in the Big War."

"You flew during the war?"

"Yeah. First I started with the Lafayette Escadrille as a volunteer. Then, after the United States entered the war, I joined up. I even got a chance to fly with Eddie Rickenbacher. You know, he was the top American ace of the Great War."

"Did you see any combat?"

"Yeah. More than I wanted. Shot down two planes and got shot at more than I care to remember. Fact was, though, we lost more pilots in accidents than in combat. Only two men out of eighteen that I started with came out alive. I was one of them. If you learn to fly with me, I'll show you some of the tricks I learned over the years."

"Of course I was scared. Only fools and dead people aren't scared of dying. I was scared every time I left the ground in those days. After all, those airplanes weren't as good as the ones they make now and there was always someone shooting at me."

Frank thought that perhaps this was a way to overcome some of his innate fear. How could he pass up this opportunity to break this debilitating cycle of fear and trepidation? And how could he convince Dottie?

As Frank approached Dottie, she asked, "How was it?"

"It was undoubtedly the most terrifying, yet exciting, thing I've done in my life. The pilot even let me fly the plane. What a feeling of freedom."

"It sounds like you really loved the experience."

"Oh, I really did."

"Well, if you like it so much, why don't you take flying lessons?"

Frank was speechless.

"No, I think that if you really love it, then you should do it."

"I'm not sure it's meant for me. It is terribly risky and will take a lot of time, money, and effort."

"It sounds like you are trying to talk yourself out of it."

"Perhaps I am."

"Listen, you need to do that for yourself and no one else."

This woman is perfect. Unknown to Frank, Dottie had overheard the entire conversation and had also perceived the thrill in Frank's voice that had been missing from so many of their previous conversations. She wanted to pave a way out of his doldrums.

She was also concerned that it would appear that she stood in the way of something he might enjoy. How could she stop him if she truly loved him? If she had said "no," then he might have resented her for standing in his way. After all, she was not competing with another woman.

"I'm going to do it," he said in an almost quivering voice.

He quickly trotted back to the biplane and told the pilot of his decision.

"When can we start?"

"That's up to you, son."

"How about next Saturday morning?"

"Let's go into my office and get you scheduled."

"By the way, sonny, I'm Sam Bullock. What's your name?"

"It's Frank Johnson."

"Well, Frank, I'm going to teach you to fly so that the airplane becomes an extension of your body. When you think roll, the airplane will roll, and when you think loop, it'll loop."

"I have to tell you, Mr. Bullock ..."

"That's Sam."

"Okay. I have to tell you, Sam, that I am really nervous about all this."

"Don't worry, kid. Flying will become second nature to you before you know it."

All the next week Frank waited with anticipation and heightened nervousness for the arrival of Saturday. He could not hold a thought in his head aside from his upcoming flying lesson. He became so entranced thinking about it that he almost forgot his standing Friday night date with Dottie. As it was, he was an hour late picking her up for a movie. However, it was her nature to be understanding and forgiving. So, since the movie already started, they went bowling instead. Frank couldn't concentrate and, as a result, had a horrible game. In fact it was the first time Dottie beat him at the game.

The next morning Frank was awake at the crack of dawn. He felt nervous pangs about the impending events of the day. His flying lesson was scheduled for 10:00 a.m. He rushed to complete his showering, shaving, and eating breakfast. He wasn't sure if his breakfast of corn flakes and orange juice would stay in his stomach. It was still nearly three hours before his lesson. So, he decided to slow down his pace and calm his frayed nerves. When eight o'clock rolled around, he decided to call Dottie to see if she wanted to go along, not necessarily to fly, but to provide moral support.

Dottie agreed, so long as they could spend the rest of the day along the beach. That was something to which Frank agreed readily.

Frank was so preoccupied with the lesson that he lost track of how fast he was driving, but immediately reigned himself in when he caught sight of a motorcycle cop issuing a ticket to another driver. He thought to himself, *That could have been me. I'd better concentrate on what I'm doing. And I really need to concentrate when I fly, too.* Now he was having second thoughts about his decision to fly.

It was nearly nine o'clock when Frank arrived to pick up Dottie. Frank met her at the front door. She was well prepared with a picnic basket full of chicken, cole slaw, and root beer. She was as excited about spending an afternoon at the beach as Frank was about flying. So long as they agreed to mutually do things that made each other happy, this would be a relationship made in heaven.

A few minutes before 10:00 a.m. they pulled up to the airport. Frank trotted ahead as Dottie chastised, "What's the hurry? You don't move that fast when I want to go someplace."

"Sorry."

Just as they arrived at the operations shack, Sam taxied his plane near the fence with another student. Sam greeted Frank and Dottie warmly and invited them inside. He would be a few minutes reviewing the flight with the student before taking Frank for his lesson. It was only five minutes, but it seemed like an hour to Frank.

"OH! Stop fidgeting, Frank. You're always in such a hurry."

Frank took a few deep breaths.

"Okay, Frank. Are you ready to hit the wild blue?"

With a quiver in his voice Frank said, "Sure." But he did not sound so sure.

Sam led Frank out to the plane.

"Before we do anything, the first thing we're gonna do is make sure this old crate is in condition to fly. This is your chance to make sure everything is where it is supposed to be and working properly. After all, when you're up there you can't get out and push."

As Sam walked around the plane explaining the preflight, Frank listened intently.

"Frank, make sure you inspect the canvas for holes and tears, especially the wings. That's where the plane gets its lift. Also be sure the ailerons—they're the controls on the trailing edge and outboard of each wing—that make the plane roll, move freely in the right direction. See, as you move the trailing edge of the aileron on the starboard wings down, the one on the port wings move up. When the starboard aileron is down, that creates more lift on that wing, while the port aileron deflection upward at the same time produces less lift. So, which way do you think the airplane will roll?"

Frank thought for a brief moment, after all, he was almost an aeronautical engineer.

"To the left."

"Good. Some people just can't figure that out."

They continued the preflight. "This is the rudder. It controls the yaw, or moves the nose left or right."

Sam quizzed Frank about the operation of the rudder just as he had with the ailerons. Next they discussed the elevator.

"This is what allows you to raise or lower the nose."

Then Frank asserted, "The elevator points the plane in the general direction you want to go, up or down, but I learned in my aeronautical engineering class that power is the real way to control the climb and descent, right?"

"Yeah, you're right! It usually takes me quite awhile to get that concept into a new student's head. It's pretty confusing because you actually control your climb and descent with power and your attitude controls your airspeed. This is counterintuitive when you compare this with how you operate your jalopy."

"Yeah, I've learned all about aerodynamics; I've just never been able to apply it before this."

"Here are a few more key points about your preflight. Make sure you have plenty of gas, and check and fill the oil as needed. Check the propeller for nicks and that it is securely fastened, and make sure those lousy starlings haven't built a nest in the engine compartment or in the carburetor intake, or you could find yourself in real trouble. This is especially important if the plane has been sitting for a while. Also, make sure the tires have decent tread and are properly inflated with air."

"How about the brakes?"

"What brakes? A lot of these older planes don't have them; so, you have to plan ahead if you want to stop. That's why when I taxi up to the ramp I cut the engine and just coast to a stop. It just takes a little practice to time it right. Next lesson you'll do the preflight and I'll watch. Okay, let's go flying."

Although Sam tended to be more of a free spirit during scenic flights, he was dead serious when it came to being a proper pilot. He made sure Frank knew all the basics of flight, like controlling his speed and altitude just by keeping a reference point on the airplane's windshield fixed on the horizon. He insisted that Frank control the plane's ground track regardless of the direction of the wind. They would follow power lines so that Frank would get used to crabbing the plane into the wind and flying in a straight line. This would set him up to make cross country flights and, more importantly, align the airplane with the runway for landing in a crosswind. Much of their time was spent making low approaches for landing, but not actually landing. Sam was making sure that Frank would not panic as the plane approached closer and closer to the ground. Sam was a stickler on airspeed control during the approach. After several lessons Sam decided Frank was ready for a landing on his own.

"Okay, Frank. I'm going to direct you down. Do exactly what I say when I say it."

Frank entered the landing pattern. As he approached a location aside the approach end of the runway, he reduced the power, raised the nose, and slowed the plane. When the airspeed dropped to eighty miles per hour he began his descent for landing. He turned the base leg and slowed the airplane to seventy-five miles per hour while carefully adjusting the power and attitude to obtain the desired result. Now it was time to turn onto the final approach for landing and slow to sixty-five miles per hour.

Sam asked, "What do you think about your set up for landing? Are you high or low? How's your airspeed. Where on the runway do you plan to touch down? Do you have enough altitude to make the runway if your engine quit now?"

There were so many questions and so little time to think. Frank understood that this was serious business. "Ah, I think it looks pretty good."

"Well, if you think so, then let's try a landing. When you're sure you have made the runway, chop the power. Now as we get closer and closer to the ground, I want you to keep the airplane from landing. Hold it off the ground as long as you can, but not too high from the ground. Otherwise, we're going to bounce around like a basketball. Also, make sure you don't over-control the rudder pedals because we don't want to get into a ground loop."

Frank did his best to make the proverbial perfect landing. It was acceptable for a first landing. You might say he had one takeoff and three landings if you count all the bounces. Not bad for a beginner. There would be plenty more flights to perfect his technique.

The next several Saturday's and, sometimes on Sunday afternoon, they would practice all the basics including stalls, landings, and emergency procedures. Then after a brief flight around the traffic pattern and landing Sam instructed Frank to stop taxiing. Sam unhitched his safety belt and began to climb out. Frank wondered to himself, *What's wrong?* Nothing was wrong; everything was right.

"The time has come, son, to do this on your own. You're ready to solo."

Frank could not believe his ears.

"I want you to make three takeoffs and landings to a full stop. Keep an eye out for other airplanes and just remember all your procedures."

All alone now, Frank advanced the throttle slightly and taxied the lumbering biplane to the end of the runway. He lined up into the wind, pushed the throttle to full power, and made a smooth takeoff. He was amazed at how much faster things seemed to happen than when Sam was along for moral support, partly because the lack of Sam's additional weight allowed the plane to lift off sooner.

Once Frank reached pattern altitude on the downwind leg, he began to calm down and catch up with his procedures. He paid careful attention to his power and attitude and nailed his airspeed on the money. Now it was time to turn onto final for the runway. This would be his last chance to make adjustments for the landing. There was a slight crosswind and Frank was using every ounce of his being to stay aligned with the runway. With the power at idle, Frank eased the control stick further and further back into his belly in his attempt to hold the airplane off the ground. He pushed on the left rudder pedal to maintain alignment with the runway center line. Then, the next thing he heard was a squeak. The wheels were down. He had landed and had not felt so much as a thud.

As Frank taxied back for Sam's critique his right leg began to shake uncontrollably. Not his left leg, just his right leg. It was caused by a combination of stress and excitement. Sam had nothing but glowing comments. Frank had soloed and he was thrilled. He still had two more take-offs and landings before his flying day would be done.

Over the next several months Frank continued to practice his maneuvers and learned how to navigate. Sam trained him how to fly cross country using *pilotage*—picking out features on the ground—and *dead reckoning*—taking into account wind drift and time between checkpoints using a mathematical approach. Literally expanding his horizons by flying cross country was an exciting, new adventure. In short order he was ready for his private pilot check ride. The flight examiner commented that he seemed like a natural pilot. He was smooth and concise with every maneuver. At that point, Frank felt a sense of purpose and thought about building upon his flight experience and possibly turning it into a profession.

Frank decided to take the next step in his flight training—instrument flying. This was an extremely challenging venture considering the limited aids to flying in instrument conditions. However, he knew he needed to do this because the New England weather did not always cooperate with the forecasters' predictions. In other words, if one wanted to know for certain what the weather would be like, then the only way to be certain was to look out the window. And what one saw was no guarantee what the weather would be like ten minutes later.

Sam really put him through the paces. They flew in all kinds of weather. Sam also required much more exacting control from his students during instrument flight training. The only conditions in which they would not fly were on extremely gusty days and during icing conditions. No one in their right mind would challenge ice. Wings could ice up, causing the airplane to virtually fall out of the sky. Or, the carburetor throat could ice up and starve the engine for air. Under those circumstances, the chance of making a safe landing while flying in the clouds was slim.

By the time Frank completed his instrument training, he knew it was the most demanding, yet satisfying and valuable training, he had received to date. Now he had the confidence to make longer cross country flights without the fear of being trapped during marginal weather conditions.

Then he was on to the next stage. Sam started to train him as a flight instructor. Instead of flying from the front seat of the Stearman where he had flown as a student and for pleasure, now he had to transition to the rear seat. It was a whole different perspective. The nose seemed to jut higher into the sky during taxi so his forward view was totally obscured. Gentle S-turns during taxi were particularly important to insure that he would not run into another airplane, person, or thing. Yet, he adapted to the change quickly and he learned how to assume the role of teacher. He actually learned much more about flying an airplane as an instructor than during any other phase of his life as an aviator. Perhaps having to explain maneuvers, flight characteristics, navigation, map reading, civil aeronautics regulations, and so on reinforced his inherent knowledge about the subject to the point that he became a knowledgeable and respected expert in the field.

Chapter 4

A New Chapter in Life

Although Frank continued to hone his flying skills, he did so concurrently while studying through the remaining two years of college. Frank was well-adapted to handling multiple tasks, and he demonstrated this by earning his aeronautical engineering degree with excellence. In fact, he would be one of the top graduates by graduating *summa cum laude*. Everyone marveled at how well he balanced his life among his education, family, love interest, flying, and church activities. He was the epitome of the saying, *If you want to get a job done, then give it to a busy person.* This was done with the understanding that busy people have to know how to manage their time effectively. That was a good description of Frank.

It was Saturday, June 10, 1939. At twenty-one years old, Frank was graduating with a college degree from a prestigious university. His family was so proud of his accomplishments. He was also glad that he had completed four tough years of study and was now ready for new challenges. His family had a cookout in their backyard to celebrate. Neighbors, close friends, and, of course, Dottie's family, were all invited. It was a joyous occasion that went well into the evening. It appeared that Frank was coming out of his shell.

Frank was anxious to put his degree to good use and build a career. But, he would take the summer off to recuperate from the stresses of college life. He also wanted to renew his relationship with Dottie whom he felt like he had ignored while he was in school.

Desiring to spend every available moment with her, he made big plans how they would spend their summer together.

For the last two years of his college life he had pondered his career options. After long deliberation he decided to start out by continuing to be a flight instructor and possibly seek employment as an airline pilot once he built up some more experience. He knew the competition for airline jobs would be stiff. So, he wanted to make himself a standout among the competition.

He could use his education and, hopefully, literally expand his flying horizons by eventually hiring on with Eastern Air Lines and flying their advanced equipment. At least he could apply for a job with them and see what would happen. Having amassed about 700 hours of flight time through pleasure, training, and flight instruction, Frank considered his chances slim. Yet, he figured that by the time the airline got around to contacting him he would have amassed significantly more flying time.

When he wasn't with Dottie, he spent every moment giving flight instruction in Plymouth. As Sam Bullock was starting to have trouble with his eyesight, he began grooming his star pupil, Frank, to take his place. Other times, Frank just went up on his own to practice aerobatics in order to build his flight time. He loved the freedom of flight and the thrill of loops, rolls, and spins. His aerobatics were so intense that he could not help but stay in the best of physical condition. He was equally comfortable flying right-side up or upside down. With all of his training and experience he had pretty much eliminated any of the initial trepidation he had about flying.

On those days when Dottie felt particularly adventuresome, she would join him on an aerial sightseeing tour of the Cape and the Islands of Martha's Vineyard and Nantucket. All the nooks and crannies of the inlets and bays lent themselves to exploration. When they spotted sail boats, Frank would sweep in low and wave to the crew. On occasion, they would even spot a whale basking on the surface just off Provincetown.

Occasionally, they would land the small plane on the packed sand beach on Monomoy Island at low tide, have a picnic lunch, and go for a brief swim. They pretty much had the island to themselves. The only other inhabitants were thousands of sea gulls breaking the silence. It was all too easy to lose track of time. Yet, they just had to be sure to take off before the tide turned. Frank didn't want to try taking off higher up the beach. There was just too much danger of flipping if the wheels dug into the soft sand. Whenever he made the flight to Monomoy Island, he would partially deflate the main tires so as to make them more adaptable to the soft conditions of the beach. Then he would always re-inflate them upon his return to Plymouth.

Whenever Dottie flew with Frank, he was always on his best behavior. No aerobatics of fancy maneuvers. He did not want to scare her off from flying with him.

Other times they would visit one of the grass strips adjacent to the beach on the Vineyard. Those made for beautiful days. They would rent bicycles and pedal their way through Edgartown or Oak Bluffs. They would loll on the beach and stop by some seafood shack for lunch. The long summer days were perfect for extended getaways. Nothing could beat a brief thirty-minute flight from Plymouth down the west side of the Cape including about five minutes over water to the island.

It was a relatively inexpensive date considering he did not have to fight Cape traffic on the weekends and take the ferry ride from Woods Hole. They had more time to spend together on the Vineyard, too. They loved the quaintness of the villages and the architecture of the homes. Planning their trips for mid-week, they avoided the crush of tourists that would crowd the island on weekends.

Occasionally, they would make the hop to Nantucket Island. The tourist trade was not quite so heavy, nor did it seem as though the island catered so much to tourists as the Vineyard did. That being the case, there just was not as much to do there aside from walking the waterfront and looking at the whaling-era homes. In any event, it seemed as though Frank had something planned for Dottie every week that involved a flying getaway.

That was a memorable summer. Graduation. New job as a flight instructor. Fun flying around the coast with Dottie. The summer was soon to end with a bang.

On Saturday morning, September 2, 1939, just prior to leaving to pick up Dottie, Frank went to the front porch to grab the newspaper. Right there on the front page it announced that Germany had invaded Poland the day before. War had begun in Europe. However, things went on normally in the States. War had not reached our shores—yet. After all, the events unfolding in Europe were thousands of miles away, separated by the expanse of an ocean, and there was no hint that they would have any profound effect on the United States of America.

They were on their way to spend the Saturday before Labor Day on Martha's Vineyard for a final summer fling. It was a mob scene of tourists doing the same. During the flight to the Vineyard, they could see the lines of traffic awaiting the ferry. The winding roadways were now a massive parking lot. They were not going anywhere fast. Frank and Dottie lolled along about a thousand feet overhead. There were no long lines waiting for them.

It was an absolutely beautiful day. They followed their usual routine of renting bicycles and spending their day along the waterfront. It could not have been a more perfect time in their young lives. They dined on a steamed clam and lobster dinner, and sipped fresh-made lemonade along the waterfront in Edgartown. The sun beat down on them warming them as a cooling breeze swept across Edgartown Harbor.

After lunch they pedaled their way to Katama Beach where they waded in the surf and hiked the beach. The warm, sugary sand felt so wonderful between their toes that they just kept going. No one else was around them. All they could hear was the sound of the surf and an occasional call from a seagull. During this time the couple talked about their future, what they wanted out of life, and how much they meant to each other. His summer with Dottie went just as he had intended. It was to be a summer for the renewal and intensification of their relationship. But, it was getting late. It was time to turn for home.

After they made their way back to town, they decided to cool off with an ice-cold frappe. No self-respecting New Englander would order a milkshake because a frappe has a richer texture derived from its ice cream base. This was probably the only point on which there was disagreement. Dottie adored strawberry and Frank would kill for chocolate. If this was the biggest conflict between them, then they had nothing to dismay. It did not get any better than this.

At about 6:30 p.m. they arrived back at the airplane. Frank did the preflight inspection and they took off for home. They passed over Oak Bluffs and saw another long line of traffic waiting for the ferries' return to the mainland. And once they returned to the mainland they could see a continuous stream of traffic running all the way from Cape Cod into Boston in the distance. It took them thirty minutes to get to the Vineyard and thirty minutes to return to Plymouth. It was sure better than sitting in traffic feeling frustrated for hours on end. There were no stop lights or stop signs. They could see afar where they were going and it was clear flying ahead of them. Travel over and above all that mess sure made sense and Dottie saw the value in that mode of transportation. She had grown to love the benefits of aviation and Frank's talents as a pilot.

Following the end of the summer, Frank picked up the pace with his flying. His days were full of flight instruction and scenic flights over Plymouth Harbor. When he wasn't out doing instruction or scenic flights, he was honing his own skills. He was working at being a precise pilot because he knew that the airlines would expect it. In order to expand his résumé, Frank also gave a fair amount of instrument instruction. He liked doing it at night because there was generally less air traffic at that time, and it made it more difficult for the student pilot who wore a hood restricting his vision to cheat by peeking. Often the air was smoother at night, as a result of fewer rising and sinking air currents.

Frank was also considering other options for his future. He thought about continuing his education by earning a master's degree or a doctorate in aeronautical design. But he realized that he needed to accrue considerable funds before doing so. He needed a real job. Flight instruction did not pay enough to support a wife or a family. He also thought about performing aerobatics while traveling around the country like the old barnstormers. But sensibility prevailed and he recognized that a steady source of income could be quite elusive if he took that career path. If we wanted to do that, he would need an airplane, and he certainly could not afford one at this stage in his life.

He was starting to lose hope as he ran out of options. Considering how remote it would be to hear from Eastern Air Lines, he was shocked when he received a large envelope from the Personnel Department of Eastern Air Lines in the mail a few days later. It read,

Dear Mr. Johnson,

I am pleased to inform you that you have been selected to interview for the position of pilot with Eastern Air Lines. Please contact our Boston office to schedule a date and time within the next two weeks.

Frank could not contain his glee as he let out a shout at the top of his lungs. He jumped up and down and spun around with excitement. His poor mother was taken completely by surprise as it sounded as though a pig was squealing after being stuck by a sharp implement. His father, who had been in the garage servicing the family car came running in to see what had happened. They were both upset with Frank for startling them so. Yet, they were congratulatory for his good fortune once they learned the reason for his outburst.

He never expected to hear from the airline so soon, let alone at all. However, the combination of his flight experience and aeronautical engineering degree pretty much guaranteed that the airline could not ignore him.

Frank tried to call Dottie right away, but some long-winded callers were tying up the telephone party line. Frank kept trying, but the callers continued talking about mundane topics like the weather, dinner last night, and their kids. Come on—Frank had something important to tell Dottie!

Consequently, after thirty minutes trying to get through to Dottie, he decided to jump in the car and drive to her house. When he got there, she was hanging laundry in the back yard. When he arrived at her home he could see her through the screen door in the back yard. So, he ran to the back of the house skipping along like a school girl. When he told Dottie about the letter, she was thrilled. She saw this improving the possibility of being married in the very near future once Frank landed a steady job with a good salary.

The next morning Frank called the Personnel Department. Within the next three weeks he was sitting in an interview. He was charming and personable and, most of all, he was knowledgeable about everything to do with aircraft operation and aerodynamics.

The interview ended about an hour after it began. The Personnel Manager told Frank that they were interviewing a pool of candidates over the next two weeks for only two positions. Thus, there would be a lot of competition. Frank felt that he had done an admirable job with the interview, but his bubble was burst a bit with the revelation about the other candidates. Now, he had to wait and wonder. There was nothing more he could do at this point.

The next several weeks dragged by although he stayed busy with his flight instruction duties and, of course, there was Dottie. She was so supportive and consoling. After all, she reminded him that he was a fresh college graduate but that he had gotten a job interview on the first try. So, he should feel proud of himself. Nevertheless, he still felt dejected and upset. He was not sleeping well.

Then the letter from Eastern Air Lines arrived. He was afraid to open it. It was a thin envelope. He remembered when he received his acceptance to MIT just how thick the envelope was. This had to be a rejection. If so, then where would his career plans go? He had a sour taste in his mouth as he tore open the end of the envelope. As luck would have it, he could not separate the sides of the envelope to reach in and pull out the letter. What torture! Finally, in desperation, he could take it no longer and he started tearing into it anyway he could and partially tore the letter itself. He started to read,

Dear Mr. Johnson,

Congratulations. You have been selected to begin training as a pilot with Eastern Air Lines. Please contact this office ...

And the letter went on with further details. Frank was speechless. How could this be? He had a dream job right out of the gate. He had to call Dottie immediately.

This time, there was no one else on the party line. When the telephone rang at Dottie's home, she thought that it was a prank call. All she could hear were yips and screams from the other end. Then she realized that it was Frank.

"Calm down, Frank. What is it?"

"I got the job! I got the job! Get yourself ready. I'm coming right over and we are going out to celebrate."

"But, Frank, it's only ten o'clock in the morning. It's a little too early to celebrate."

"Okay, but I'm going to come over anyway."

"That's fine, but don't try to hurry because I don't want you to have an accident."

Frank anxiously awaited the start of his training with the airline on November 6th. Having freshly experienced the rigors of earning his degree, Frank took to the airline training with little difficulty. The book learning for many trainees was tedious, but for Frank much of it was a review of material he already understood extremely well. He breezed through the aerodynamics and had no trouble with aircraft systems including hydraulics, gyroscopic, pitot-static, controls, and avionics. After all, he had experience designing just such systems, at least in the classroom and the lab.

Upon completing the classroom instruction, now the fun would begin. He would get his hands on some of the actual heavy equipment. Much to his chagrin, though, was the strict procedural training. This tended to take some of the fun out of flying. But Frank had his mind straight. He knew it needed to be done. The training included such mundane things as how to greet passengers. It was all necessary to make the paying public comfortable with the business of flying.

Of course, most time was spent on emergency procedures. He had to know how to feather a propeller, discharge a fire extinguisher, make an emergency landing, fight an onboard fire, cross-feed fuel, isolate a hydraulic leak, lower the landing gear using the hand crank, and every other contingency. Frank was determined to do his best—and he did.

Before he knew it, training was completed and he was the co-pilot flying a combination of freight and passengers on some late-night runs between Boston and New York City. This schedule went on for about six months. Then Frank was able to get a more agreeable daytime schedule. Due to his schedule he was able to spend a lot of time at home. Partly this was due to the fact that he also got a lot of time off between assignments. So, he still got to spend time with Dottie.

Frank's assignments expanded, too. He found himself flying up and down the eastern seaboard. He loved it. He was seeing new places, new things, and meeting people from all over the country. As he flew with various captains, he became known among them for his attention to detail and his ability.

Meanwhile, Dottie finished her nursing degree. She was now pursuing her credentials as a registered nurse while working at the

Weymouth Hospital in South Weymouth. Their careers were burgeoning and they both felt fulfilled and elated that they were looking to successful futures.

Finally, Frank learned in mid-October 1941, that after almost two years of sitting in the copilot seat, he would be moved into the left seat, captain at last. This was a major milestone in his career.

The only drawback would be the fact that he would have to go back to flying some of the less desirable schedules until he built up his seniority among the other captains. That would be okay. He had survived such a schedule as a copilot; he could do the same as a pilot. Largely, he would suffer through it because he was going to receive a higher salary as a result. He saw himself as being the top dog, eventually. It would take some time, but he was on his way.

Although Frank had a busy schedule flying with the airline, he never gave up on flying for pleasure with Dottie. If anything he was able to do more pleasure flying because he could afford it with his new salary. Of course, he did not blow his salary on just flying. He was planning ahead and saving quite a nest egg for his life with Dottie. In fact, he was planning to ask Dottie's parents for her hand in marriage and propose to her on Christmas day. He was already shopping for an engagement ring.

Furthermore, Frank had not given up his flight instruction duties at the Plymouth airport. To the contrary, he found himself more in demand as a flight instructor because students saw training with him as an established airline pilot as being a first step to getting an airline job themselves. After all, he had made the leap to the airlines and had experience how to get there. Yet, his education placed him in a unique situation and certainly had something to do with it, too, which gave him an edge over the competition.

In addition to his airline flights along the eastern seaboard, they started to extend to more and more locations as well. There were even trips to Bermuda and Florida. Those excursions were especially welcome during the cold winter months of the northeast. Occasionally, Frank would return from Florida with a sack of fresh oranges and from Bermuda with perfume for his mother, Dottie, and Dottie's mother. He liked Bermuda so much that he considered going there for his honeymoon; so long as Dottie agreed. It seemed like a world apart, yet it was only 700 miles from their local paradise, Martha's Vineyard.

Perhaps they could take a cruise or just take the airline there on their honeymoon.

Over the last couple of years he had earned the respect of his crew mates and the administrators at Eastern Air Lines. There was no question that he would have a long career with the airlines. Frank got used to flying in all kinds of weather conditions. He had seen them all, turbulence, rain, sleet, snow, and fog. He had also landed on grass, asphalt, concrete, ice- and snow-covered, and unimproved runways. This was a great training ground for him as he became accustomed to all types of flying and all kinds of conditions.

He realized how fortunate he was and he never took for granted how he had been blessed. He was flying the most sophisticated and newest equipment and he was being paid to do it. His hard work and dedication were paying off.

There were also rumors floating around the airline that in a couple of years they would be upgrading their aircraft from the iconic twin-engine DC-3 to the four-engine DC-4. Frank could not wait to get his hands on that. It would be more powerful, faster, more comfortable, and have superior load-carrying capability. Things were looking great.

He had his degree in hand, a great, well-paying job with a great future, and plans to get married once he saved enough money to buy a home. Life could not have been sweeter.

Chapter 5

Preparing for War

It started out as a typical Sunday morning in December. A cold, clear day in the low thirties; it felt much colder due to the wind-chill from the steady, stiff breezes. As was his habit, each Sunday morning Frank drove to pick up Dottie for church at her parent's home in North Weymouth. The heater was set to maximum temperature, cranking out the hot air so that the car would be warm enough to make the drive tolerable for Dottie. He would drive her to church every Sunday. Frank was a fixture around her home; he was already considered a part of the family. Although they had talked about marriage, there was no definite date set. Among everyone they knew it was a foregone conclusion that they would be wed. And Frank was definitely working towards popping the question.

Sunday dinners were shared by alternating between their parents' homes. This Sunday, December 7, 1941, would be spent with Dottie's parents. The day would not be a typical one.

Following a lovely dinner of roast beef, mashed potatoes, and green beans, the family sat around conversing while sipping hot coffee and eating freshly-baked apple pie. Who could possibly have room for apple pie after that huge meal but, then again, who could pass it up? Around the Stoddard household, if apple pie sat around for more than a few minutes Dottie's father, Eddie, would claim it as his own. He was a short, portly man—probably the result of too many extra slices of apple pie. He was always a jovial, generous sort, and supportive of Frank's relationship with his only daughter. Frank was like the son he never had.

Sometimes Frank would help Eddie work on their family car while they sipped iced tea. It was a beat up heap that was covered with splotches of rust. Eddie was not the best mechanic and he did not understand the concept of preventative maintenance. Consequently, Frank did his best to help him keep the old jalopy running. Perhaps this is why Frank drove Dottie to church each Sunday—to keep her from being stranded in the broken down family car, or just to keep her from feeling embarrassed from riding in the town eyesore.

Other times Frank and Eddie would just hang out like a couple of pals. They would take a walk to the local ball field to watch the kids play baseball or football depending on the season. Or Eddie would lie in the hammock while Frank mowed his lawn. Frank knew how to ingratiate himself with Eddie.

On this particular Sunday, the radio played softly in the background. It was the big band era with the music of Harry James and Glenn Miller being the big hits. Frank particularly liked the comedy routines of Spike Jones and His City Slickers. Mrs. Stoddard decided that she wanted something a little more sedate playing in the background so that conversation could be conducted without too much interference from the radio. So, she found the Philadelphia Philharmonic playing on one of the radio stations.

The family was so enrapt with the spirited conversation that they almost missed the news flash at 2:30 in the afternoon. It was the same message being heard across the country at that time. The Japanese had bombed U.S. military bases at Pearl Harbor, Hawaii. How could this have happened? The first news cited hundreds killed or wounded. But, where was Pearl Harbor? Dottie's dad pulled out an atlas and located Oahu, Hawaii on it. It was just a speck in the vast Pacific Ocean and thousands of miles from the west coast of the United States.

Frank looked around at Dottie's family. Their eyes told the story. Dottie's mother, Ann, had tears welling up in her eyes. Dottie was visibly trembling. Frank hugged her to comfort her. And this was the first time ever he saw Eddie brought to anger. Eddie had fought in the trenches in France during what would be known as the First World War, now that there would be a second. He knew that a war of this magnitude would cost the lives of many a fine man. What he had hoped would be joy for him on this earth was his fervent belief that the war to end all wars would truly be just that. But it was not to be so. This would be bigger, more destructive, and truly a world war.

The rest of the day was spent in somber reflection as they listened to the continuous news flashes. All military personnel on leave were being called back to duty. *Duty,* Frank thought to himself, *I have a duty to beat back this foe. I'm scared stiff but I have to do my part.*

Frank had some deeper concerns, too. He was worried about the status of his two younger brothers. Danny, the middle brother, was half way towards earning a degree in history at the University of Massachusetts in Amherst. And the youngest brother, Billy, had just graduated from high school and was working as an apprentice mechanic at a local printing company. Frank considered the likelihood of them being drafted, and it seemed all too certain.

Back in his bedroom that night, Frank's mind was racing. He knew what he was going to have to do; he had to enlist. Yet he was shaking with fear at the prospects of going into harm's way. It was one thing to fly in the battle-free skies over the U.S. and quite another to be a target for a trigger-happy enemy pilot or *ack-ack* gunner. He could not sleep a wink and tossed and turned throughout the night.

The problem was how would he tell Dottie that they would have to put a hold on their plans? Then another thought crept into his mind. If he fought, there would be no guarantee he would return. Then again, he would probably be drafted anyway. So why not take some control of his destiny and have a choice in how he would serve.

Having made up his mind, the next day he drove to Dottie's home to tell her of his decision. He was not sure how Dottie would take it, but he felt led to do it because he felt it was right.

On the way he listened avidly to President Franklin Delano Roosevelt's declaration of war on the Empire of Japan. It wasn't long after that Germany, a fellow Axis member with Japan, declared war on the United States. This was going to be a big one.

Frank arrived at Dottie's home and slowly walked to the front door. He was still mulling in his head how he wanted to tell her. He knocked on the door, and Mr. Stoddard answered. He still looked sullen. He invited Frank into the living room. Just twenty-four hours earlier, life was great. Everything was right with the world. Christmas was just around the corner along with the long-awaited proposal. Now it was like the funeral of a beloved member of the family.

Frank asked if Dottie was home.

"Frank, the way you asked that, it sounds serious."

"It is, sir."

"Let me get her for you."

Dottie came flitting down the stairs. She always seemed excited to see Frank. However, her joy turned to dismay as she cast her eyes on Frank's countenance.

"What's the matter, Frank?"

"I have something to tell you. I don't want to hurt you, but I have to tell you."

"What's happened?"

"Well, this war has happened, and I have to do my part. I've decided to enlist."

"You can't. We're planning to get married and start a family."

"Hon, with the current state in the world, it just wouldn't be fair to you to get married, have a child, then turn you into a widow because I got drafted and killed. By enlisting I will at least have some control over how I serve."

Eddie chimed in, "You know, Dottie, he makes a lot of sense. I've seen it before. Once a war like this starts up, every able-bodied man is called into service. Whatever you do, son, stay out of the trenches."

"Oh, I plan to, sir. I plan to join the Army Air Forces as a pilot. The way I've got it figured, I have a college degree and have been a flight instructor and airline pilot, with all the special flight training I received from Sam Bullock, I should be a pretty desirable candidate for any flight program."

"When do you plan to enlist?"

"I'm driving downtown to the enlistment office now."

"Have you told your parents?"

"Yes, at breakfast. My mom dropped a couple of eggs when I told her."

"How did your dad take it?"

"As well as could be expected. He seemed to be proud."

Dottie was having difficulty listening to all this talk of going off to war. Her life was taking a dramatic change in direction. Yet, she remained calm and stoic. This woman came from good stock.

As Frank was leaving to drive to the enlistment office, Dottie hugged him like a vise and kissed him passionately while whispering, "When you leave, you'd better write."

"Honey, I'm just going to enlist. I'm not going off to war right now."

With that she turned and quickly ran upstairs to have herself a good cry out of Frank's sight.

When Frank arrived downtown, he was astonished to see a line of men of all shapes, sizes, and ages that extended down the street from the enlistment office. It seems he was not the only one to feel a driven sense of duty. Many of these men would be brothers in arms against a ruthless, merciless, and murderous foe.

By the time Frank made it inside the enlistment office three hours had passed. He filled out the paperwork and handed it to the staff sergeant, who read it over.

"So, you're a college boy and a pilot. Well, if you pass the physical and aptitude tests you'll probably be sent to flight school, but there are no guarantees that you'll graduate. It's pretty tough with the physical training, classroom exercises, and flight training. A lot of guys wash out."

"I don't plan to wash out."

"Good attitude, son. Okay go through that door and you'll get a preliminary medical exam to see if you're fit for service. If you are, then you'll get your reporting papers within the next couple of months."

"Two months?"

"Yeah, two months. You'll learn that in the military, all paperwork is done in triplicate. Besides, you've seen all the guys we have to process, and this is happening across the country. So, it takes time."

Frank passed into the next room where he stripped down to his shorts for every manner of probing, jabbing, and tapping. It was like a tout trying to pick out the best thoroughbred for a race. The only difference being that this would be a race for his life and the life of his country.

A team of doctors checked his pulse, blood pressure, temperature, teeth, ears, and eyes. He was made to hop on one leg, bend over, turn his head and cough, and any other demeaning activity that can be imagined. When the examination was complete, he was given a clean bill of health and determined to be fit for service. His eyes were twenty-ten and every other vital sign was as perfect as any young man could hope for as he prepared to train for war.

He also took a test to determine his aptitude for flight training. With his credentials, it was a total waste of time. A short time later he was notified of his acceptance into flight training.

Another two months passed before he received a telegram ordering him to report to Kessler Field in Biloxi, Mississippi for basic training in ten days. Evidently, the military had a sense of humor sending a boy from the frigid northeast to the sweltering south. He was going a thousand miles south and he would be allowed only one suitcase. Everything else would be provided for him by the Army. There was not a lot of time to prepare. It would take almost that long to transit the country by rail and whatever other means of transportation would be required.

His parents decided to throw him a going away party. Their home was filled to capacity with all their neighbors, friends, and family since it was now mid-February and there was no way that the party could overflow into the yard; New England winters are just too cold for that. Boyhood friends stopped by to wish him well. Some had already joined the service; others were waiting to be drafted. Still others had skills necessary to support the war effort at home. Somehow each would find a way to serve their country in its time of need.

Each person stopped by, bringing all manner of potluck food and drink. Frank plowed into it figuring that, based on the rumors, Army food wouldn't be too appetizing. Besides, with all the physical training he was about to endure, he needed to build up his strength.

Although the home was packed solid with well-wishers, Frank and Dottie had eyes only for each other. They had no idea how long it would be before they would see each other again. Some optimists thought the war would be over in a year or eighteen months. The pessimists thought it would go on for years without any assurance that the United States and its allies would prevail. Frank had already made up his mind that he would make it back and he told Dottie so.

The following Monday, Frank's parents drove him to the train station for his trip to Biloxi, Mississippi. Dottie and her family met him there. This scene was being repeated all over the country. Of the two million men who were to ship out, more than 400,000 would not make the return trip, and many more would come back physically and emotionally wounded. Their lives would be changed forever.

As the conductor called for final boarding, Frank had to pry loose Dottie's hug on him. She did not want to let him go. But Frank had to go. He quickly gave final hugs to his mother and Mrs. Stoddard, and handshakes to his father, brothers, and Mr. Stoddard. He jumped onto the train as it started pulling out of the station bound for the next phase of his life and a new adventure.

As the locomotive chugged along, conversation on board became spirited. Every other young man on board bragged as to how he would single-handedly win the war. Frank listened politely as he knew better. The young men with whom he traveled came from all walks of life and with all manner of experience. Some had worked on dairy farms, one or two worked in the family business, others worked in factories, most were fresh out of high school, and relatively few had a college education. The jobs provided by the Army would be just as varied. Fortunately for Frank, the Army had already agreed that his unique flight experience made him a prime candidate for flight school following basic and officer training. Once completing the cadet stage of his training he would be commissioned as a second lieutenant. He had taken Eddie's advice; he would stay out of the trenches.

When the train finally pulled into the station, the Army had a green bus waiting to transport them to the base. As was typical, the dehumanizing phase of their training began with the barking drill sergeants ordering them to grab their belongings, get on the bus, find a seat, and shut up. Army life had begun on the usual sour note from a non-commissioned officer.

Upon arriving at the camp, the sergeants continued to scream at them to fall into line and march to their home, the barracks, for the next twelve weeks. This was not the Hilton or home. It was a barren, corrugated steel structure that echoed whenever it rained. And heaven help you get any sleep if there was any hail. Speaking of sleep— everyone had different sleeping habits. Some had to clear their sinuses and others should have, based on the intolerable snoring that resonated in that large tin can of a building.

Immediately upon their arrival there were a myriad of medical tests which included so many vaccinations that some men fainted as a result. As a budding combat pilot, Frank was most concerned about his eyesight. It was twenty-ten, better than the standard twenty-twenty. This meant Frank might have the advantage of seeing his adversaries before they could see him. Nothing concerning his medical history would keep him from the air. What Frank feared most was the possibility of being assigned as a navigator or bombardier, or as a pilot or co-pilot in a bomber or transport plane. He wanted a fighter. Straight and level flight did not appeal to him. Besides, he wanted to be able to shoot back.

The first six weeks of basic training were grueling. Sit ups, push ups, obstacle courses, running, and the pre-dawn hike with full packs. He felt that this was not a good use of his talents; yet, he understood that this was required of everyone and that the Army wanted to make sure everyone was in peak physical condition to fight an equally well-trained enemy. He missed home, but he was kept far too busy to dwell on it for long.

One activity that Frank enjoyed was the firing range. They used Springfield rifles from the Great War. Actually, the rifles were manufactured back in 1903, well before the First World War. The old days of shooting tin cans and rats paid off. He attained expert marksman status. The sergeant tried to convince him to train as a rifleman in an infantry company, but he flatly told the sergeant that he would rather shoot at airplanes than directly at people. Yes, there were people in those planes; however, it was a bit less personal than shooting someone face-to-face.

During this period letters to Dottie were less frequent than he had planned. His days were long, busy, and exhausting. He had all he could do to climb into bed at night and be ready for a 4:00 a.m. call to assembly the next morning.

Finally, the torture of basic training was over. He was now off to officer training, which soon would be followed by flight training. This was what he yearned for. Yet, there was no guarantee that he would not wash out or be stuck in a bomber. Not that there was anything wrong with bombers. Obviously, they had a major part to play in this modern-era war. But Frank liked the speed, maneuverability, and firepower associated with the agile fighters. So, Frank made sure that he did his best to reach his goal to fly fighters. For his flight training, he was off to sunny northern California, Lincoln to be exact. Lincoln was a satellite training field for Mather Air Base.

Just as with the airlines, the military placed a lot of stock in classroom instruction before handing over a sophisticated and expensive aircraft to a cadet. So, as before, hours were spent in the classroom slogging through the physics and mathematics of flight. This included calculating fuel requirements for a mission profile which took into account warm up, taxi, take off, climb to altitude, cruise, action, return to base, and landing. And just as with the airline, the military stressed emergency procedures. This was all second nature to Frank. With much of the classroom instruction behind him, it was finally time to take to the air.

It was a beautiful California morning, not only because of the weather, but because this would be his maiden flight as an Army Air Force cadet. After a brief pre-flight meeting with the instructors, he and about a dozen other cadets headed off to the flight line to prepare their mounts to take to the air.

Their ride was to be the venerable tube and fabric Stearman PT-13D Kaydet biplane. The "PT" stands for primary trainer. It had a basic silver paint job with standard military markings. Its power plant was a Lycoming R-680 rated at 220 horsepower. Frank already had about 400 hours of flight time in Stearmans before his enlistment. Nonetheless, he had to follow protocol and qualify to fly the Stearman according to military procedures. There was some good news about these Stearmans that differed from the one he flew back in Plymouth. At least these airplanes had brakes.

His instructor watched Frank closely as he performed the pre-flight inspection. Considering his experience, he had the technique down pat. Many young cadets found out early that tail wheel airplanes with a narrow wheel base tend to ground loop quite easily. The plane can only be turned by applying differential braking, although it does have a tendency to weathervane, that is, turn its nose into the wind if the pilot is caught napping. A ground loop often occurred during landing as the cadet attempted to transition from flight control to ground control. Upon touching the ground the plane would quickly turn off its centerline, either due to under- or over-control of the rudder pedals. Many a wingtip would be scraped or bent as a result. A more severe outcome might cause the plane to flip, injuring or killing the pilot. Frank always controlled any plane he flew as though it was flying all the time, even when on the ground.

Prior to jumping into the cockpit, Frank told the instructor of his flight experience. The skeptical instructor advised Frank that he would do the take-off then give Frank a chance to prove himself at a safe altitude. It wasn't long before the instructor was totally convinced as Frank put the trainer though its paces. He had the plane doing slips, rolls, loops, lazy-eights, hammerhead stalls, and spins. The landing could not have been better, a real "squeaker."

Upon exiting the plane his instructor took him aside and said, "Son, you're wasting your time and mine here. I'm going to talk to the major and see if we can't bump you up to advanced flight training."

Frank was thrilled. This meant newer, more powerful aircraft, and a faster route to his goal to fly fighters.

The North American AT-6 Texan was a whole new story in Frank's flight training as a military pilot. Here was a powerful airplane constructed of aluminum without the view hindering upper wing of a biplane, and it was far more complex with more instruments, systems, and retractable landing gear. This advanced stage of flight training would be more demanding than flying the venerable Stearman. The AT-6 became known for its ability to ruin a cadet's career as a pilot. It was heavier and inherently more stable than the Stearman; however, landings were another story. More of the ground was hidden during ground operations and during landing flare than in the Stearman. And the closely set main landing gear was notorious for contributing to ground loops when the pilot failed to continue to fly the airplane, even on the ground. But this much could be said about the AT-6. If you could fly it, then you could master any of the front line fighters in the military inventory.

During this phase of his flight training, Frank learned about formation flying and the correct four-finger position consisting of four airplanes of two groupings each with a wingman protecting his leader. He also had to concentrate on more precise flying, although that was expected of him with the airlines, too. But the most fun for him was finally getting the opportunity to use his skill with aerobatics. In this area he far exceeded the abilities of other cadets and, in many cases, the instructors. The training that he had received from Sam Bullock would prove to be invaluable. As the cadets trained in mock combat they found that no one could stay on Frank's tail, nor could he be shaken from anyone else's six-o'clock position.

This close formation and simulated combat flying were not without their inherent dangers. It was on a clear, sunny day and the air was a smooth as a pond free of ripples. Frank flew the lead in an echelon formation of four AT-6s. All aircraft were flying straight and level … nothing fancy, when Frank heard the screeching and tearing of metal. He immediately called a break in the formation, but the damage was already done. Two of the AT-6s were on their way down. The right wing had separated from the number three aircraft. It was spinning down uncontrollably. The pilot never had a chance. He was pinned in his seat by the G-force. The number four aircraft had its engine ripped from the mount. The pilot managed to bail out and land safely. An investigation by a board of inquiry found that the surviving pilot failed to maintain proper separation and was sightseeing when he should have had his attention locked onto the number three aircraft. He was summarily washed out of the flight program and transferred to the infantry.

This event shook Frank to the core. He was now reliving his years of fear. He started to be tentative during some of his aerobatic maneuvers. But, within a few days he began to work through his fears as he convinced himself that he had to perform to his utmost ability if he expected to survive the war and not have a detrimental effect on his fellow pilots.

This was especially important as he was entering some of the most demanding training—instrument flying. Some training was done on the ground using the famous Link trainer. Why it had to look like one of those airplanes hanging from cables at an amusement park is anyone's guess. Why did it need wings anyhow? It was never intended to fly, and the trainee was completely sealed in it without any external references. So, he could not see if it had wings or not. In any case, it could have been an apple crate and the pilot would have been none the wiser.

Instrument training did not cause any consternation for Frank as he had had experience with it both with the airlines and as an instructor back in Plymouth. This was just another hurdle to jump on his way to flying fighters.

As he neared the end of his advanced training, discussions began about the next level of training. Frank clearly had in his mind on this next step. Yet, with the military, the cadet's goal may not match that of the military's plans for the cadet's future.

As a result of his history of flying the big iron with the airlines, Frank's superiors intended for him to continue with bomber flight training. As best as he could respectfully argue with his superiors, he finally convinced them that his aerobatic experience would best be served by flying fighters. Also, the marksmanship he displayed during basic training in conjunction with his superior vision could only enhance the package that comes with being a fighter pilot. His instructors supported his efforts by telling the commanding officer that it would be a waste of Frank's talents to put him in a lumbering bomber just flying straight and level. After reviewing Frank's record some more, the commander agreed.

Now it was off to Mather Air Base in Sacramento, only about ten miles from Lincoln. His next challenge would be the high performance Bell P-39 Airacobra. It was the first true fighter he would fly. The Airacobra was odd from a conventional standpoint. Other front line fighters in the U.S. Army Air Force's inventory were tail-draggers and most, save the Curtiss P-40 Warhawk, had radial engines. The Airacobra had a nose wheel and a twelve cylinder Allison in-line engine. Radial engines were air-cooled, while the Allison engine, also used in the Warhawk, was liquid-cooled.

These features, however, were not the most noteworthy. Rather, it was the complex arrangement of the engine which was located behind the pilot coupled with a drive shaft running between the pilot's legs and a troublesome cannon that was geared to the drive shaft and fired through the propeller spinner, that made the airplane a standout, and not necessarily in a good way. There were continuous problems with the cannon and, as it turned out, most airplanes were shipped to Russia as Lend-Lease aircraft. The Russians made some good use of them by employing them as tank busters. There were also horror stories from some of the old time mechanics who had seen P-39s auger into the ground. Under those circumstances, the engine would just keep driving forward through the cockpit. In the end, all that would be found of the pilot sometimes were his feet in his shoes.

At least the P-39 was a step up in performance and maneuverability from the trainers. It could do a bit better than 300 miles per hour in level flight. This is about twice the speed of the AT-6. It was not just the speed and maneuverability that made flying the P-39 fun; it was gunnery practice. It was time to check out the fire power of this baby.

The increase in speed meant that everything would happen faster. An unprepared pilot could easily fall behind the aircraft and get into big trouble. It was especially busy upon entering the landing pattern with setting up the proper configuration including setting propeller pitch, manifold pressure, fuel mixture, wing flaps, cowling and coolant flaps, and landing gear. Needless to say, although he knew the time was coming for this step in his training, Frank had some reservations. The first time he stepped into the P-39 he felt a heightened sense of nervousness. Upon being strapped into his seat by the crew chief, he sat for a few minutes just trying to calm himself. He found that he could control his tremors by inhaling deeply and exhaling slowly. This became a standard regimen for getting himself calmed down. It was a technique that worked more often than not.

The pilots were briefed to head to a gunnery range about thirty miles north of the base. Here ground targets were set up to gauge the pilots' accuracy. They had all been given training on deflection shots and leading their targets. Frank knew that this would be challenging because, unlike a stationary shooter aiming at a stationary target, this would involve controlling an airplane moving through space at about 300 miles per hour shooting at a stationary target. Eventually, once they mastered this type of gunnery, they would begin shooting at moving targets. Of course there would be another big difference between this and real aerial combat; no one would be shooting back.

It was one thing to be an excellent pilot or shot, but quite another to combine the two. Fortunately, Frank's comfort and aptitude in the airplane, and his uncanny marksmanship, gave him the greatest satisfaction and joy of any training to date. He particularly liked to come in low over the irregular surface of the ground, weaving among the hills, and finally lining up on his target. It reminded him of shooting rats at the town dump.

During some of his flights to and from the gunnery range he would weave in and around the Sutter Buttes. Being the smallest, free-standing mountain range in the world, what made them unique is the way in which they seemed to spring up from Sacramento's Central Valley floor. The rugged volcanic peaks seemed to be out of place; yet, they provided a great playground for airplanes seeking to maneuver using ground terrain for cover. Nonetheless, pilots had to maintain a safe distance from them to avoid swirling eddies of air from throwing them into the unforgiving rock face.

During his time at Mather Frank continued to write his family, especially Dottie. They still discussed marriage and she made him promise not to do anything foolhardy or to volunteer for any dangerous missions. She must have had a feeling in her heart that he would be going overseas soon. Face it, Uncle Sam was not investing all this time and money into training Frank for him to stay stateside and shoot up the California Central Valley.

So long as Frank remained stateside, his parents and Dottie could rest easy. Nonetheless, there remained the specter of him being shipped overseas at a moment's notice. When that happened he would be incommunicado for security reasons until he arrived at his destination.

Occasionally, there would be a weekend pass into Sacramento. The young cadets would jump a bus and head into town en masse. At this time, Sacramento seemed like such a cow town compared to the urbane city of Boston near Frank's home. He was expecting a lot more activity. After all, this was the capitol of California. But the city had not yet hit its stride to deal with the influx of the huge population of soldiers and Army Air Force cadets. Frank was disappointed as it seemed to lend credence to the saying, *They roll up the sidewalks at night around here.*

One weekend, he, and a group of a dozen fellow cadets, took the bus to San Francisco. It was much livelier there, although it seemed to be over-run with sailors. Frank and his friends felt a little out of place. But Frank felt more at home in San Francisco. It sat on a bay, like Boston, had islands sprinkled throughout the Bay, though far fewer than Boston, and it had hills albeit much steeper than Boston's Beacon Hill. But they were similar in so many ways, and it was nice to smell the salt air again. More than anything else, Frank wanted some fresh seafood. The men found a decent restaurant on the waterfront for supper and sat down for platters full of sweet, dungeoness crab, tender slices of abalone, and piles of succulent shrimp. He had not eaten this well since he left home. As he ate, Frank gazed across San Francisco Bay towards Alcatraz Island and over towards the Golden Gate Bridge. It was partially engulfed in a layer of fog such that it looked surreal and dreamlike. The fog seemed to boil in and around this great man-made wonder constructed of steel and wire. Frank had never seen anything so awe-inspiring and picturesque.

As the sun started to set behind the Bridge and into the Pacific, it was time to find sleeping accommodations. They tried to get a hotel room, but they were booked solid. So, they just took the last bus back to Sacramento so that they could sleep in their own bunks. Regardless, they all had a wonderful day and a nice escape from the day-to-day training schedule.

Frank was also developing some strong friendships among his comrades-in-arms. Of the dozen or so cadets who had been transferred to Mather with Frank, ten remained. The others washed out during gunnery practice. They just didn't seem to be able to coordinate flying a plane and shooting at the same time. This did not mean that they did not earn their pilot wings. One transferred to bomber training where he could fly the plane and let someone else do the shooting or drop the bombs. The other would fly the Douglas C-47 Goony Bird, a tried-and-true transport. The remaining ten pilots earned their wings and their second lieutenant bar.

Now that their training was done, they awaited their orders. In the meantime, during jaunts away from the base on some weekends, the remaining pilots would often hit the bars and dives. Frank was not into this as he did not want to do anything to dishonor his family, Dottie, or the uniform. He preferred to relax at a movie or hit a hamburger joint for something other than military cuisine. Another pilot in the group felt the same way.

Scotty Winslow, a young man from St. Louis, Missouri, was the son of a Baptist minister. He had always enjoyed aviation. In fact, he spent some time as a crop duster. He was used to flying low and slow. But now he enjoyed the speed of fighters. So, he and Frank just seemed to find a mutual reason to enjoy each other's company and share their common interests.

You would think that being the son of a minister would contradict his choice to be a fighter pilot. It is not so strange if you consider that his motive was to protect his family from an imminent invasion by the Axis powers. At that time in history, nothing was certain about the outcome of the war. It was anybody's game. Quite frankly, at that time the Axis powers were winning.

Scotty was also serious about a girl back home. Yet, although he was in love, he did not allow it to interfere with his training to the best of his ability. Frank liked that about Scotty. Many times Frank and Scotty engaged in healthy competition as they tried to outdo each other during various stages of their training. As it turned out, you could not call either one of them the loser. They were obviously both winners in so many ways. This rivalry never came between them. To the contrary, it only served to strengthen their friendship and respect for one another throughout the war.

As with most freshly minted pilots, this group was no different than all the others who went before them or who were training elsewhere across the United States. They wanted action. At that time, there were three theaters in the war. There was the Pacific Theater in which the Allies concentrated on subduing the Japanese within that enormous ocean and the myriad islands dotting it. Then, there was the China-Burma-India Theater where the Allies were trying the beat back the Japanese who were entrenched in those regions and brutalizing the inhabitants. Finally, there was the European Theater which consisted of the European continent and countries largely surrounding the Mediterranean. The goal here was to repel the Italians and Germans.

The new pilots had no idea where they would go. Although the Pacific was largely the realm of the U.S. Navy, there was still the chance for an assignment to one of the atolls or Australia. While they waited, they continued to train intensely.

As Frank awaited his overseas assignment his nerves felt like elastic bands being stretched to their limit. It was a case where it would have been better to know than be in a state of constant worry. He had difficulty falling asleep and any sleep he got was restless and left him feeling unrefreshed. Finally, after five weeks passed, word came. Frank, Scotty, and two others would go to England to serve with the Eighth Air Force, the Mighty Eighth. They were to leave immediately with no outside contact. Their immediate families would be notified of nothing more than they were on their way to their next assignment. They would receive more information later.

Chapter 6

Overseas

Frank had always been able to handle demanding maneuvers required to do aerobatics. He had no problem with pulling gs. But the transit of the Atlantic Ocean on the *Queen Mary* was another story. Like so many other service men, he could not tolerate the constant rocking and rolling of the seas. It may seem like an idiosyncrasy, but Frank could easily adjust to abrupt aerobatics and flying inside clouds without any outside visual reference and never suffer the ill effects of motion sickness. To the contrary, rolling of the ship was an entirely different story. He could not keep down any food and the seasickness of others around him only exacerbated the problem. While the *Queen Mary* maintained top speed, which allowed it to outrun German U-boats without zigzagging, it seemed that the crossing would never end.

Nevertheless, during the Atlantic crossing few soldiers and airmen were very comfortable as a result of those two debilitating factors—worry about U-boat attack and seasickness.

Even after reaching port in Liverpool, England and stepping ashore, Frank felt like he was still rolling with the waves, and so did his stomach. He was sure that he lost fifteen pounds as a result of being unable to eat. There was no time to dwell on his persistent sickness; he had to report to his base of operations. Several deuce-and-a-half ton trucks were there to meet the arriving pilots and maintenance crews. It would be a long, slow drive to their airfield with nearly everyone continuing to feel a lingering seasickness. The term "getting one's sea legs" did not contain the same importance as "getting one's sea stomach" to Frank.

Upon arriving at their base near the sleepy village of Steeple Morden and forty miles north of London, the pilots reported to the commanding officer, Lt. Col. William Cummings. It was November 1943 and Lt. Col Cummings had been in command since November 1942. He was a seasoned, no nonsense, combat pilot, and he expected the same of the pilots under his command. Following introductions, the men were directed to stow their gear and report to briefing. Colonel Cummings wanted to make it clear to the pilots just what they were up against.

When Colonel Cummings walked into the briefing hut, everyone snapped to attention. He fired the message straight from the hip. Eighth Air Force, especially the bombers, was being slaughtered. Fighters were taking big losses, too.

"You new pilots," he began, "have been flying P-39s stateside. Well, you've been caught in the middle. You'll be transitioning to the Republic P-47 Thunderbolt. It's a beast of an airplane. It's pulled through the sky by a two thousand horsepower engine at better the 400 miles per hour. So, between now and the next mission I want you new men to spend every available hour familiarizing yourself with them. Additionally, depending on your ability to survive each mission, I expect you to continue to train until you become proficient. You have to be better than the competition. Check the board for your assigned aircraft number. One other thing, I am pairing up each one of you with a combat veteran. You can learn a lot from them; so follow their lead."

Frank did not have any previous experience with the Thunderbolt. His first meeting with the airplane left him awestruck. It was massive as single engine fighters go. The whole plane was built around its engine, the Pratt & Whitney R-2800 Double Wasp. It also swung a huge four-blade propeller.

Known affectionately as the Jug, due to its resemblance to an old-time milk bottle, the Thunderbolt had already earned a reputation for being tough. Republic built a winner. It could take all kinds of punishment and still complete its mission and deliver its pilot home safely. There were even reports that Thunderbolts safely returned from missions after having engine cylinders shot off. So, the combination of airframe and engine made it almost invincible.

While it could not turn with the more agile German fighters, it could surely out-dive them and out-roll them too. Just point the nose towards the ground and let her rip. The sheer mass and power of the airplane allowed it to accelerate away from its nearest competition. Therefore, it was best not to engage in a turning battle with the enemy. Rather, the accepted tactic was to make a sweeping pass and keep on going. Climbing was another story. There were times Frank thought he was going to have to get out and push. In any event, the airplane would come into its own as a premier ground attack platform.

Frank decided that Colonel Cummings' order to get as much time in the Thunderbolt as possible was a great idea. He always liked an excuse to fly, especially when it involved one of America's top fighters. He wanted to find out just what it could do. But he also had some trepidation stepping into such a high performance fighter without formal instruction.

Frank's early trials with the aircraft followed the usual protocol whenever a pilot began to fly any new aircraft. First, he read the pilot's operating handbook in order to understand the operational limitations. Once he was comfortable with all the documentation, he signed the plane out for his maiden flight in it.

Upon climbing into this monster, he sat there familiarizing himself with all the gauges, instruments, and controls. They were going to keep him busy. Unlike the P-39, the view over the P-47's nose was virtually nonexistent. Flying this airplane would be a whole new ballgame. It would not be for the faint of heart.

Once he was comfortable that he could find everything and operate the systems, he energized the starter. As he counted six propeller blades passing his sight he engaged the ignition switch and the engine came to life. The power and noise were overwhelming.

Taxiing away from the ramp he made sweeping S-turns so that he could check his route for obstructions. This was standard operating procedure for any long-nosed tail-dragger where forward view was limited.

As he did his pre-takeoff run up, he could feel the P-47 strain at the brakes. It wanted to fly. Could he handle all this power? There was only one way to find out the answer to that question.

Frank was understandably nervous. As he inched the throttle forward, he felt like he was getting a kick in the rear end. That Pratt &

Whitney engine really had some get up and go. He took off normally and climbed to altitude to find out how it handled before trying anything too demanding. On his first flight, Frank climbed to 10,000 feet and got used to the aircraft in various configurations—landing gear retracted then extended, then flaps retracted and extended, and combinations of the two. He tried assorted power settings and power on and power off stalls until he felt comfortable with the flying characteristics of his new mount.

Then Frank decided to put the airplane through its paces. He thought he would try something simple. So, he rolled the plane inverted to start a split-S maneuver. The next thing he knew the airspeed was winding up fast and the altitude was winding down even faster. He was committed to completing the maneuver. He pulled back the power and started to pull back hard on the control stick. The control stick was feeling stiff. He continued to pull. The g-force started to build. He could feel himself being squashed into the seat with almost unimaginable force. Yet, he continued to pull on the stick. Finally, the plane gradually recovered from the maneuver. In a few short seconds, although it seemed like minutes, he leveled at eight hundred feet. It was fortunate that he did not start the maneuver any lower, or his first flight in the Thunderbolt would have been his last. Frank had a new respect for this monster and, quite frankly, he had scared the heck out of himself. He was shaking like a leaf. He considered calling it quits, but knew he could not because to do so would have dire consequences of being known as a coward and a quitter.

By nurturing the airplane and proper planning, Frank found that he could do virtually any maneuver safely even at much lower altitudes. Frank continued to practice at every opportunity. He also arranged with some of the combat veterans to put him through the paces of mock aerial combat. Initially, he started these combat exercises against one foe. After becoming proficient he arranged to face two mock enemy aircraft because that is how real combat tends to occur. You find yourself on the tail of one adversary while his wingman sneaks up behind you and shoots you in the rear. Frank wanted to be ready for the reality of combat.

The Thunderbolt was an outstanding ground attack aircraft. Its heavy armor and eight Browning .50-caliber machine guns meant the airplane could withstand brutal punishment as well as deliver it. The strengths built into the airframe and armament naturally led to its use in ground attack missions. Thus, Frank and the other new pilots needed to master the art of ground level attacks.

Ground attacks were dangerous and scary. Operating within a few feet of the ground left very little room for error. Mistakes could lead to flaming crashes and no altitude for a safe bailout. Frank was justifiably frightened at those prospects. Yet, he would bite his lip and make his low level runs at the targets. It became easier with practice, but the risk was tremendous.

There was a lot of low level flying, and not exactly all of it was justified. Colonel Cummings received many a complaint from an irate farmer because his cows had gone dry as a result of loud, low, strafing passes over their pastures. Or, worse yet, one farmer's wife was terrified when a flight of Thunderbolts operating at near full throttle passed within feet of the family's privy, while his wife was in there.

Colonel Cummings did his best to appease the enraged townspeople, most of whom knew the purpose of such activities, by offering compensation for dry cows and abject apologies to the farmer's missus along with a promise to relocate the practice area. Finally, he issued an edict that any pilot identified as engaged in unauthorized maneuvers would be grounded. Further, he established strict practice areas well away from the township. Nevertheless, there were always some who tested the system, and those few suffered the wrath of Colonel Cummings. He was true to his word.

After several weeks in England, Frank received some troubling news. His brother Danny had been drafted. Eventually, he would wind up in the Pacific Theater of operation on a destroyer. His younger brother, Billy, was drafted a short time later. After technical training he became one of the revered aircraft mechanics. Frank wondered if his brother Billy would be assigned to his base, but no such luck. After completing his training at Chanute Field, Illinois, the Army Air Force saw fit to send him to Alaska to service aircraft guarding the Aleutians. He would be cold, but he would be safe.

At least there was some good news for Frank, a promotion to first lieutenant. Now he wasn't at the bottom of the barrel in the officer pool. He had yet to fly his first combat mission and he was getting antsy and also a bit nervous. However, there was no way to rush the winter weather. It was miserable. It was so bad that the seagulls were grounded, too.

Finally, after what seemed like weeks, his 355th Fighter Group got the go-ahead. It would be a mission to bomb submarine pens in France. High altitude bombing had been pretty dismal with little damage to the reinforced concrete dry docks. It was someone's idea to try lower level bombing to see if it would be more effective. At least they hoped it would be more accurate. Frank felt excited and sick at the same time. He would be wingman for veteran combat pilot Major Henry Corcoran with the 354th Fighter Squadron, callsign "Haywood."

As they walked to their planes, Major Corcoran reminded Frank of his duty to stick with him as his wingman and to watch their six o'clock for enemy planes sneaking in from the rear. Frank knew what he had to do. No matter what, he would not let Major Corcoran down.

Their flight was off the ground by 7:00 a.m. and they formed up with the remainder of the Fighter Group at 10,000 feet. This would not be a high altitude mission. It was a ground attack. In this case, the lower the better was ideal for added accuracy. Their Thunderbolts were loaded with two 1,000-pound bombs each.

Frank felt nervousness in his gut and he had a bitter taste in his mouth. This would be his first mission. He did not know if he was ready, if he would run if he came under attack, or if he could shoot and try to kill someone, even if it was the enemy who was trying to kill him. He just didn't know. During the entire cruise phase of the flight his mind kept returning to the fear that continued gnawing at him. His stomach became more unsettled. He thought he was going to be sick so he started to look for something in which he could vomit. He finally settled on his map case. But he managed to hold his composure and the contents of his stomach.

The flight across the Channel progressed rather quickly. Their target lay dead ahead. Then the attack began. Frank followed Major Corcoran down keeping on his tail for the bombing run. Heavy ground fire was coming up to meet them. They maintained their line to the target, not making so much as a flinch trying to avoid the fire-red, oncoming projectiles. Finally, they were over the target and dropped their load followed by a sharp climbing turn to the left.

Frank felt the shock wave from the first explosion. Then others followed quickly thereafter. They had done their job; it was time to return to base. They would not know until there were reconnaissance photos taken if they had had any effect on the submarine pens.

Then without much warning a call came over the radio.

"Bandits! Four o'clock high!"

There they were swooping down on them from above—about two dozen Messerschmitt Bf-109s. The Group began climbing for altitude in an attempt to negate the German's altitude advantage. As the German aircraft approached, the Allied flight turned headlong into them. Frank stayed just behind Major Corcoran's right wing. He was where he was supposed to be.

Before he knew what happened, the flight of Bf-109s went screaming by them firing their cannon and machine guns. Two Thunderbolts were hit and going down over the English Channel. If the pilots managed to bail out, then it would be a race to see who could recover them first, the Germans or the Allies. The Bf-109s, being smaller and more maneuverable and flown by some veterans who had seen aerial combat since the Spanish Civil War, could easily turn within a smaller radius than the huge Thunderbolt.

The whole sky seemed to be a massive disarray of action. Even so, Frank stayed with Major Corcoran. Eventually, Major Corcoran was able to position himself behind a Bf-109 and tried to line up for a shot. This being Frank's first combat experience, he was trying to catch up within his mind all of his training. Then he remembered. Cover your six. He looked over his shoulder first right, then left, and there it was. Another Bf-109 was bearing down on their flight from slightly above and behind. What could he do? He could not abandon Major Corcoran. Yet, he could not leave himself and Major Corcoran vulnerable to be shot down without a fight.

So, he yelled out over the radio, "Bandit six o'clock!"

He was terrified. He was right in the Bf-109's sights. Bullets whizzed by his plane. He froze for a second. A few more bullets whizzed by. Then just as quickly he snapped out of it.

His mind began processing the information faster than the speed of light. Taking quick action he quickly and adeptly pulled into a barrel roll. Up and over and behind the German he went. Before the German knew what happened, their positions were reversed. Frank was now on his tail and slightly above his prey. It all happened so fast that the

German had no time to take evasive action. Then Frank had one of his questions answered. Could he shoot down another airplane?

The answer, yes. He pressed the trigger on his control stick and peppered the Bf-109 along the left wing. With slight movement of his rudder pedals, he continued to hit the Bf-109 along its fuselage and across the right wing. The German had had enough, he was hitting the silk. It was over in a matter of seconds. In fact, it happened so fast that Frank never really lost his position in support of Major Corcoran who continued to pursue the other Bf-109. Unfortunately for Major Corcoran, the German pilot performed a quick reversal and beat his way out of there. So, he missed his opportunity for a kill.

The flight of Thunderbolts continued home. Frank survived his first combat, had his first kill, and realized that he could do this. But it bothered him that he had frozen for a moment. This was an entirely different game than what he had practiced back in the states or with his introduction to the Thunderbolt. There was shooting involved and he could get killed. Reality finally set in. Upon returning to base, he sat trembling in his cockpit for a while. It was uncontrollable and he could not seem to stop. So, he rolled back the canopy and started taking some deep breaths from his oxygen mask. After a few minutes he started to regain his composure. Then he climbed out of the cockpit and ran behind the nearest building where he proceeded to vomit his guts out. Is this what it would be like every time?

He would continue to be scared. There was not a mission where he would not experience fear. But what is courage? He reasoned it is not not being scared. It is overcoming your fear and going on with what needs to be done anyway. How would he continue to handle it?

During their interrogation by the intelligence officer, Major Corcoran complimented Frank on his actions. He commended Frank for his beautiful maneuver to gain an advantage on the German pilot. Frank felt that he just did what he was supposed to do, what he was trained to do. Major Corcoran was duly impressed, so much so that he recommended Frank for a citation. Subsequently, he was awarded a Bronze Star.

It was the job of the fighters to escort the bombers and protect them from enemy fighters. Sadly, however, the escort fighters of the day, the P-38 Lightning and the P-47 Thunderbolt were anything but fuel efficient. Their range was limited. The Germans knew this and planned their defensive action accordingly. As the escort fighters began running low on fuel and approaching the maximum outbound range they could see the German fighters circling in the distance. They looked like vultures ready to swoop on their victims. And swoop they would.

As the American fighters turned for home, they witnessed a heart-sickening display. They looked over their shoulders and felt helpless. They watched in horror as German fighters engulfed their prey and shot them out of the sky.

Even on the shorter missions over French soil, they could only help the bombers so much. As the bombers approached their target, the German fighters would swarm all over them. Then they would withdraw. As the bombers continued on their mission, they would be faced with flak. They looked like harmless puffs of black smoke, but they were full of insidious shards of metal meant to tear at the aluminum skin of aircraft and their crews. This also gave time for the enemy fighters to refuel and rearm and meet the bombers on the return flight. Obviously, it was much more expeditious to meet the bombers before they loosed their load, but there was no reason to allow them to return another day, either. The Allied fighters could help protect their bombers from enemy fighters, but they were helpless when it came to flak.

At least Frank could do everything in his power to knock down the Luftwaffe aircraft. And he excelled at that. Early in the war, the German Luftwaffe was comprised of aces who literally had a hundred victories versus the opposition. With air battles normally taking place over German occupied territories, even if they were shot down, they would parachute into "friendly" hands and be flying the next day. To the contrary, Allied pilots shot down could, at best, expect a long tenure in a prisoner of war camp. Some of these Luftwaffe pilots had been at it for years. So, they had refined their skills and knew how to best beat their adversaries.

There was one advantage U.S. pilots had. Generally, after a certain number of missions, usually 25 for bomber crews and 250 hours for fighter pilots, they would be sent home to train new pilots how to wage an effective air war against their foes. The tricks of the trade would be passed on to the next generation of fighter pilots. This was an extremely effective method that was deployed to its fullest potential. American pilots were the best trained pilots of the war. As the war progressed, however, the U.S. Army Air Force increased the number of missions or hours required to complete a tour of duty.

For Frank, missions continued off and on depending upon the weather. It is a common adage that *the war was long periods of boredom interspersed with occasional occurrences of sheer terror.* It was no different for Frank. Having seen the ability of the German pilots, Frank had no misgivings about their ability as fighter pilots. Often he wondered if he was operating outside his ability.

If there was one thing constantly eating away at his insides, then it was that he would fail to perform his duties as expected. He would wake up in the middle of the night with night terrors. The nightmares didn't repeat themselves. It seemed to be always something different, like a cockpit fire, or a wing being shot off, or being trapped and unable to bail out, or being out of position to help a comrade. Each time, just before his final demise, he would awaken soaked with sweat while shivering uncontrollably at the same time. His biggest fear was that he was a coward. He was tormented by this over and over, yet he went on.

For Frank it was not so much that fear set in during the course of the air battle, because he was far too busy to be afraid. Yet, he had almost paralyzing fear as he prepared for battle and flew into it. And surprisingly, it was on the journeys home that the full realization of what had just happened came into focus. It could have just as easily been him as the victim lest some minor change occurred during the battle. It was only then that stark terror hit him. Sometimes he felt sick to his stomach. Other times, he felt the shakes. The more missions he flew, the more he felt fear tearing out his insides. He was often sick to his stomach before each mission. Once, a fellow pilot saw him vomiting behind their barracks. Frank shrugged it off to something he ate. What Frank did not know was that other pilots were experiencing the same turmoil and each one was handling it differently.

Yes, Frank was well known back home for his derring-do. But those were all kid's stunts. The worst that would generally happen to him as the result of a mishap might be some bruising, bleeding, or a tanned rear end. This arena was different. Here a guy could get killed. Worse yet, he could get someone else killed if he froze at the wrong time or failed to do his job. Furthermore, since his boyhood friend, David Billings, lost his arm, he was never one to take unnecessary risks. That single event had a profound effect on his life.

He just could not make the fear go away. In some ways he was thankful because he rationalized that it gave him an edge over his foes by getting his adrenaline flowing. It was sometimes a miniscule advantage over one's adversary that meant the difference between life and death. Often it was nothing more than luck.

Perhaps it was the adrenaline pumped into his body by the fear that gave him an edge but, whatever it was, it was enough to sharpen his reflexes and focus his mind on whatever he was doing. Quite frankly, his skill with aerobatics and marksmanship set him apart from most other pilots. Sam Bullock's training back in Plymouth was serving him well.

It was especially during the longer missions when he felt fear creep its way into his mind. There was too much time to dwell on what could happen, but it also gave Frank time to formulate how to deal with almost any situation that would arise during combat.

If you talk to combat veterans, you get a general sense that the infantry soldier bemoaned his dismal conditions, particularly when on foreign soil. He had to live in filthy conditions while eating cold rations and seeing the killing up close and personal. To the contrary, the airman would do his business and be home to his bed later in the day while enjoying a hot meal. What is typically forgotten is the fact that while ground troops had to slog it out face-to-face with the enemy and lived in appalling conditions, they did not have to fight every day. Alternately, airmen could find themselves continuously in combat depending on the weather. So, there were advantages and disadvantages with each. Both groups suffered and both groups did their part to win the war and, frankly, there was respect one for the other.

As Frank's Thunderbolt rumbled along, his mind ran through various combat scenarios but, in the meantime he kept his head on a swivel and continued to seek the glint of sunlight reflecting off the surface of an enemy airplane in the distance, thus giving itself way. Then there it was—a flight of Bf-109s directly ahead of the bomber formation. But there was a bigger problem, another flight of FW-190s behind them and about 2,000 feet higher. Frank called his sighting over the radio. The Group commander directed them to climb and, if possible, get some altitude advantage over the FW-190s. Their first responsibility was to protect the bombers. The pilots of the Bf-109s planned to make a head on attack at maximum rate of closure and roll over to do a split-S, regain altitude and make subsequent attacks. Then the FW-190s would swoop in from above. It was up to the Thunderbolts to disrupt their plan. The Group commander ordered Major Corcoran to the 354th Squadron and head off the Bf-109s while he took the 357th and 358th Squadrons to meet the FW-190s head on.

It was a melee. Enemy aircraft darted in and out of the bomber formation. When a Bf-109 pulled up on the tail of a B-17 the tail gunner would holler over the intercom, "Bump!" With that the bomber pilot would make a quick movement of the control column forward or backward to throw off his adversary's aim. Sometimes it worked. Many times it didn't. The Thunderbolts did everything they could to disrupt the attack. It was all chaos. Frank stayed close with Major Corcoran. Tracers flew in every direction from friend and foe alike.

Then it happened. Major Corcoran was hit and it was bad. Flames were pouring out from his airplane's cowling, the canopy was shot to pieces, and a huge section of the horizontal stabilizer was shot away. He was going down. Frank followed hollering over the intercom for the Major to bail out, but there was no response. The flames continued to engulf the fuselage and then BANG! There was nothing but a hole in the sky where his plane had been.

What could Frank have done to prevent this? Probably not much as Major Corcoran had fallen victim from the friendly fire of a B-17's guns. Frank tried to regain his composure. Tears welled up in his eyes. He liked and respected Major Corcoran and now he was gone and Frank was on his own. This, in turn, lit a fire in his belly. In an instant he pulled up to get back into the fight. As anger raged within him he gave his plane full throttle and climbed back into the foray determined to seek retribution. Yes, his squadron mate was shot down by friendly fire, but he still blamed the enemy for it.

At that moment his anger overtook his fear. He hated not only the Nazis, but all Germans. He would make them pay dearly for this crime. He was determined to destroy the Luftwaffe single-handedly, and the Third Reich right along with it. While this new-found anger for the enemy helped him to compensate for his fear while engaged in the heat of battle, it continued to haunt him whenever he was not enrapt in battle.

Now he was alone, he was no longer a wingman. Yet, perhaps being on his own would work to his advantage. At least for the rest of this mission he could fly his own way and pick his own targets. That is what he did. He would pick out an enemy plane over which he knew he had the advantage due to his position. Then he would make a diving run at them anywhere from their four o'clock to eight o'clock position and blast away. He would roll and bank and climb to make sure no one was on his tail. Then he would do it again. He was a man possessed. He made three passes and shot down two Bf-109s and one FW-190. The enemy withdrew. Not a bad day. But it was a bad day. He had lost his leader and a man he respected.

He had intercepted direct attacks on a couple of disabled B-17s that would have been easy meat for the enemy planes had it not been for his actions. He purposely put himself in the line of fire by taking positions between the B-17s and the enemy fighters in order to protect the lumbering bombers. Now it was over and he was on his way back to base and had some time to try to calm his frayed nerves.

Back at base, Frank was devastated and depressed. This was the first loss of someone close to him. He had dined with Major Corcoran and, of course, had a close flying relationship with him. So, it hit him hard. But, at least something positive came out of this negative incident. Frank's prowess as a fighter pilot had not gone unnoticed. In fact, the B-17 crews had even shared their accounts of his actions and how he was their savior. As a result, his bravery in beating back the enemy was rewarded with a Distinguished Flying Cross (DFC). This was one of the most prestigious medals awarded by the United States. Frank was honored but continued to be saddened at Major Corcoran's loss.

Based on Frank's initiative and leadership, Colonel Cummings promoted him to Captain. He would now be a flight leader, and as luck would have it, Scotty Winslow would be his wingman. These two were so much alike that the pairing could not have been sweeter. They had been through flight training together and they had similar interests. Now they could keep an eye out for each other.

After a while, Frank started to work his way out of his depression. Perhaps it was the regular letters from Dottie that comforted him and lifted his spirits. Or maybe it was talking to the chaplain. Part of Frank's anxiety was not just the fact that he had lost someone close to him, but it was that he had killed and he was worried about the fate of his eternal soul. When he tried to sleep he would be overwhelmed and tormented by his thoughts. The chaplain was a kind, patient, and wise man of God. He told Frank that often the Sixth Commandment is misinterpreted. It does not say "Thou shalt not kill." It says "Thou shalt not murder." This helped Frank resolve his issues and go on from there.

Back home, Frank's parents followed any and all news related to the Eighth Air Force and, more specifically, the 355th Fighter Group. They constantly worried about and prayed for Frank's safety. They continued to hear reports about the devastating attrition rate of the bomber forces. Things were going badly. His father always tried to read the newspaper before his wife, just in case there was some bad news about Frank. In that way, he could filter and soften the news before his wife learned about it. His mother clipped every newspaper and magazine article about the air war that she could find. Much to her consternation, there was never any news about her beloved son. She did not know if this was good or bad.

Upon Frank's arrival overseas, Dottie had to deal with continuous bouts of insomnia. She tried to keep herself busy at the hospital and around the house in order to divert her attention to something other than Frank's hazardous duty. Sometimes it worked. Yet, often in the quiet of the evening she could not help but drift off to thoughts of him and his circumstances. Her deep love for him and separation caused her grief and tormented her innermost being throughout much of the war. Yet, she continued to write letters of encouragement to him almost daily.

Over the next few weeks, missions came and went. Sometimes they would be escort missions. Other times they would be ground attack missions. Frank preferred the escort missions where he could meet the enemy head on, but he accepted the need for ground attacks, too. Frank continued to grow his tally of victims steadily. He did not set out to kill. He merely wanted to destroy the plane not the pilot. But in the heat of combat you cannot be too selective. Things happen fast and events become a blur. At this point Frank already had eight kills marked under his canopy using the infamous swastika. They were all air-to-air kills. But he and his fellow pilots felt disheartened by the fact that they still could not escort the bombers on their long missions into Germany. That was about to change.

The bombers continued to take a pounding. Something needed to be done to protect them all the way to their targets deep within

Germany. Eventually, the Lightnings and Thunderbolts would be replaced by a radical new fighter which used aerodynamics as opposed to sheer power to create its high speed—the North American P-51 Mustang. Early on, the Mustang was used in Africa and Italy as a dive bomber. At that time it was designated as the A-36 Apache. It had a V-12 Allison engine which produced great low altitude performance, but lost power at altitude where most dogfights and escort missions took place. It was not until the British mated their superior Rolls Royce Merlin engine to the Mustang's airframe that the plane was converted into the famous thoroughbred as it is known today. The Mustang was fast and maneuverable. The P-51B/C had a radical laminar flow wing and plenty of firepower with four Browning .50-caliber machine guns. Most noteworthy, though, was its range. It consumed half the fuel of either the Lightning or Thunderbolt. Finally, the German fighters could be met head on, and they could escort the bombers all the way to Berlin. Yet, the 355th Group had to await delivery of the Mustang. For now, they would continue to use the venerable Thunderbolt with great effectiveness.

While he awaited arrival of the P-51, Frank set about designing his P-47's nose art. He settled on a swooping bald eagle holding a banner in its talons with his airplane's name, "Freedom Fighter." What better name could there possibly be than that? When the painting was completed by one of the talented members of his ground crew, his plane really stood out as a testament to what he believed his role was in this war.

Frank respected his ground crew. They were all a team. The crew chief was a Master Sergeant (MSgt) by the name of Bud Riley. He was a middle-aged man who was a career aircraft mechanic and who knew airplanes inside and out. He could fix anything and took great pride in his work. And he held all other members of the crew accountable for keeping the airplane operating at peak efficiency. You could tell a member of the ground crew from a few telltale signs. For example, there was always grime under their fingernails. Another sign were burned fingertips. In order to determine if all the cylinders were firing, it was faster to quickly touch the exhaust pipe of each cylinder. If it was hot it was firing properly; if not, then they would pull the spark plugs to clean, replace, or regap them. It was crude but quick and effective.

The flight crews took care of everything including engine and system overhauls, armament, fuel, oil, warm up, installation of film in the gun camera, and keeping the aircraft clean. They kept oleo struts inflated, checked tires and brakes, and hydraulics operating properly. They also repaired battle damage. Often they worked in the most appalling conditions throughout the night to have the aircraft ready for the next day's mission. There was a kindred spirit between the pilot and his ground crew. Frank appreciated every member of his ground crew and he knew that they prayed for his safe return on every mission. They were there to greet him every time he safely returned to base. Of course there was some friendly bantering between Frank and his crew chief. The chief would tell him to take care of HIS plane or not to come back. Frank would retort with, "What do you mean YOUR plane?"

The ground crew was proud of Frank. They knew that their work on his plane was not for naught. Frank put all of their hard work and dedication to good use. He made sure to acknowledge the efforts of his crew for contributing to a successful mission. They deserved it as did so many other ground crews throughout the war in all theaters of operation.

Frank was mutually as proud and respectful of his ground crew. Whenever he went into one of the nearby villages he would return with little treats for them. Sometimes it would be fresh fruit or pastries or little mementos. Whatever he did for them he never thought it was enough. These men with all their technical expertise deserved credit for keeping the armada flying and the pilots confident in the performance of their aircraft. Frank felt a close kindredship with these special men.

Based on his performance and leadership, Colonel Cummings felt it was time to give Frank even more responsibility and promoted him to the rank of Major. Frank would take over as squadron commander from Major Daniels, who had been severely wounded during a ground attack mission. His aircraft had been damaged by flak yet he still managed to get it back to base and do a belly landing. Major Daniels would be sent stateside to recover.

Frank took over the responsibility of leadership without hesitation. He instilled in his squadron an intense drive to be aggressive but not foolish. His main mantra was "protect the bombers" and only once they were safely on their way home would they look for targets of opportunity.

Chapter 7

Losses

Wars cannot be fought without losses. It may be easy to dissociate from losses that have no direct effect because there is no personal attachment. However, once they strike close to home in the form of a family member, friend, or close acquaintance, then it becomes significantly more meaningful and painful.

The loss of Major Corcoran was only the beginning of losses that Frank would experience. The worst was yet to come. Missions were frequent. Limited only by the weather, both over England and at the target, missions were planned at every available occasion. Pressure needed to continue to be applied on the enemy's resources. There was little opportunity for Frank to rest or to gather his composure. The combination of constant fear and being worn down by almost daily air battles were taking their toll on his health.

Quite often Frank found his squadron trying to defend bombers that were greatly outnumbered by enemy aircraft. They had a habit of attacking from any direction attempting to find weaknesses in the bombers' defensive formation. More often than not, the circling German buzzards remained just out of range of Allied fighters. This was often frustrating to the Allied pilots who wanted to help and were itchy for action.

Each time a B-17 Flying Fortress or B-24 Liberator went down the fate of ten lives was in question. Would they be killed, wounded, captured, or escape? Too many times the bomber would burst into flames and no parachutes spotted. Other times, one or two parachutes could be seen as crewmen made their escape from a spinning, flaming bomber. However, fighter pilots, like Frank, were too busy to know the exact fate of those pilots who landed safely on the ground. Normally, the only way to be certain was communication from the International Red Cross, who ensured that the Geneva Conventions were followed with respect to prisoners of war.

Missing air crews left a haunting question among their surviving crew and family members. Were they dead or alive? Not knowing the fate of a loved one meant many sleepless nights, worry, and years of speculation about what happened to them. This was especially true in the Pacific Theater where the Japanese did not adhere to the Geneva Conventions. There they committed heinous acts of cruelty and barbarism on prisoners-of war and the general populace..

All too often new pilots joining the Group thought they could win the war single-handedly. In their first role as wingmen it was their responsibility to cover their lead pilot as he pressed an attack. Although it was not widespread, some of these pilots were undisciplined and had the impression that they were hotshot pilots even before seeing their first combat. Considering the fact that most pilots were young, in their early 20s, this macho behavior was somewhat understandable. At that age, they saw themselves as invincible.

They would see a target in the distance that looked like easy prey. So, they would break out of formation and head for their first kill. No sooner would they tear into their opponent then the next thing they knew they heard the plinking of projectiles hitting their aluminum aircraft as cannon fire ripped through them. In a matter of seconds, it was all over. Unfortunately for them, they would be the kill. In their exuberance and inexperience they would forsake common sense.

From their years of combat experience, the Germans had developed superb attack tactics. They had the habit of sweeping into the bomber formation while firing their cannons. Then they would roll on their back and dive away in a split-S. This presented only a brief target for the bombers' gunners.

Firepower from Nazi aircraft could be devastating. The Bf-109 was mounted with a 30-millimeter cannon as well as two 13-millimeter machine guns, and the FW-190 sported a 20-millimeter cannon and two 13-millimeter machine guns. The fire rate of the cannon was slow compared to the Browning .50-caliber machine guns used on American fighters. But it hit with explosive force and a single hit could sever a wing spar. American fighters used an overwhelming spray of ammunition onto the target. For example, the P-47 boasted eight. With the later arrival of the P-51B/C, four .50-caliber machine guns were used. This was followed later with delivery of the P-51D with six .50-caliber machine guns.

American fighter plane designers and builders also took additional steps to protect pilots and planes. Armor plating was installed at critical places throughout the airplane like behind the pilot's seat, at the firewall, and elsewhere where there were critical components. Of course, the whole plane could not be armored like a tank due to weight restrictions. The windscreen was also built up with laminations producing a bullet-resistant shield in front of the cockpit. Another extraordinarily helpful protective feature was the self-sealing fuel tank.

Missions over France fell within the fighters' range. This meant that there was an opportunity to mix it up with the enemy. In any case, German pilots shot down over France could expect recovery from their own kind. Conversely, Allied pilots could expect capture and a long stay in a prisoner of war camp. Sometimes, if they were lucky, they would be rescued by the French Resistance. Even with that, there was no guarantee they could elude German patrols or that they would make it back to England.

On one mission over northern France, Frank watched a Thunderbolt pilot bail out after the outer ten feet of a wing was blown off. Frank saw him land safely on the ground. Then he saw several vehicles racing towards the downed pilot. He was destined to spend the remainder of the war in a prisoner of war camp. Frank decided to give him some help. So, he signaled Scotty of his intentions. They were going to break up the Nazi's party and help the pilot get some distance from them. The Germans never saw the P-47s coming up behind them. Frank and Scotty raked them with machine gun fire. They were stopped short in their tracks and tried to take cover. In the meantime, the downed pilot ran for a sunken road and made his way northwest along a hedge row. Frank and Scotty circled the area as long as they could but, eventually, had to leave as their fuel ran low. Frank never knew the outcome. The pilot could have made it back to friendly soil, or captured, or killed. Frank only knew he and Scotty did what they could to help.

During the running air battles over France, Frank saw many of his fellow pilots lost. Some bailed out; others did not. With aircraft coming from all directions midair collisions were common between friend and foe alike. During one such engagement two flights of Thunderbolts were each chasing a Bf-109. The Bf-109s crossed each other's path. The pilots of the four Thunderbolts were so locked onto their respective target that they did not see what was developing. A plane from one flight slammed into the two Thunderbolts in the other flight. Two of the planes disintegrated and the third plane spun through the clouds. Frank spotted the pilot jump clear and open his parachute.

Then Frank noticed one of those same Bf-109s starting to dive on the parachute. He had heard about this dastardly habit by some of the enemy. Now he was seeing it first hand. Rage took over. He skillfully rolled his plane and rushed to help his fallen comrade. His gigantic plane was accelerating fast. The German was closing on his target. Frank was still a distance off and was not within effective firing range. But he started firing anyway. He thought that he could drive the German off his intended target. Evidently, the German spotted him because he broke off the attack. Frank decided that he was not going to let this louse get away and do this to some other helpless Allied pilot. So, he used his momentum to climb to meet his adversary. He approached from the Bf-109's four o'clock position and began firing. He could see his rounds flashing off the Bf-109's aluminum wings and fuselage. The German pilot tried to evade the withering machine gun fire, but Frank stayed on his tail. The German rolled to dive away, and Frank followed. This German was doomed. Frank kept firing in short bursts and continued to get hits on the enemy plane.

Finally, the German decided he had had enough. He climbed to gain altitude, opened his canopy, and jumped. His parachute opened about six thousand feet above the ground.

Frank decided to make an impression on this pilot. As the German drifted downward, Frank banked into a gentle turn towards him. Frank constantly looked around to make sure no one was sneaking up on him. He lined up on his target. He had a perfect bead on him. As he approached the German at 350 miles per hour, he waggled his wings and pulled off to one side. Unlike the German, Frank could not bring himself to shoot at a helpless human being, regardless how vile the person. He wanted to put the fear of God into that pilot and cause him to think twice before he pulled the same stunt again.

Frank actually had some fleeting thoughts about shooting his adversary. Better yet, he thought about turning his parachute into Swiss cheese. That would give the German a little more time to consider what he had done as he plummeted to his death. After all, Frank hated Germans. But Frank was not the type of person who could kill someone in cold blood. Perhaps he would have responded differently if the German had been successful in his attack. If that had been the case, Frank was not so certain if he could have controlled his rage.

What Frank feared most was burns from a fire. He felt that being shot or caught in an explosion would be quick and relatively painless. But fire was another story. He had seen burned comrades and it was a horrible sight. That was not the end of it because they had to suffer through months of pain, recovery, and skin grafts. They would never look the same again regardless the skill of the surgeon.

Frank saw some pilots exit airplanes with engine and cockpit fires while they were too low to the ground, and the pilot knew it. But, rather than suffer through the intolerable flames, they jumped to their deaths anyway.

Frank even saw one pilot of a German aircraft jump from his burning aircraft and open his parachute only to see it aflame. Needless to say, he did not make a happy landing.

Bearing in mind his fear of being trapped in a burning aircraft, Frank even considered using the .45-caliber semi-automatic pistol that he carried to end his suffering quickly. However, he dismissed that option as he felt that it would be a grave sin to do so and it would be counter to his moral upbringing. He tried to put the thoughts of a flaming aircraft out of his mind.

In any event, Frank saw more of his comrades meet their end than he cared to remember. Many would be lost to ground fire. Most pilots felt helpless against ground fire. At least with air-to-air combat they could meet their foe plane-to-plane and pilot-to-pilot. To the contrary, ground fire was ubiquitous. Anti-aircraft guns were everywhere and they were devastating. Even the P-47 could take only so much. Ground fire during ground attacks was particularly dangerous because it gave little time and altitude to bail out of a damaged airplane. Too many times Frank saw pilots try to bail out of a burning airplane too close to the ground. They would jump clear, but their parachutes would not open fully.

Some of the most heart-wrenching losses occurred during landing accidents. If landing gear failed to extend, most adept pilots could make a safe belly landing. However, after extending the gear if one wheel lowered and the other did not that would create a problem, especially if the one good wheel could not be retracted. Now the pilot had to gingerly hold the wing with the bad gear off the ground until it no longer provided any lift. If he did not, then there was the potential for a catastrophic ground loop. Frank saw all too many airplanes cartwheeling or flipping wing over wing down the runway only to burst into flames.

The loss of hydraulic pressure could cause a number of problems, too. For example, flaps could not be lowered. This increased approach and landing speed. Couple this with damaged brakes and you compounded the problem because the combination of high speed and no stopping ability caused the runway ahead of the pilot to disappear quickly. Sometimes the only solution was to push the stick forward and nose the propeller into the ground using friction created by the dragging propeller to help stop the speeding and hulking airplane. This often led to disastrous consequences. If the propeller dug in too much, then the plane could nose onto its back, crushing the canopy and injuring or killing the pilot.

During one such incident, Frank was just preparing to land. He had done a low pass on the runway preparing to break into landing sequence. A P-47 was making its final approach with serious battle damage. As Frank was flying his downwind leg of the pattern he saw the P-47 touch down—fast. The runway was disappearing quickly and the P-47 was not slowing enough to stop before it reached the end of the runway. So, the pilot decided to nose his plane forward. The propeller jammed into the runway and jolted to a stop with the blades twisted like a licorice stick. All was going according to plan with the exception that the airplane was approaching a small berm at the end of the runway. As it hit, there was an explosion of dirt. The P-47 flipped forward and onto its back. Emergency crews rushed to the pilot's aid along with an auxiliary aircraft derrick. The overturned aircraft was covered with foam to prevent a fire, and the rescue crew set about trying to extract the injured pilot. Straps were place around one of the wings and the derrick lifted the wing to give the rescue crew access to the pilot. He was extracted and rushed to the infirmary. He survived, but would be paralyzed with a broken neck. Such was the legacy of war. Some scars would persist well after the war was long over.

In many cases, it would have been safer for the pilot to just bail out over the air base. But, they were dedicated airmen who wanted to return their aircraft to fly again another day. In some cases they just did not know what the extent of the damage was, but at least they would try to land.

Frequently, they would be lost as a result of accidents which Frank felt were inexcusable. Pilots were prohibited from doing victory rolls by the commanding officer. Still, some pulled the stunt without realizing that their controls had been damaged during combat. They could not predict that just at that moment a control cable would snap and they would instantaneously slam into the ground into a pillar of flames. It was needless and sad. They would experience a moment of elation in their victory celebration followed immediately by a split-second of terror.

Frank felt angry with them for allowing that to happen. They were good pilots who had survived combat, but died by doing something so foolish—good planes and good pilots wasted.

Consequently, the enemy continued to take an awful toll on Allied aircraft. Their pilots were excellent and ground batteries covered all airspace surrounding critical industries making them virtually impenetrable. If nothing could be done about ground fire at least something had to be done to mitigate the threat from Nazi aircraft.

At this point of his military career, Frank was thankful that he did not have the unpleasant job of writing to parents or wives about the loss of a loved one. How do you tell someone that the young man who was sent off to war will not be returning home? He wanted to make sure that he did his best to prevent his family and Dottie from receiving a similar letter.

He decided that he had to try to put his fear in the background, to look for an advantage in every attack, and to be aggressive. Now, if only the enemy would cooperate.

Chapter 8

The Big Day

It was February 22nd 1944. Frank had been on escort missions for each of the previous four days. He had mixed it up with a few planes here and there. But most of the time, as soon as his adversary was aware he was at a disadvantage, he quickly took evasive action and scooted out of the area. Frank got in a few shots, but other pilots were having more luck getting kills.

This particular day it was cold and clear; overall it was a beautiful winter day. It is one day that was part of what would be known as Big Week. And it would be a big day for Frank, too.

The flight proceeded normally towards the fighter's limit to deliver the bombers to central Germany. They would escort the mixture of B-17 and B-24 bombers to targets in Schweinfurt. The main target would be the ball bearing factories. Most war machines needed ball bearings for smooth operation. It was hoped that knocking out those factories would halt production of planes, tanks, and other vehicles.

The bombers flew at 20,000 feet using their standard box formation to obtain the best protection from their guns. The fighters crisscrossed about 5,000 feet above them. The contrails produced by their engines etched their paths in the frigid air. It was like a roadmap in the sky. It was beautiful, but also potentially deadly because it pointed the enemy aircraft gunners and interceptors directly where to find them. Yet, there was no way to prevent it.

They had one trick up their sleeve. Their course was set towards Berlin then diverted south at the last minute so as to throw off the Nazis. Hopefully, the ruse would delay the fighter attack and they could accomplish their task unmolested by them. They knew that they would still have to face the flak.

The flight droned along. The Group had already turned southwest towards its target. Frank was getting cold and stiff. He tried to stretch to loosen up and to get the blood flowing. Constantly he and his wingman weaved in and out above the bombers looking for the telltale signs of enemy aircraft. There was no sign of them. Perhaps the trick had worked.

The minutes ticked past. Frank's anxiety was building the closer he got to the target. They were approaching Schweinfurt. They could see the city through the industrial haze that hung over it. Then there was a puff of black smoke. A few seconds later the sky started to darken from puffs of black smoke. Flak!

There was nothing the fighters could do to combat flak or help the bombers. They were on their own. Rather than needlessly getting hit by flak, the fighters did all they could to avoid it by remaining at a higher altitude or exiting the area.

The bombers were on their bomb run to the target. There was no way they could take evasive action now. Each aircraft was under the direct control of their bombardier. He was flying the plane via the revolutionary Norden bomb sight. The flak was becoming more intense and concentrated. Gunners were zeroing in on their prey. Flak did not need to make a direct hit to cause damage or take down a whole bomber. The black smoke was just the ominous sign of what was to come, the shards of flying, hellacious metal tearing at metal and bodies. It would cut through the thin aluminum skin of the bombers, slice hydraulic, fuel, or oil lines, maim and kill crews, and take out control cables. The bombers were built tough, but they could only take so much.

Frank watched the battle unfold below him. It was all one-sided and he could do nothing to help. The first line of bombers was ready to drop its load and trailing flights would follow suit. They were getting pounded. Then away they went. The bombs started to rain down on Schweinfurt. Subsequent flights continued on their bomb runs. The flak continued to meet them with black puffs thickening in the sky and obscuring their view more and more.

A B-24 was hit right in the wing root and directly through a fuel tank. The wing erupted into flames and the whole left wing tore upwards away from the fuselage. The bomber swirled in a left-hand spiral as it plummeted to earth. The forces generated by the spiraling action literally pinned the crew within the aircraft and no one made it out.

Then another bomber was hit. Its outboard starboard propeller was sheared off, but it continued flying its bombing run. Still another bomber was hit. A large portion of horizontal stabilizer was gone. The crew struggled to maintain control. That could be a real problem if they made it as far as the trip home when they would likely be jumped by enemy fighters. Fighters, like birds of prey, would seek out damaged or straggling bombers.

Planes continued to be hit by the devastating barrage of flak. Another bomber, a B-17 began to lose control and start down. A control cable must have been cut or the flight crew disabled, but it was definitely on its way down. Frank observed dark specks exiting the bomb bay and out the hatches. Men were hitting the silk. At least they were getting out. *Thank God*, he thought.

After the bombers completed their attack they started a slow, wide turn to the north, then to the west heading for home. Their fighter escorts started to link up with them to await what was to come next— enemy fighters.

There was no way the Nazis were going to fly into their own flak. So, they waited patiently for the bombers to exit the area. They did not care so much about the Allied fighters. They were not the ones doing the damage. It was the bombers they wanted. Right now it did not matter to them that the bombers had already done their damage. Their goal was to prevent their return the next day.

All of a sudden the black puffs ceased. That was good news in the sense that the bombers no longer had to contend with it and wend their way through the murderous onslaught. But it also signaled that attacks from the enemy fighters were at hand. All eyes on the bombers and Allied fighters kept a close look out for them. Then there they were, a swarm of them. And in they came on their diving run.

The bombers started to make rapid climbs and descents within their individual formations in an attempt to throw off their foes' aim. They would "bump" up and "bump" down whenever the tail gunner alerted the pilot that he saw a fighter closing from the rear.

Now the Allied fighters could go to work. They moved in, as the Westerns say, "to head them off at the pass." Frank and his wingman, Scotty, worked as one. Being the lead, Frank was the primary shooter while Scotty protected his back side. Scotty was a dedicated and effective wingman. Frank respected Scotty, and vice versa.

Frank spotted a FW-190 lining up on a wounded B-24. Thinking he had some easy pickings, the German pilot closed in for the kill. Unfortunately for the German, he had developed tunnel vision. He was concentrating so intently on his prey that he forgot the first rule of a fighter pilot—keep your head on a swivel—look around. Hunter had become prey to Frank's guns. The FW-190 was torn to shreds—number one.

As the Nazi bailed out Frank could see him making what appeared to be an obscene gesture at him. The sky was full of fighters. Frank had his pick of targets. His next ones would be a pair of Bf-109s below and slightly to his left. He rolled his Thunderbolt to the left and started a shallow dive while trying to lead his targets. He swooped in above them while raking across them both with a dense peppering of projectiles. Using just short bursts from his eight .50-caliber machine guns, he demolished them both in short order—numbers two and three.

During the attack on the bombers Frank witnessed one of the most heart-wrenching sights of the war. It was during the heat of the air battle where the mix of Bf-109s and FW-190s filled the sky. Danger came from every angle. You not only had to worry about being shot down by the enemy, but if you crossed the guns of one of your own, you ran the risk of being hit by friendly fire. The air was so thick with airplanes that you also had to worry about airborne collisions. They were not at all uncommon, and one happened directly in front of him. While it rattled Frank a bit, at least it was two enemy aircraft.

Furthermore, you'd better keep turning and looking over your shoulder to make sure that the enemy didn't sneak up your tail and put some cannon fire through your rear end. Many American fighter pilots installed a mirror above their windshield to provide a little more protection from a rear attack. Situational awareness was critical if you wanted to survive such conditions.

With all the targets of opportunity, Frank couldn't help hitting something. He was having a field day. He made a broadside, diving attack on another Bf-109 and quickly dispatched it. The engine was on fire. He didn't have time to see if the pilot bailed out before he spotted his next target, still another Bf-109. Once he had shot down the previous Bf-109, he found himself in perfect position with a mildly climbing rear quarter shot. A short burst from his machine guns tore through the Messerschmitt's wing spar. When it separated from the fuselage the Bf-109 spun rapidly out of sight—numbers four and five.

As Frank scanned the sky, he observed two FW-190s causing a bit too much grief for a bomber crew. He gave his Pratt & Whitney engine full throttle and climbed to meet them head-on. As he did so, a few tracer bullets from the B-17 gunners whizzed by him. It was a little too close for comfort, but he pressed his attack. As he approached the altitude of the FW-190s, he dropped the Thunderbolt's nose and his gun sight fell on one of the FW-190s. As it did, he pulled the trigger and continued his turn into the next victim. He could see flashes as bullets penetrated virtually every inch of the FW-190. It must have looked hopeless to the FW-190 pilot because he jettisoned his canopy and quickly exited the cockpit. This was number six.

As he turned to chase the remaining FW-190, he looked up. Overhead was a stricken B-17. Its bomb bay was open and its left wing was on fire. He could clearly see through the open bomb bay and spotted a crew man reaching for his parachute. Just as the hand grasped the chute, the plane exploded into a ball of flames and debris. Frank had to rapidly maneuver to avoid flying projectiles of aluminum and other bits of shrapnel. He felt sick. But he could not let it get to him. There was still a battle all around him. He had more resolve than ever to beat back the Nazi horde.

He whipped the Thunderbolt on its back and pulled hard on the stick. His fighter accelerated to 450 miles per hour as he locked his eyes onto another target. The experience of the B-17 explosion pumped up his adrenaline. Frank could feel a sense of invincibility overtake him. He also felt more alert and his reflexes were keener, too. A flight of two FW-190s appeared dead ahead. He swung his plane right then left to get a better shot. As his Thunderbolt's nose passed the closer FW-190, he pulled the trigger and raked it with a steady stream of fire from his machine guns. He never let up his fire while continuing his turn onto the next FW-190. He could see hits all along the side of the fuselage. Pilots from both planes bailed out of what could have been flaming coffins. These were victims seven and eight.

His attention was next drawn to an air battle developing between another P-47 and FW-190. Only the Thunderbolt was on the receiving end. It was Scotty, he had gotten separated from Frank while trying to protect their flight from a rear attack and had gotten into trouble himself. Frank snapped his Thunderbolt into a steep turn and dive to help out his buddy. Scotty in his Thunderbolt was trying all of his tricks to shake the FW-190 off his tail, but this German was no novice. Frank just hoped he could close within firing range to drive the German flyer off. However, as Frank closed the gap and began to fire, his machine guns ran dry. He was out of ammo.

Frank couldn't relent on his pursuit. By now, the combatants were maneuvering at treetop level. There was no room for error at such a low altitude and high speed. Frank continued his pursuit. He closed on his target and from slightly above it. Shortly, he was directly above it and began to descend. He moved in closer and closer to the FW-190 until the German pilot, who had been locked onto his target, finally looked up and saw his predicament. The propeller from Frank's P-47 was inches from the FW-190's canopy. If the German tried to climb or turn, he would run into the spinning prop. He was sure to be sliced into mincemeat. He tried to slow down, but Frank quickly responded by retarding his throttle and dropping a notch of flaps. Now, the German couldn't accelerate or he would run into the propeller. His options were running out.

Frank decided upon a new tactic to end this dangerous stalemate quickly—one way or the other. He continued to inch his airplane's propeller closer and closer to his adversary's canopy while slowing his aircraft more and more. As he retarded the throttle towards idle, he lowered his flaps. Hopefully, his strategy would pay off. He was close to the ground and dangerously close to a stall while within inches of the FW-190's canopy.

Then he noticed what he was waiting for—the FW-190 started to buffet. With the quickening events, and a propeller spinning only inches from his head, the German pilot did not think to lower his flaps, too. There was no room to recover from a stall at this altitude. His only choice was to try to make a controlled crash landing and hope for the best. Frank kept inching his Thunderbolt closer and closer until the German finally relented. The FW-190 skidded a few hundred feet before coming to a stop with dust swirling all around it. As Frank applied full power, he climbed and banked the Thunderbolt while looking over his shoulder to see the wrecked German airplane with one of its wings separated from the fuselage. Frank thought to himself, *Thank God that's over!*

Surely the German felt the same way, too. Frank circled for a moment overhead and saw the German jump out of his twisted airplane. Once he cleared the aircraft he looked skyward and saluted Frank. This German was one of the chivalrous ilk who appreciated the skills of a better pilot. Frank made a low pass and waved his wings in response. Then he pulled up to rejoin the Group.

Frank was an ace in a day, eight planes shot down in one day plus another one without the benefit of machine guns. Scotty was certainly appreciative of Frank's efforts and unselfish act of heroism.

At this point, there wasn't much more he could do. The German fighters had to return to their airfields due to a lack of fuel. The bombers had completed their bombing run and were returning to their bases in England. Frank was out of ammo. So, he just climbed back to his cruise altitude. At least he could look threatening to any enemy daring enough to go at it again. However, at this point he was happy just to have some cover from the bombers' and Scotty's guns, should the need arise.

It was not just a good day for Frank. Eighth Air Force had done some real damage to their target and to Germany's fighter forces. It turned out to be not only a winning day but a truly successful week for the Eighth Air Force. The air campaign changed dramatically from that point forward. The Allies had won air superiority.

Now that he was cruising along in relative quiet, except for the beautiful rumble of the Pratt and Whitney engine, it finally hit him. His adrenaline level was approaching normal and he found himself trembling uncontrollably. His legs were shaking so much he had to take his feet off the rudder pedals. He thought to himself, *What in heaven's name just happened?* Frank just realized that what he had done could have turned out much differently had the German panicked and climbed into him. Frank threw up a simple praise, *Well, thank the good Lord that the German remained composed enough to make a rational decision about his options and not take me out in the process.*

With the aftermath of this lull period, fear struck him with a vengeance. So much so, that he could not wait to return to base before he felt so nauseated he could contain it no longer. Since his first bouts with vomiting Frank decided it would be prudent for him to carry something to contain it as opposed to his map case. He reached into his flight jacket and pulled out an airsickness bag just in time and let go. The whole cockpit reeked. Feeling sick from the smell, he wanted to throw the bag out but he could not do so because it would have smashed on the side of his plane. Worse yet, it could hit a propeller and obscure the view out the windshield of a trailing plane. So, he opened the air vent to let in some fresh air. He also cranked up the heater to compensate for the cold air rushing into the cockpit. It would still be cold, but at least the stench would be dispersed. He was starting to feel better.

Upon returning to base the ground crew was excited to see black powder smudges around the machine gun barrels. It was obvious evidence that the airplane in their charge had seen action. Not only had it seen action, but it had returned home safely.

During the debriefing Frank gave his account of the mission. In his usual, understated manner, he itemized the enemy aircraft that he encountered, the altitude and heading at which each one was met, and the outcome. He mentioned that he had shot down four Bf-109s and four FW-190s and managed to scare a FW-190 into crash landing. The debriefer was skeptical of his recollections. While impressive, it wasn't until other pilots were debriefed that the true magnitude of his mission came to light.

Scotty Winslow was interviewed and told the debriefer how Frank had blasted one enemy plane after the other out of the sky. Then he related how he himself had a FW-190 on his tail that he could not shake. Had it not been for Frank, he surely would have been lost.

Then it became time for intelligence to review Frank's gun camera footage. It was only after it was analyzed that they realized what an exceptional piece of flying took place during the air battle. The claims were true. This was no ordinary aerial confrontation. It was like highlights of aerial combat were spliced into a single film. Only they did not need to be spliced. They had all been shot from a single camera during one mission.

The sworn statements and gun camera footage were forwarded to General Ira Eaker's headquarters for review. Subsequently, the footage was rushed to the Pentagon. It would make excellent fodder for the public relations people. Within the month the film would be shown at theaters in newsreels all over the country. Nothing built a fire in the American public's mind than resounding victories over the Axis. Naturally, at the end of the newsreel there was the standard message, "Buy Bonds for Victory." There was an immediate spike in bond sales everywhere the newsreel was shown.

The order came down immediately that Frank had earned another Distinguished Service Cross as well as a Distinguished Flying Cross. He had earned a reputation as a formidable and skilled combat pilot. There was no one better. Yet, Frank had his own doubts about his courage as fear constantly tried to subvert him. He was confused about his own feelings. So long as he could disconnect from his fear during combat by substituting anger, then he would be okay. He certainly possessed the skill. Now, it was a matter of winning the battle against fear within himself.

Frank was beginning to feel the onset of nervous exhaustion. He had been flying missions almost daily for the last month. He faced death on more of those days than he cared to remember. Thinking back to his early days of flight training, he pondered Sam Bullock's words. When Frank asked him about how much combat he had seen during World War I, Sam's response was, "More than I wanted." Frank knew now what Sam meant. He, too, had seen more than enough.

The next day, the mission was cancelled due to fog and rain over his base. It was a welcome respite and allowed Frank to get himself rested and more composed. But the following day it was another mission as usual. Combat can be feast or famine. This time it was feast depending on your point of view. Frank saw a few enemy aircraft ahead of the bomber flight, but by the time he got there they had already been dispersed by other fighters. To him, it was like a feast for not being placed directly in harm's way. It would be like this for the next few missions. He needed a rest anyway.

The problem was the fact that he never knew what to expect. One day it would seem to be shaping up like a routine, low demand mission and all hell would break loose. Other days he would enter enemy territory expecting the worst, and nothing would happen. That in itself caused extreme anxiety.

Chapter 9

Between the Action

Although the intensity of aerial combat could be overwhelming, at least there were some periods of respite. Whenever the weather forecast over bombing targets indicated obscure conditions, missions would be scrubbed. The English weather, mainly the fog, caused the cancellation of many a mission. There was always the danger of aircraft colliding with one another during their climb out, even though each aircraft would take a slightly different heading to avoid such collisions. It happened all too often.

While many of his fellow pilots engaged in regular poker games, crap shooting, or general raucousness to release pent up tension, Frank tended to use his time more constructively. He liked to walk around the base and photograph scenes from everyday life. Not only did he create quite an album of normal daily activities, but also of the nose art from the Group's aircraft. The nose art ranged from cartoon characters like Donald Duck and Bugs Bunny, names of girlfriends, wives' names, obscure idioms, and even extended to the unquestionably obscene. Innumerable pieces of artwork had to be censored prior to the aircrafts' return to the states and civilization. You had to wonder if any of the pilots with this artistic expression could ever show pictures of their wartime steed to their parents or girls, or would they have been too embarrassed?

Frank continued to use the screaming eagle with the "Freedom Fighter" emblem on all of his personal planes. He would never be embarrassed for its message. Meanwhile, the Group was transitioning from the P-47 Thunderbolt to the P-51B/C Mustang. Now they would have the longer legs needed to make it to Berlin and back. As soon as he received his new plane, he had an artist on his ground crew copy his "Freedom Fighter" moniker to it, too.

Frank was also a voracious reader. He had his parents mail books to him from time to time. Whenever he went to town, he would stop by the little bookstore below a row of apartment flats. Sometimes he would leave with four or five books. He particularly liked to read stories that allowed himself some sort of escapism, like *Robinson Crusoe* or *Treasure Island*. Often, he would buy a travelogue about some exotic island—anything to take his mind off the war and his almost daily brushes with death. He thought about the possibility of settling in such serene surroundings after the war. But he would come back to earth and realize it was a pie-in-the-sky dream. After all, what would he do— paddle an outrigger canoe in the pursuit of fish, dance to the beat of war drums in a grass skirt, or just lie on the beach drinking coconut milk? Reality would kick in. He needed to earn a living and eventually support a family. Nonetheless the diversions were therapeutic.

The base also had an officers' club. It was the standard hangout when they could not get a pass to go into town. Frank really disliked how some of the men became so belligerent after a few drinks, or how others just drank until they collapsed in a drunken stupor. He felt that many of them were just trying to stave off depression or fear. But who was he to tell them how to behave? So long as it did not affect their missions he felt he had no right to confront them about their behavior— except once.

Frank and Scotty were known as teetotalers among their group. Occasionally, it led to some friendly ribbing from their fellow pilots. They took it in stride. However, a situation developed when a newly assigned pilot was being harassed by a First Lieutenant who was really laying into the youngster about his manhood because he did not drink. He kept goading the young pilot to take a drink and the youngster kept refusing. Finally, it escalated to the point that the Lieutenant said in a drunken slur, "Well, little boy, if you ain't gonna drink it, you can wear it."

With that he threw a beer on the pilot's uniform. A Major in the officers' club said and did nothing to intercede on the escalating situation. Frank had seen enough. He would not allow this demeaning behavior to continue unchecked. He jumped up and grabbed the Lieutenant by the lapel and pulled him into his face. He ordered the Lieutenant to snap to attention. The Lieutenant stood as best he could, but he was so unsteady that he looked like a willow swaying in a stiff breeze. Frank got right in his face and told the Lieutenant to apologize to the young pilot and, furthermore, to pay him to have his uniform cleaned.

The Lieutenant started to get surly. He said he would not apologize; he was just having some fun. And he certainly would not pay to have the pilot's uniform cleaned. Frank said he had two choices. He could do as ordered, or he would be sent to the guardhouse under arrest for insubordination. Perhaps the Lieutenant did not think he had anything to lose at this point. As Frank turned away, he caught sight of a fist out of the corner of his eye. By sheer reflex he dodged it, while tossing the drunken Lieutenant to the floor through a crash of tables and chairs. The Lieutenant was out cold.

Frank ordered a couple of the Lieutenant's drinking buddies to take him back to his quarters to sleep it off. It did not end there. Early the next morning Frank ordered the hapless Lieutenant to stand before the base commander to face the consequences of his actions. As he stood there, he fought back the urge to be sick from a major hangover. In the end, he was sent to the guardhouse for ten days, ordered to pay his victim's dry cleaning costs, and demoted to Second Lieutenant. Upon his release from the guardhouse, he was transferred to another Group.

Times at the officers' club did not regularly turn violent. Usually, it was one time where the men could let off a little steam by telling stories about home, romantic exploits, and jokes. As would be expected, most of the jokes were off color or about the "Japs" or the "Krauts." As off-color as they may have been, they were funny. It was a chance to have a hearty laugh amidst the dark days of war.

One of the men must have had a joke book because he always seemed to have a funny story. Not everyone can tell a joke to great effect, but he could. He would act it out, contort his face, and use voice inflections to make his tales entertaining and hysterical. This guy had a future in comedy, so long as he survived the war.

Other activities included darts, horseshoes, and pool. There would always be some betting associated with these games. Periodically, a new pilot would join the Group who would be challenged to a game of pool. Invariably, they would be beaten—at least the first few games. Then, once the bet had grown to be worthwhile, they would literally mop the floor with the competition. Some of those guys were so good they must have grown up in a pool hall. You could never tell by looking at them who could be a ringer. You had to keep a watchful eye especially for the guy with the baby face. They were the most dangerous when it came to playing someone for a sucker because no one suspected them of being such skillful players.

Sometimes the men would gather to pitch horseshoes during their leisure time. Usually, the players would bet a few dollars or a pack of cigarettes on the outcome of the game. Several of the men were real professionals at it. They became so adept at cleaning out the competition's pockets that eventually everyone became wise and refused to play against them. So, it became a common rule to require them to pair up with another player so that everyone would have a fair chance.

Frank did not believe in gambling, not necessarily for religious reasons, but because it was an irresponsible use of his money. Therefore, he usually waited until the horseshoe court was clear. Scotty and Frank would play each other for nothing more than a leisurely game and some healthy competition.

Whenever he had a break Frank usually spent the early evening hours nearly every day writing letters home to Dottie and his family. He tended to write mostly about his visits to historical sites in London and the surrounding countryside. Dottie wrote regularly, too. She was continuously worried about his safety and their future. This was another reason Frank said little about his missions, to protect her from the true horror of war.

At least servicemen stationed in England had it better than the foot soldiers who often found themselves sleeping in a mud hole or cutting a slit trench out of frozen ground like those in the Italian campaign. There were also hot meals that didn't come out of a can. And there was London. Even though it was a city under siege, later from buzz bomb attacks, London was still a city of life. There was entertainment and shopping. There was a pub on every corner. It was a chance to escape from the terror of war.

Visits to museums, like the famed British Museum, weren't all that exciting to him because most of the valuable collections he had read about in college had been moved to protective vaults and underground storage to safeguard them from bombing. Still, there was a lot of history associated with the city. He made sure to visit the Tower of London, Westminster Abbey, Big Ben, Trafalgar Square, and Saint Paul's Cathedral. It was also nice just walking along the streets among so many old buildings. Unfortunately, he saw far too much devastation, too. Earlier attacks by German bombs had wreaked havoc within the ancient city.

There were also occasional USO shows and social gatherings. He remembered once following D-Day that Bob Hope brought his entourage to the base and they had a wonderful time, with the exception that concurrently a German V-1 buzz bomb was heard overhead. As long as you could hear it, you were okay. But once the engine cut out, down it would come. At this particular time, anti-aircraft artillery brought it down harmlessly. Everyone cheered. They were small and fast and difficult to hit. So, the gunnery crews did a great job. The show went on without a hitch after that. It was an enjoyable time and great escapism from the war.

As a Major, Frank had certain privileges, such as being able to requisition a car to go to town. But that didn't mean he had *carte blanche*. After all there were a lot of other officers who outranked him but, at least, he wasn't a lowly lieutenant. Normally, he could find four or five other officers who were ready to go to town to blow off some steam, or just get away from the airfield.

Sometimes, he just wanted to escape to someplace quiet. One of the men in his squadron, Jack Leslie, studied archeology at Harvard University. So, one day he and Frank drove up to Stonehenge. It was eerie and impressive and one heck of a big calendar. Jack explained that it was built by the Druids, whoever they were? They had moved the stones from other locations. At the time they didn't know where. Only a few others were visiting and the quiet was deafening. It was nice to separate himself from the roar of an engine or the noise of London. The air was crisp and clean and the countryside beautiful. The history lesson was over and it was time to head back to base.

He acted like a regular tourist snapping photos and visiting every site popular with the tourists. He liked to walk alone along the Thames. Sometimes Scotty would join him and they would talk about their futures. They talked about their plans after the war as though there was no possibility they would be marred by injury or death. Rarely did they discuss their missions. It was time to feel free of the bonds of the war.

Often Frank would take the opportunity to catch up on some sleep. During his quiet times he would reminisce about his childhood and teen years. Those were fairly carefree times. He reflected on his special times with friends and, particularly, those times with Dottie.

On this day he harkened back to one of his family summers on the Cape. His father had just bought a piece of waterfront property in Dennisport about a year into the Great Depression. His rental properties were doing well. So, he decided that he could not lose money by investing in property right on the beach. He would move the family to the beach house as soon as the boys were out of school for the summer. They would stay there until the Labor Day weekend and he would commute back there each weekend after completing his work week at the power plant. During the week he would stay in the family home in South Weymouth.

He continued to recollect that this was child's heaven. Frank and his brothers had miles of beaches and inlets to explore along with picturesque salt marshes. Waterfowl thrived in the environment. He liked to relax on the deck or down at the beach just watching the seabirds fly overhead. It was fascinating how they used the wind currents with little or no effort. He would be held spellbound for what seemed like hours.

It was also nice to enjoy the cooling breezes from the salt air while everyone inland was sweltering during the hot, humid nights. Frank wondered why he constantly returned to this scene in his life. But as he analyzed it, he came to the conclusion that it was exotic, carefree, and restful. What better scene to recall.

When the opportunity presented itself he also enjoyed escaping to the surrounding English countryside and little villages. Sometimes he just wanted to be alone, but he also enjoyed the company of Scotty. They liked to hit the local pubs. Neither drank, but they enjoyed socializing with the local citizenry and some of the food. For example, Frank could not bring himself to try steak and kidney pie. However, he liked fish and chips. Food was generally better than at the base.

Sometimes the local girls would come into the pubs and try to flirt with them in the hopes of getting U.S. servicemen to buy them drinks or give them chocolate, cigarettes, or nylons. But Frank and

Scotty were dedicated to their girls back home. They had no intention of taking up an affair. Usually after eating they would engage in a dart throwing contest with the locals. There was always some friendly betting. The old timers were good, but not quite as accurate as Frank and Scotty. If Frank or Scotty lost, then they would buy a round of ale although they never drank themselves. If they won, then the locals would buy them each a couple of root beers.

Several times Frank was invited into English homes for Sunday dinner. The English people had been asked to reach out to American servicemen to help them feel more at home and welcome. Unfortunately, there were those British servicemen who disdained the Americans because they always seemed to be on the prowl for English maidens. After all, they looked very smart in their uniforms and they were paid better than their British counterparts. It was often reported that the British servicemen disliked the Americans because they were "over-paid, over-sexed, and over here."

Frank also enjoyed the English custom of high tea. The pilots at Steeple Morden were invited to a local estate for tea. The owner, Earl Dennis Balfour, a stylish man in his mid-sixties, wanted to show his appreciation to them for helping his country fight back the Prussian horde. The estate was enormous. It must have been 2,000 acres of well manicured gardens and lawns. It looked like a picture postcard.

When they arrived they were greeted by a butler who took their caps and showed them to the sitting room. Frank could hear music being played in the adjoining parlor. There was a string quartet playing the classics. Floors were lined with ornate marble and the walls consisted of fine, highly polished woods. Nearly every square foot of space was filled with any number of rare antiques and the walls were covered with tapestries and paintings. It looked like a museum.

Frank walked around the room and hallway imbibing all the spectacular works of art as he considered the lavish surroundings. He thought about all the excess and how all this extravagant display ought to be in a museum where everyone could enjoy it and share in the experience.

Then the butler came to the room's entry and announced that tea was served. The men did not know what to expect. Upon entering the parlor, some men stood while others took chairs. The Earl's staff delivered trays of tea pots and cups and others containing absolutely fabulous displays of pastries, finger sandwiches, and *petit fours*. This was living and Frank could easily adjust to this lifestyle. He had not felt more relaxed in ages. In fact, he was so comfortable that he almost fell asleep in one of the overstuffed chairs.

The Earl was very interested in learning about each and every pilot's life back home, what they did for work, and what their plans were when they returned. He was a great, caring gentleman. The men were truly appreciative of what he did for them by giving them this little respite from the dirty work of war. The men were reluctant to leave, but they knew they must. They all gave a hearty thanks to the Earl as they left, but the Earl felt heartsick because he knew that many of his guests would not make it home to fulfill their hopes and dreams.

Upon his return to base, Frank reflected on the wonderful, relaxing day he had enjoying high tea. While in this reflective mood, he decided to write a letter to Dottie.

Frank never wrote about his missions. The censors would have made mincemeat out of his letter had he done so. Instead, he wrote about his visits to town or the countryside. Dottie was probably getting the impression that he was a constant tourist. But Frank could not bother her with his troubles. And she certainly would not understand his anxiety, depression, and terror. Therefore, he always tried to cast a positive light in his letters to her.

Such were his letters —

My Dearest Dottie,

It was a miserable, bone-chilling, foggy day. Yet, it turned into an absolutely wonderful day because of the excellent comradeship of my fellow pilots. It was a day of total relaxation. We all visited a spectacular estate owned by Earl Dennis Balfour. He truly represents a prime example of an English gentleman.

The estate is enormous. The gardens are spread throughout the property and you would not believe the splashes of color from the spring blossoms. I wish you were here to share this with me. The gurgling from the fountains and many brooks reminds me of the waves lapping on the seashore of Plymouth back home.

We were catered with every manner of pastry and sweet and, of course, English tea. It was all very proper. We were made to feel like royalty. I guess that the English really appreciate the help we are trying to give them in the form of equipment and men.

I am back at the base now. Tomorrow I begin anew with the mundane tasks of military life. I have done a fair amount of flying; so much so as to make me feel a little fatigued. This day of rest and relaxation was more than welcome. Aside from that, I am happy and healthy.

Well, I must hit the sack as I will probably do a little flying tomorrow. I'll have to wait and see what the weather looks like.

You are constantly in my thoughts and prayers and you have all my love and devotion.

Your Adoring Admirer,

Frank

He hoped the upbeat tone of his letters would help Dottie and his family not to worry. There was no reason to let them know of the almost constant danger. Each time he went on a mission, there was a risk of being wounded, maimed for life, killed, or captured. He knew that he had been fortunate up to that point. Yet, with all the pilots around him who had suffered their fates, he came to the sad realization that he was flying on borrowed time. But, he was also determined to take some control of his destiny. He reminded himself to remain alert and aggressive.

Whenever the pilots rested in their barracks they listened to records playing hits of the era. There was one musical standard in particular that always caused Frank to hearken back to thoughts about Dottie—it was the strains of *Don't Sit Under the Apple Tree*. Assuredly it was also the one song that evoked a similar reaction in every soldier with a girl back home, faithful or otherwise. Undoubtedly, whenever Dottie heard that song, her thoughts extended to Frank, too.

Unknown to him there were some really big life events awaiting him in the near future and they would test his innermost self-confidence.

Although he was praying for his family back home, he hoped they were praying for him, too.

Chapter 10

D-Day

Beginning about the third week in May, the air bases and other military installations around England were locked down. No one could enter or leave unless they had specific orders to do so. Quite frankly, it took an act of God to make that happen. Missions continued to be flown. They covered a wide array of targets throughout northwestern Europe. The Allies did not want to give away their intended target for the impending invasion. It seemed to all the men, Frank included, that the lockdown was just going on and on. But, the weather and tides were not cooperating.

With the way things were going, it would be autumn before the invasion would be mounted. There was no way to keep it secret that long. Chances would need to be taken by Allied Supreme Headquarters.

With all the safeguards put in place by Field Marshall Erwin Rommel along the Atlantic Wall, the Allies wanted to attack while the tide was low. According to the invasion planners, it would mean a more murderous run by the infantry up an open beach, but the alternative of running a landing craft atop a mined beach defense more than compensated for the risk. Besides, with all the preliminary bombing by Allied bombers, there should be innumerable craters in which the liberating soldiers could seek refuge from a rain of machine gun fire, mortar shells, and artillery. It was also believed that strong-points would be blasted to oblivion by the Allied bombers, too.

It would be learned as the invasion began, however, that the strong-points were more reinforced than originally believed and bombing accuracy had been so abysmal that most of them hit too far inland to be of any use for cover on the beach. The invading soldiers would be easy targets for the waiting Germans, especially on Omaha Beach.

Frank's missions leading up to D-Day included bombing missions and attacks on airfields. He also searched for any other targets of opportunity. This was not so easy. German artillery and tanks were well camouflaged. He and his fellow pilots looked for any sign of movement among the hedge rows. They also tried to spot the glimmer off a piece of metal that might give away a position. But it was nearly impossible to spot the German positions if they did not want to be seen.

Sometimes, intelligence information gleaned from the French Resistance helped with mission planning. Their on-the-ground surveillance helped to pinpoint the best targets. Sometimes, fighters would use that information to blast a clump of trees only to flush out return fire from a hidden cluster of tanks or artillery position.

Multiple sorties were flown daily due to their close proximity of the targets to fighter and bomber bases. They would make their runs to the targets, drop their load of bombs, empty their machine guns, and return to base within the hour. Ground crews were being run ragged. They had to prepare aircraft for the next mission as quickly as possible, and it was around the clock. Planes needed to be refueled and rearmed. Gun cameras had to be loaded with fresh film. Windshields needed to be cleaned. Sometimes minor engine service was required, like spark plug replacement. There were even quick repairs made as a result of battle damage. Although ground crews were safely ensconced in England, they were instrumental in supporting the overall effort for the invasion of Europe.

During this period, there were only occasional encounters between Allied and Axis aircraft. The slaughter of Nazi planes during Big Week and subsequent attacks on airfields had effectively cleared the skies of them for this all-important invasion.

This went on day after day as weather permitted. Frank thought that the Germans had to be completely confused about the primary target. Air missions were striking everywhere, including Normandy and Pas-de-Calais. Supreme Command did not want to give away Normandy as the point of invasion by omitting it from the list of targets. Some smart intelligence officer in the German High Command surely would have figured it out then.

Sometimes Frank felt like he was dropping bombs just so he would not have to return to base with them. Occasionally, he would hit something. For all he knew he was destroying nothing more than chicken coops or outhouses.

Finally, the long-awaited day arrived, June 6, 1944. Frank's Fighter Group would be flying cover missions looking for enemy movements towards the beaches of Normandy as well as enemy aircraft. His plane was loaded with two 500-pound bombs and the normal complement of .50-caliber ammunition. He would go in, make his attack, and head back to base to rearm and refuel. This went on all day. As the ground forces were trying to break their way past the beach defenses, the fighters and bombers did their best to hold back a possible counterattack. There were points all along the front that they attacked throughout the day.

Specifically, they were looking for tanks and artillery pieces. But they shot at anything that looked like a German defensive position or vehicle. The big prize, however, was the tanks. The ideal way to attack a column of tanks was to knock out the lead and trailing tanks. Then you could take your time picking off the ones in between them. This was especially potent on the narrow roadways considering the Germans had flooded much of the surrounding areas. They essentially hurt their own ability to maneuver out of such situations as a result of this tactic. Except for some minor skirmishes, the airplane-versus-tank battles were few and far between.

Frank concentrated on sporadic targets. He hit what appeared to be a matériel storage depot outside St. Lo where he dropped his bombs and strafed the area. A few vehicles caught fire but nothing blew up. So, he returned to base for another load of armament.

Dottie awoke on the morning of June 6th to the news of the invasion. As she sat at her kitchen table drinking a cup of coffee looking out her back window at the freshly bloomed roses, terror started to overtake her. It was a beautiful day, but her thoughts and prayers extended to not only Frank, but to every young man participating in the invasion. She wondered what trials and tribulations they would face. She knew within her being that the enemy would do everything within their power to repel the invasion forces. Frank had said nothing to her about the impending invasion; so, this was a complete surprise as it was meant to be.

She remained glued to the radio and called Frank's parents to see if they had any news about him. They had not heard a word from him or about him in the last two weeks. Dottie immediately began to compose a letter to Frank pleading with him to let her know what was happening and how he was doing. She knew that he was restricted concerning the information he could share about the invasion, but she just wanted some consolation from the love of her life.

Frank's parents were equally as worried. They spent the day listening intently to the radio and the continuous news flashes about the invasion's progress. It was like torture awaiting the final result. There were no guarantees that the invasion would succeed. They, too, worried about their son's fate as they thought that the Germans would throw every available airplane against them. And Frank would be in the middle of it all. They all waited anxiously for the outcome, and each of their silent prayers was not so silent anymore. None of them would sleep well that night.

On other flights he, along with Scotty on his wing, would come in low and fast skimming along the tree tops and hoping to spot targets below the trees' canopy. If they espied anything questionable they would fire a few machine gun rounds hoping to stir the pot a little and evoke a response.

Twice it produced a retaliatory retort. The first involved a German half-track. Once Frank and Scotty confirmed their target they blasted it to pieces. The second one was almost a tragedy. As fate would have it, they started firing on a hidden position where they noticed some movement.

Then they noticed a soldier run into the clearing waving his arms wildly at them. They were firing on members of the U.S. 82nd Airborne Division who had parachuted behind enemy lines early that night. Fortunately, no one was hit. So, Frank and Scotty waggled their wings to let the frantic paratroopers know they understood they were friends. Frank and Scotty swept the area around the 82nd to ensure there were no lingering enemy positions nearby to cause them trouble.

In the process, they spotted the flashes created by an artillery emplacement. They turned to make their attack. As they did, Frank noticed what looked like brilliant red balls coming at him. It was tracers from ground fire. Frank and Scotty opened up on the source of the fire and the artillery piece. As they passed the target both planes dropped their bombs. It was a direct hit. Frank looked over his shoulder and saw the big gun propelled into the air.

Then there was a call over the radio. It was Scotty.

"I've been hit! My coolant temperature is rising. It's the radiator."

It would not be long before his engine overheated and seized. Frank directed Scotty to climb and head for the coast. Frank could see glycol coolant flowing from a large hole below the Mustang's ram air scoop which housed the radiator. Frank did not know if Scotty could make it all the way back to mainland England, but at least they would try.

Frank took up position behind Scotty as his wingman so that he could keep an eye on him. The coolant temperature continued to rise. He could see the coolant continue to stream out below the belly scoop. They both feared that the Mustang had no chance of making it across the Channel. So Frank asked Scotty if he preferred to bail out or ditch his plane. Once the decision was made, the plan was to do so as close as possible to a nearby Allied ship thus expediting his recovery.

Scotty decided to ditch because he worried about getting pulled under the surface of the water by the parachute. He knew that he had only about three seconds to get out of his plane before it sank in the English Channel. No sooner had Scotty made his choice, then the engine quit. He was almost over Omaha Beach. He was not about to attempt a crash landing on Omaha Beach as he would find himself in a murderous crossfire. Therefore, he set up for best glide speed and headed down to the water. He picked out a likely ship nearby, but he wanted to be sure that he was not placing himself between any of the ships firing on enemy emplacements on the beach and inland targets.

Once he found a likely candidate, he began spiraling and checking the wind direction by looking at the telltale signs on the surface of the water. He lined up into the wind, dropped his flaps, tightened his safety harness, and slid back his canopy. Before hitting the water just above stall speed, he kicked in left rudder and lowered the left wing to cause his airplane to skid on the surface. He did not want to land straight ahead as that could cause him to nose over and be trapped in the cockpit under water.

As soon as he hit the water, Frank saw water spray up all around it. Scotty immediately jumped out of the cockpit and onto the wing and slid into the water and inflated his life raft and Mae West life preserver. In a matter of a few seconds his airplane was headed to the bottom of the Channel. Frank circled overhead to make sure his comrade was safe. One of the small ships must have noticed that Scotty was in trouble because it launched a small boat to retrieve him. Scotty was wet and cold, but safe. Frank was elated that his best friend was okay.

As far as being one of the biggest events of the war, it turned out to be fairly normal and uneventful for Frank. It was a far different story for the men fighting and dying on the ground.

An organized counterattack just never materialized. As is turned out, the German High Command was convinced that Normandy was a diversionary attack and that the main thrust would come at the Pas-de-Calais. Fortunately, they were wrong.

Frank had his concerns about the use of the Mustang as a ground attack weapon, but he managed to get through it with only minor flak damage to his rudder. The fabric covering was easily repaired by his ground crew and he lost no time returning to action. He had one consolation. At least he was close enough to the English Channel, which was squarely in control by Allied naval forces, that he could ditch close to a vessel and expect recovery within a few minutes.

His concern about the Mustang's susceptibility to ground fire was his biggest worry about the airplane. But, he loved every other attribute about it. The plane climbed like a rocket. It could maneuver with the best the German's could throw at him. The fuel economy was excellent compared to other American and British fighters. Its firepower was devastating. Its cockpit was comfortable and roomy. And it was fun to fly. The mating of the supercharged Packard-built Rolls Royce Merlin engine with the airframe made it a real winner. Frank was elated that he had one as his very own to fly.

Frank was disappointed that he had not done more to support the invasion. Yet, he was also comforted that air cover did its part to prevent an aerial counter-attack. He was also thankful that he was not a foot soldier because he knew they we facing a tenacious enemy bent on destroying them and keeping them from gaining a foothold on the European continent.

Some of the beaches met relatively little resistance compared to Omaha Beach. Omaha was a slaughter until individual bands of heroic soldiers penetrated the Atlantic Wall. On Utah Beach brave Rangers scaled the sheer cliffs while facing the onslaught of machine gun fire, hand grenades, and the cliffs themselves to try to flank the enemy.

The British, Canadians, and French quickly secured the Juno, Sword, and Gold Beaches and began their movement inland. The British had hoped to capture Caen within a day or so. But, it would be thirty days later before they could defeat German forces holding the town.

With all this drama unfolding below them, all the pilots of the fighters could do in many cases was act as casual observers to the events unfolding below them. In so many ways, Frank felt detached from this nightmare scene.

By the time of the D-Day invasion much of the Luftwaffe's effectiveness had already been knocked out. At this point in the war, coordinated ground support by air was limited, too. As would be demonstrated just a few weeks later during a bombing mission in support of the breakout, friendly fire would kill a large number of ground troops due to such a lack of coordination and planning. But the Allied Air Forces could still disrupt enemy actions by hitting ground troops, supply trains and convoys, tanks, and gun emplacements.

As it turned out, the German Luftwaffe could only manage a couple of sorties. It was reported later that a disgusted and angry Reichsmarschall Hermann Göring said, "On D-Day British planes were green, American planes were silver, and German planes were invisible."

Troops were trying to move their way inland. For the most part, they did not reach their first day's objectives. In some cases, those first day's objectives would take a full month to bring to fruition.

As the Allies were expanding their foothold in Normandy in mid-June, a new Nazi threat emerged—the V-1 buzz bomb. These flying bombs got their name from the unique sound made by its pulsejet engine, that is, until the engine stopped, causing it to plummet to earth and explode on impact. They also received the British nickname of "doodlebugs." Over six thousand innocent residents were killed as a result. Some were even directed at Allied troops on the European continent.

While anti-aircraft guns could shoot them down, there was still the danger of them falling into congested areas and exploding. It was up to the British Royal and U.S. Army Air Forces to locate and destroy them before they could be fired towards England. A couple of other tactics worked, too. The first approach involved shooting them down. They were small and difficult to hit and, considering the high explosives packed in the warhead, it was extremely dangerous for the pilot doing the shooting. The second method required nerves of steel. The pilot would pull alongside the V-1 and use the wingtip of his airplane to upset the gyro-navigational system of the buzz-bomb. The goal here was to force it down over remote sections of the English countryside or over the English Channel.

Consequently, it would be much easier to eliminate them on the ground. So, the 355th Fighter Group, among others, received the call to hit the northern coastal areas of France, Belgium, and the Netherlands to seek-and-destroy the V-1s and supporting equipment. Many of the missions relied on intelligence reports from resistance fighters in those countries to provide accurate target positions.

The 355th Fighter Group was assigned its first mission versus the "buzz bombs" towards the end of June. Without the detailed intelligence reports and reconnaissance photographs, it would be extremely difficult to spot such small targets from the air. This mission would use a combination of 500-pound bombs and machine gun fire.

Once the target was located, the plan was to come in low in a steady stream of bombing runs with guns ablaze in order to carpet the area with destruction. His squadron's specific target area was located in and around Dunkerque, France. Frank, carrying reconnaissance photos, kept a keen lookout for geographical and physical features to help him pinpoint the telltale signs of launch sites. They were nothing more than short rail ramps; so, they would not be easy to find and they could be camouflaged, too.

Considering the possibility that the site would be virtually invisible from the air, Frank was under orders to strike the target area regardless of visual contact with the actual launch system. He was looking for a spot nestled among some dunes just off the beach. It would be marked by a small dirt road leading up to it and immediately to its west was an adjacent canal.

As Frank cruised along at six thousand feet, he strained to match the features on the ground with those on his photograph and map. Then he started to pick out the key checkpoints, *Okay, there was Dunkerque. Now, just east of Dunkerque should be the canal, the beach, and the roadway leading to the beach and the target. There they were.*

Frank continued to fly east about twenty miles in order to throw off defensive positions around the target. Perhaps they would think that the flight of Mustangs had another target and that they would be safe from attack. Upon reaching twenty miles east of the target, Frank signaled the squadron that they were ready for their attack. They were all to follow in a line behind him.

He rolled his airplane into a split-S and started to build up speed for the attack. The other planes followed one after the other. After he rolled his wings level, he continued to make a steep descent to one hundred feet. The target area lay directly ahead. There was a small tower in the distance that he used to help align his attack.

As he approached the site, he started firing his machine guns and when he got closer he pulled the bomb release. It was bombs away. Upon contact with the ground, they skipped a little. One bounced, hit the ground and hit the ground again. There was an enormous explosion, more than would be expected from just two bombs. They must have hit their mark. As the other planes continued to sweep the area, there were many more secondary explosions. They must have hit a combination of fuel and V-1 storage facilities. It looked like bottle rockets flying through the air. It would have looked even more impressive at night. As a matter of safety for the remaining fighters, Frank called off the attack. Otherwise, subsequent airplanes could have been taken down by flying debris. Frank was satisfied that the Nazis would not be using this launch site again in the very near future. Mission accomplished.

Following D-Day, Frank continued to support air missions. He escorted bombers to help breakout the troops from the area around Saint Lo. Due to a failure of the leaders of the ground war and air war to gain agreement about a plan of attack, on July 24th most bombing runs were made perpendicular to the advancing infantry as opposed to parallel to it. Bombing accuracy was also hindered by poor visibility. This meant that bombs that fell short of their intended aim point killed a hundred and wounded five hundred infantry as a result of friendly fire.

This was devastating news and demonstrated the need to develop better coordination between ground troops and air support. Frank would remember this and apply the lessons learned to future missions. With the Allies moving deeper and deeper into enemy territory, it became more likely that there would be more frequent interactions between forces on the ground and those in the air. It became imperative that new tactics had to be developed to keep those close contacts from turning into unnecessary massacres of friendly forces while trying to support them.

Chapter 11

Operation Market Garden

No one wanted the war to go on any longer than absolutely necessary. After all, even once the Germans and Italians were completely defeated, the Empire of Japan remained as a formidable adversary. Although the island hopping campaign was progressing, much of the focus continued with the European war. Furthermore, promises had been made by Franklin Roosevelt and Winston Churchill to maintain a concerted effort on the western front of Germany in order to relieve the pressure on the eastern front at the urging of Russia's leader, Josef Stalin.

After much political posturing by British Field Marshal Bernard Montgomery with Supreme Commander Dwight Eisenhower, he pushed for his plan to drive into the Netherlands to capture the port of Antwerp. This was contrary to Generals Omar Bradley's and George S. Patton's plan to move due east along a broad front into the industrialized central Rhineland.

Montgomery reasoned that overland supply from the Normandy beachhead was slowing the Allied advance. That was certainly a legitimate rationale. The port of Antwerp would provide a necessary outlet to the sea and adequate port facilities to expedite the movement of those supplies to forward troops. However, Bradley believed that supplies could be transported by C-47 Dakotas in order to keep the front lines moving forward into Germany.

American servicemen did not like the idea of Eisenhower selling out to who they opined was an overrated commander. They thought that Montgomery had lost his edge following his victories against Erwin Rommel's Afrika Corps at El Alamein in Northern Africa. General Patton was able to achieve greater results in Sicily, and now in Europe. Patton had already demonstrated to the world his ability to read the Germans' minds and develop a strategy to outwit and punch through them. Now, it seemed to most soldiers that their forces were being diverted from the German prize for a side trip in order to placate Montgomery.

This would be the biggest airborne operation of the war. The 355th Fighter Group would provide aerial cover for the 82nd Airborne Division's C-47 Dakotas in order to guard against enemy fighters. The C-47s would be coming in low and slow. Many were also towing troop-laden gliders. Two squadrons of Mustangs would provide low cover and hit ground targets as appropriate.

It was early Sunday, September 17, 1944. Frank thought how he would normally try to be in chapel at this time. Whenever there was not a Sunday mission, Frank would be there with Scotty. They both felt comforted that having an eternal hope was absolutely necessary should they be killed in action. Furthermore, Frank was still troubled that he was killing other human beings, even though it was the enemy and justified according to the rules of war. He needed the solace he received from the chaplain's sermons. Somehow he could place this whole nasty war into the proper context with Biblical principles. Nonetheless, Frank needed to be reminded that this was a war against an enemy so insidious that the evil could not be matched throughout all previous history.

Frank believed that even if there was only a ten percent chance of God's existence, it was still better odds that not believing in Him and eternal life at all. It gave him solace and comforted him. He also knew that his faith in God and eternal life should have allayed his constant fear. After all, true trust in God should have replaced his fearful feelings. But, he could not help himself. It was something deeper within himself. Perhaps it was a psychological problem. Maybe he was going mad. Yet, he thought to himself, *If I was really going mad, could I rationalize my feelings this way. Wouldn't an insane person just accept his condition unknowingly and go on thinking everything was right and okay?*

So, Frank tried to cloak himself in his religious beliefs. He continually tried to use Scripture, chapel, prayer, and heart-to-heart talks with the chaplain to help him understand his feelings. He felt comfortable talking to the chaplain, and comforted by him, too. The chaplain, a middle-aged, balding gentleman, assured Frank that he was not going mad. Doubts about God's existence were normal. After all, belief in God was based entirely on faith rather than sight.

Frank really did not have a problem with the existence of God. His doubts were about himself and how his fears could coexist with a strong belief in God. He also worried about his unresolved anger against the Germans. The chaplain told him that man was imperfect and that the sin nature would always be there. The chaplain was not inferring that Frank was living in sin, but that sin exists in all humans. The chaplain recommended that Frank continue to pray, attend chapel, and talk to him about his concerns. Whenever Frank walked away from one of these sessions with the chaplain, he always felt better, and his soul was refreshed. This Sunday there would be no chapel, but he still prayed. Duty prevailed. Yet, he felt a special calmness this particular day.

The flight took them over the North Sea. All the pilots and maintenance crews took special precautions to make sure the Mustangs were operating in peak condition. After all, nobody wanted to bail out into that frigid body of water. Every time Frank flew over the North Sea he thought about the possibility of being shot down and lost at sea. What would go through his family's or Dottie's minds should his body be lost forever. It did not pay to worry about such things. At least they weren't over the open Sea very long.

Arriving near the 82nd's drop point, flak intensified but did not seem to be very accurate. Frank saw a couple of gliders that were hit and spun down almost in slow motion. The 82nd jumped and landed within a few hundred yards of its target. Frank's squadron circled overhead. To his surprise, no enemy aircraft made an appearance. It was amazing to look down from above and see a sky full of parachutes drifting to earth, then, once they hit the ground to see the earth littered with them.

It was a relatively uneventful day for Frank and his squadron. It was a welcome respite from aerial combat. Upon returning to base, he stopped by the mess hall for his evening meal. Then he went for a walk out to his plane. He stood there for a while gazing at the stars just considering his future and the universe in general. Following this brief interlude, he returned to his quarters where he wrote letters home before he fell asleep.

The first letter he wrote to his parents sounded too fatalistic. Since he had flown so many missions to this point he began to feel thoughts tearing at him from within that his number would soon be up. But he could not express those feelings to his parents or Dottie. So, he tore it up and started anew. Again, he focused on pleasant thoughts, like the picturesque scenery and fascinating architecture of Holland that passed below him. The letter to his parents expressed just general thoughts about the war, separation from family, and daily extracurricular activities. He never touched upon his missions.

His letter to Dottie proved to be a bit more introspective.

Dearest Dottie,

It seems so long since I last wrote you. I remain in excellent health and spirit but I miss you within the depths of my being.

Our separation has caused me to appreciate your company all the more. This war has been going on too long and my sole prayer is to return to you so that we can live our lives in peace and tranquility.

I fondly recall our last summer together. The flights to the Cape and the Islands were made complete only because you were there to share them with me.

My spare time has been spent visiting some of the small communities surrounding the base and an occasional tour of London. However, most of the time my duties keep me close to the base. So, during my down time I take photos of the planes and personnel for my scrapbook. Sometimes I play darts or horseshoes. My aim is pretty good, but not as good as some of the other players. Yet, I manage to hold my own.

Well, it is late and I had a busy day so I need to hit the sack.

Your living
Frank

Yes, he had written "living" not "loving." He did not mean to do it. Perhaps it was a Freudian slip. Or it was his current hope and prayer. Or it was just acknowledging his current state. Whatever, he could only read the letter years later and wonder about the state of his mind when he first wrote it.

The next day, Frank was on another escort mission that almost did not take off due to a thick layer of fog over much of southern England. However, by mid-morning the sky was clear as the sun melted away the fog. His squadron would be supporting a second airborne drop on Grave, Holland.

Again, Frank kept an eye out for enemy aircraft. However, most of the activity was occurring on the ground. As he circled overhead at about 8,000 feet, he spotted some movement out of the corner of his eye. It was a Nazi staff car and four motorcycles, two with sidecars. He reasoned that someone important was being escorted out of the area. He signaled to Scotty, his wingman, that they were going after them. They rolled to reverse their direction to line up for the attack.

Evidently, the staff car personnel spotted the attack and tried to take evasive action. During the first pass they could see their machine gun bullets tear up the roadway and close in on the automobile. The car swerved as did the motorcycles. Although Frank and Scotty were concentrating on the staff car, the two trailing motorcycles went down. The car was being peppered with machine gun fire and ran into a ditch. As he made a steep turn, Frank saw two individuals jump out of the front seat and what looked like a high ranking officer jump out of the rear seat into the ditch. The two motorcycle drivers sought cover with them, too.

The German soldiers returned fire with their machine guns. Frank lined up again. Although he didn't like the idea of shooting down people on the ground, he could not allow a possible command officer to escape. He began firing and raking the area. He could not see much because the bullet strikes were tearing up the ground and brush creating a plume of dust and dirt. After the dust died down, he could see the results of his fire. It looked like one of the staff officers and both motorcycle drivers were down. The two remaining officers tried to make their way into some ground cover. He saw them duck into some nearby thick brush.

He called Scotty on the radio and directed him to circle overhead and look for them to make a dash out of the brush. As Scotty climbed into position, Frank lined up for an attack on the brush. He opened up with everything he had concentrating his fire on the brush where he had seen the Germans seek cover. The next thing he saw was both bodies flying out the other end. They were finished.

Frank didn't enjoy this type of warfare, but it was necessary. He felt sickened by it. It was not the typical sickness he felt as a result of his nerves. This is the closest he came to killing another person face-to-face and he detested it. He prayed he would never have to do it again.

It was because of the possibility of events like this that prompted him to become a pilot as opposed to a foot soldier. The only way he could see himself going to war was if he could keep it impersonal. It was a whole lot different killing at a distance. It was antiseptic.

When Frank returned to base, he went to chapel and prayed for himself and for those he had killed. He talked to the chaplain about the events of the day. The chaplain's kind, understanding nature helped him come to terms with his religious convictions and what seemed to be a contradiction to those convictions. Then, he went to see the base doctor to get something to help him sleep. He was tormented throughout the night with nightmares and they continued off and on for about another ten days. Finally, he resolved what had happened and started to sleep normally.

As his final mission during Operation Market Garden, Frank was charged with escorting flights of C-47s dropping supplies for the 82nd Airborne Division at Overasselt. He and everyone else hoped that this would reinforce them enough to turn around the course of the battle. But it was futile.

Unexpectedly, German forces in Holland were stronger than anticipated by Montgomery. Furthermore, the linkup between the Polish Brigade and British XXX Corps failed to materialize. It was a total mess. The whole campaign collapsed. It was an utter failure. The Dutch who had so willingly welcomed the Allies would now suffer the wrath of and retribution from the Germans. There would be mass reprisals against them for aiding the Allies.

While Frank may have respected Montgomery at one time, he could not help but despise what had happened. He also questioned Eisenhower's decision to allow a foreigner to take control of a campaign involving American troops. Why in the world would he have diverted all the positive energy from Patton's successful sweep towards Germany into such a boondoggle as this?

Of course he was out of the loop when it came to playing all the politics between the two major Allies, the British and Americans. Eisenhower had to make decisions based on diplomacy in order to keep these two forces fighting in unison. After all, it is always easier to use twenty-twenty hindsight to show where a plan went wrong. If it had succeeded, then perhaps the war would have been shortened and Montgomery would have been a big hero. But in reality, he had to live with his mistake. Unfortunately, a lot of good men died because of his pride and false assumptions.

Frank felt that he could do very little during this campaign. The German Luftwaffe never came up to meet them in any great numbers and, due to his orders to provide air cover, there was not much he could do to support the ground troops. That was left to the Thunderbolts.

The plan to shorten the war had all gone for naught. It would go on. Frank's battles would go on, too—his air battles and the battle within himself.

Chapter 12

Mundane Missions

While it was the combat missions and the pilots who flew them that got the glory, more often than not, most missions were long, boring, and tedious. They involved hours of flying at altitude using an oxygen mask, which caused skin irritation, and sub-freezing conditions that could cause serious frost-bite. This was especially prevalent during escort missions when flying above the bomber formations. These missions were monotonous when there were no encounters with enemy aircraft.

All too often, when Frank returned from these types of missions, his ground crew would have to help him out of the cockpit. He was cold and his joints were stiff from sitting in one position for so long. Even when he could get out of the cockpit on his own, it took him a while to get his blood flowing to his legs again. He could not seem to get warm. Usually he would head straight to the mess hall after the debriefing session to get a hot cup of coffee, soup, or anything else that could warm his insides.

Sometimes it was so cold that wounded pilots would find the bleeding stopped because the wounds would freeze as opposed to coagulating. Then, as they descended into warmer air, they would start to bleed again when they needed most to concentrate on landing. Unlike the pleasure flying he enjoyed over coastal Massachusetts, this, on the other hand, was real work in the harshest conditions.

Even while flying with Eastern Air Lines, he never flew that high. He did not need to use oxygen on most flights and it never got that cold. First of all, the passengers would never have tolerated it or stood for it. Wars always seem to be fought under the most adverse conditions possible.

During combat, adrenalin started flowing. Perhaps this was a benefit in overcoming extreme adversity. Whatever happened, everything besides the target fell out of focus, including suffering, thoughts about loved ones, and feelings about one's mortality. There was intense concentration on the target. The target was everything. That kind of tunnel vision, however, could get one killed.

Missions were not conducted every day. Frank, and his fellow pilots, found themselves on the ground more often than they flew. Sometimes an airplane would be down for maintenance or repairs. Even under the best of conditions, warbirds like the P-47 or P-51 were lucky if they could get 300 hours out of their engine before it needed an overhaul. Quite often, that was not a big worry because in all likelihood the plane could be lost before it needed an engine overhaul, as macabre as it may sound.

Then there was battle damage or accidents. Frequently, sheet aluminum parts were custom made depending on the damage. This could mean the ground crew would have to fabricate a rib, stringer, panel, or other more complicated parts. Other times, fuel tanks needed to be replaced, damaged instruments installed and calibrated, and canopies removed, repaired, and reinstalled. This work all took time. Besides, the crews working the repair depots were not magicians, just close to it.

There were occasions when the continent was forecast to be socked in but the skies over England were CAVU—ceiling and visibility unlimited. Frank would requisition his plane to wring out his kinks if he sat on the ground too long. These were great opportunities to see England from the air. He used those times to fly over Ireland and gaze upon the verdant rolling hills and ancient castles and thatched roofs. It was splendid. On other occasions he headed north to Scotland. There was so much beauty and so much to see. He reconnoitered all the nooks and crannies along the coast seeking spots that would make for some great exploring and fishing.

England was interesting from the standpoint that he flew over a number of towns and cities that bore the same names as places back home in New England. There were Swansea, Gloucester, Ipswich, Newport, Plymouth, Reading, Brighton, and Weymouth. The names were evidence of the strong historical ties to England and its influence on the early settling of the United States of America.

Flying over some of the expansive estates made them appear all the more impressive. They consisted of huge tracts of land, dense forests, at least one large manse, smaller servant quarters and guest houses, and gardens with such intricate designs and a splendid array of colors. Such spectacular perspectives could be visible only from the air. Perhaps he would return to see the sights from the ground after the war.

As often as an airplane was on the ground for maintenance or repair, it was grounded more frequently due to the weather. English weather was notorious for being quite miserable. Fog always seemed to be a problem. While taking off under such conditions was hazardous at best, landing in them was far worse. If there turned out to be a mechanical problem requiring a return to base, it was virtually impossible. If the airplane could make it to an alternate base, then there was a chance. However, if the problem was catastrophic, like an engine failure, then the pilot needed to get down right away. Some situations dictated that he had no choice, the plane was going down regardless of the pilot's actions, and his options to locate fogless skies disappeared quickly. He was going down in the blind with an uncertain outcome. Often it would not be good. Ultimately, the only choice was to bail out following an attempt to direct the injured aircraft away from populated areas. If the pilot was forced to ditch, then there was no guarantee that the plane would crash into uninhabited territory. Frank could not live with himself if he caused the death of innocents.

It was often the rule that Allied planes arriving over their target found it completely obscured by clouds. Then it was off to the alternate. If that was obscured too, then there might be secondary alternate. Bombers never wanted to return to base and land with a load of bombs. Therefore, it was common to drop them over the English Channel or North Sea. There were even instances of just dropping them on anything below the cloud layer. The target could have been any rolling stock from locomotives down to baby carriages.

There were areas designated over the English Channel to salvo bombs that could not be dropped on targets. It is believed that Big Band leader Glenn Miller's airplane was felled by being hit by a falling bomb or the concussion created by the explosion in just such as area.

As the war progressed, there were fewer and fewer altercations or chance meetings. Early in the war, missions were not so long. The Thunderbolt had limited range. Its Pratt & Whitney engine thirsted for fuel. It would burn close to 200 gallons per hour. So, the mission might have a duration of about three hours.

However, as the war progressed the Allies started to install drop tanks to extend the range of its fighters. The main purpose of doing this was to permit them to escort the bombers deep into Germany. When the P-51 Mustang, which had about twice the range of the Thunderbolt, was added to the inventory, coupled with drop tanks, missions were extended to about eight hours. With the extreme conditions, this made for a very long day.

Frank would find himself droning along on long missions with the constant hum of the engine in the background. The sound of the engine was always comforting. But, it was exhausting and demanding duty. There was no such thing as an autopilot on these World War II fighters. It was all hand flying in formation. Unlike a bomber, it was not like he could get up and walk around to stretch his legs. He could not share flying responsibilities with a co-pilot. And the choice about relieving himself was limited to the relief tube. He was strapped in as tight as he could make his harness. He could not so much as squirm in his seat. After all, once he entered combat, there was no time to adjust or tighten the harness. He could not afford to be slapping around the inside the cockpit during abrupt combat maneuvers.

So, in tallying up the time sitting on the ground due to weather or maintenance or flying to and from the target versus actual combat, it becomes readily apparent that relatively little time was spent in actual combat. But, although it comprised the least amount of time related to total flying hours, it was certainly the combat that was the most memorable and, quite frankly, the whole purpose for the fighter's existence in the first place.

Did Frank mind these mundane missions? Not really. They were great respites from the combat missions. But, like most other pilots trained for combat, he got itchy to see some action. He was still afraid; yet, he knew he had a job to do. The sooner it was done, the sooner he could get home to Dottie and his family.

One of the key attributes necessary to make an effective fighter pilot was, and still is, aggressiveness. Yes, it takes excellent flying skills, adept aerobatics, and good aim. But those traits were no good without a pilot who was willing to confront the enemy head on. Although Frank suffered from acute fear, he had all those positive attributes. His anger towards the Germans tended to negate the effects of what could have been debilitating fear.

Anyone who was a fighter pilot who was passive, tentative, or lacked the flying skills needed to find a new career. Otherwise, someone, namely the enemy, would find one for him. Consequently, it would not be one he would like, like prisoner of war, maimed, crippled, or permanently dead.

Not everyone who trained as a fighter pilot was truly a fighter pilot. Large numbers of recruits were admitted to flight school. A reasonable percentage of those could learn to fly an airplane with the proper training. However, a significant number also washed out. Not everyone could tolerate aerobatics either. Others found it virtually impossible to coordinate flying an airplane while doing aerobatics on the tail of an adversary while trying to shoot them down. Still others could not handle the complexity of the day's modern fighters. Finally, even combining all of these talents did not guarantee a fighter pilot who was willing to fight. It took one additional trait—courage.

Frank would find out all too soon that there were some pilots out there willing to usurp their comrades solely for the purpose of self-preservation. There was a certain, special comradeship among fighter pilots. They watched out for and protected each other. But there were some who were in it only for the personal glory, the medals, to be an ace, for bragging rights, and would sacrifice a fellow pilot to achieve those prizes. Enter one Ted Holenski.

Chapter 13

The Pseudo-Hero

Due to continued attrition from accidents and combat, replacement pilots were being shipped overseas to fill missing slots at a fairly steady rate. One replacement pilot added to the 355th was a second-generation Polish-American named Ted Holenski. He was a stocky five feet, eight inches tall and weighed 180 pounds. A young man of twenty-two years old, he looked much older. His head was square with a jutting lower jaw. In profile his chin stuck out further than his nose, which had been broken and flattened against his face several times during brawls. He looked mean, and he was. He had a large scar over his left eye, evidence of a knife fight when he was seventeen.

He had lived all his life in Chicago with the exception of his military service. He was intelligent, at least intelligent enough to get accepted into flight school; however, much of that intelligence was misdirected into counterproductive activities.

Ted had trained as a fighter pilot; however, he marginally made it through flight training. In fact, he had been held back in the states in order to gain additional experience. But his progress had pretty much stagnated. He could fly reasonably well, but his formation flying was atrocious. His gunnery was also less than ideal. Finally, the inevitable need for replacement pilots grew to the point that his superiors finally shipped him overseas.

Unlike the competent Polish pilots who flew with the British RAF during the Battle of Britain, Ted just did not seem to possess the same characteristics of his fellow men from the old country. They were fighting to liberate their country from Nazi rule. Ted's goal was to serve Ted.

Ted related that his father was a drunkard and an abuser. He spent more time in jails than out of them. Ted's own behavior was a propagation of that of his no-account father who was never there to administer proper discipline or counsel to his son. So it seemed predictable, whether by nature or nurture, that Ted inherited many of his father's behavioral traits. As he grew up in Chicago's slums, he joined and, eventually, led neighborhood gangs who preyed on the weak and unsuspecting. He was proud of his affiliation with them, too. His bravado was apparent whenever he was surrounded by his lackeys. Known among gang members as "Hellboy" Holenski, due to his insatiable cruelty, he carried any number of illegal weapons like switchblades, blackjacks, or brass knuckles, and firearms whenever they became available. He lusted to hurt people, apparently from his lack of fatherly direction, despite the fact that his mother loved him.

His idea of fun was hanging out at the local gambling establishments. Then he and his gang would target some poor fop dressed in spats and white gloves, who looked like he had money in his pockets. As he was leaving they would grab him and throw him into an adjacent alley. With a knife at his throat, the unfortunate victim was relieved of his cash and jewelry. It was like a pack of vicious wolves surrounding a wounded fawn. There was no chance of escape. The gang was strength. More than that, it was courage. Ted never operated without them.

It was common for Ted and his cronies to use their intimidation on anyone who appeared to display any signs of weakness. It did not matter to him who they preyed upon, young or old, male or female. If they could turn a quick buck, they would use their powers of persuasion to convince their target to relinquish their valuables, either voluntarily or by force. It did not bother Ted if he had to beat them to get whatever he wanted. In fact, he relished the thought of using a little violence anytime he could do so. It was how he displayed his power. It made him feel important.

When he enlisted in the Army Air Force, he kept his history hidden from them. Had they known of his past, surely he would have been rejected as unfit for service. He was not a nice person. He was downright nasty and antisocial. He was in this war for personal glory, and he had a lust for killing without conscience.

Ted bragged about his gang activities openly, probably with the expectation that he would instill fear in his fellow pilots or anyone else within earshot. The only problem was the fact that most of them had seen combat, faced death, and were certainly not intimidated by him.

Every two weeks, almost like clockwork, his mother would mail homemade salami to him. It was nice that someone thought enough of him to send him a regular gift. But there were some negative consequences. He always smelled like his pungent salami. His clothes reeked of it. The odor was trapped in his hair and on his skin. He sweated salami. And his ground crew openly complained that his cockpit smelled like a delicatessen. It was awful. During trips into town, no one wanted to sit next to him in a jeep or bus. Furthermore, guys trying to pick up girls shunned him like the plague because his stench did nothing to induce romantic feelings from the ladies.

Several nicknames for him were bandied about the barracks. First, someone came up with "Hot Dog" Holenski. Then, there was Ted "The Salami" Holenski, but that one just didn't have a mellifluous sound to it. Eventually, he earned a new nickname, "Hot Links" Holenski which, by unanimous decision is the one that stuck like glue.

When he heard someone refer to him as "Hot Links" he went nuts. He ranted and he raved. But he could not fight everyone; he was outnumbered and the pilots were sticking together. So, he would gripe and moan and make idle threats. The other men had figured him out. By himself, he was a barking dog with no bite. Practical jokes were only funny to him if he was not on the receiving end.

Additionally, he never had anything good or kind to say about anybody. Consequently, no one wanted anything to do with him.

On the contrary, Frank got along with everyone because he tried to nurture the new men and share his knowledge as to how to the deal with the Germans in combat. Frank was well respected and there was no question about his courage, except by "Hot Links."

Whenever the pilots went to mess, few of the veteran pilots ever sat with Ted. It wasn't just that he was gruff, if that wasn't enough. He also ate like an absolute pig. It seemed that more food wound up on him than in him. He would also belch openly and as loudly as he could. It was not that he ever tried to suppress it either. The sound resounded throughout the mess hall. Then he would comment loudly how good it sounded and felt to relieve all that pressure. He would make some woman a great husband.

One day Ted decided to play his advantage of size and meanness with a newly assigned young Second Lieutenant. The young man was the same height as Ted, but about thirty pounds lighter. He was trim and had a boyish appearance. He did everything he could to pick a fight which the young man tried to avoid. Eventually, Ted cornered him and he was pressed to defend himself. Ted reared back to throw a punch. But, Ted should have done a little research into his victim's background. As it turned out, he had been a boxer. Ted was outmatched. The young Lieutenant quickly dispatched him with a couple of quick jabs to the face followed by an upper cut to what turned out to be Ted's glass jaw. He was out colder than a mackerel. The men were pleased with the outcome and no charges were filed against either man. They hoped that this result would prompt a change in Ted's behavior. However, that was wishful thinking.

In order to evaluate Ted's flying ability, Frank assigned him to fly in his own flight of four planes, flying as wingman with Lieutenant Paul Marston, on a short mission along the northern Netherlands coast looking for enemy ships and coastal movements. Scotty took up his normal position as Frank's wingman, right where he belonged and felt most comfortable.

Lieutenant Marston was a quiet, likable guy. He was a precise and smooth pilot whose maneuvers looked like they were choreographed. Paul was well-educated, having earned a degree in agriculture from University of Maine in Orono. He had just started graduate school and probably could have obtained a deferment from military service, but he felt compelled to serve. Shortly before shipping overseas, he hastily married his college sweetheart. They knew that there was a chance he would not return, but they were willing to take that risk.

During his spare time Paul indulged in collecting teapots for his young wife at home in Maine. It seems that tea was her beverage of choice. They hoped to enjoy the relaxed, soothing habit of afternoon tea upon his return to the states after the war. Whenever he visited any of the local villages he stopped by tea shops to buy porcelain or ceramic tea sets in all manner of shapes, sizes, and colors for her. He sent her a carefully wrapped package containing the artistic treasures almost every month along with a supply of tea. By war's end, they would own quite an extensive collection to enjoy together, so long as he survived.

On the way to the proposed target, Ted complained of a rough running engine. Frank told him to switch to a different fuel tank and to check his mixture. Ted complained even more vociferously that he was having mechanical trouble. Then Frank told him to check his magnetos. Still Ted complained. So, Frank authorized him to return to base early. Nothing much happened anyway because their target area was covered by a thick layer of fog.

Although there was no action, upon their return to base Frank was suffering from one of his typical bouts of fear. He was trembling and had to run behind a supply hut to vomit. Ted saw this and could not wait to try to build himself up by pulling Frank down. Every other pilot in the Group had come to know that Frank suffered from extreme anxiety and fear. But they also knew that it never interfered with him doing his job. They trusted him and they never questioned his courage. They each had their own way of dealing with fear. They understood that this was Frank's way of managing his fear.

Ted, on the other hand, saw this as a sign of weakness and cowardice. He overtly challenged Frank's position of leadership saying that someone with the shakes had no business leading a flight. "Hot Links" asserted that he never went into combat afraid. The fact was, he had never really been in combat. This mission was his first and he had not seen so much as a sparrow.

The other pilots told him he needed to keep his complaints to himself. Frank had already proven himself in battle and, until he did the same, he should just keep quiet. Frank largely ignored him. Yet, there were times when Ted tried to instigate a confrontation. But, when Frank did not back down, Ted found some excuse to break it off. For example, he would say he had to talk to his ground crew about a mechanical gripe, or some other excuse to avoid standing up to someone alone.

Speaking of the ground crew—all the pilots understood the hard work done by their ground crews. They respected them and treated them honorably. On the other hand, Ted treated them like servants. He snapped orders and totally disrespected them. The crew chief was once heard to say to his fellow ground crew member, "Maybe we should just forget to charge his machine guns or loosen a hydraulic line and then we'll see who's in charge here."

It was not a good idea to make enemies of men who were there to ensure your safety and did so much to support the pilots' efforts. Ted just did not get it. He was too caught up with his egomania.

The following day, the same mission as previously scheduled was underway. Frank's formation was set up identically, too. Like clockwork, Ted's Merlin engine began to "act up" again. Frank began to suspect that Ted was not being truthful about his situation. Ted begged and pleaded to return to base. Finally, Frank relented, but he had every intention of investigating this further upon his return to base.

Once again, the target was obscured, this time with heavy clouds. It was another fool's errand. It was back to base and Frank focused on Ted's claim. Frank was going to find out one way or another if there was truly an engine problem.

Upon the return to base, Frank immediately went to Ted's crew chief and asked him about the status of the airplane. The crew chief told Frank that Ted complained of a rough-running engine. Furthermore, each time they had checked fuel filters, the condition of the oil, coolant flow, belly scoop shutters, fuel flow, ignition wires, carburetor, magnetos, and pulled the spark plugs. They couldn't find a thing wrong. They had even done ground run ups and the engine appeared to operate normally.

Frank told the ground crew to fuel the plane. He was going to take it for a test flight. The ground crew was delighted. They felt as though they were chasing gremlins.

Doing his preflight run up, Frank found no anomalies. The throttle operated smoothly and the engine was responsive. Take off and climb out were normal. He climbed to 20,000 feet and began flying under the same conditions as had been present during the previous two missions. He stayed up for almost three hours and the Merlin just purred the whole time.

After he landed, he returned the airplane back to its hardstand to be serviced. He gave his report about the engine's flawless performance to the crew chief. He was satisfied that the Merlin was operating without a hitch.

Frank was in a huff. He hurriedly scurried to the barracks and went right up to Ted. Telling him to snap to attention, Frank ordered him outside. Once in a deserted part of the airfield, Frank told Ted exactly what he thought about his "engine problems." He had not been deluded by Ted's overt lies. Furthermore, Ted would be flying the next mission. No excuse about engine problems would be accepted. If he turned and ran, then Frank would shoot him down himself.

Of course, Ted tried to claim that he was telling the truth. But, Frank knew better. Upon Ted's return to the barracks, he claimed that Frank was jealous of him and being unfair. The other pilots just told him to shut up.

Several days later, the three squadrons of Mustangs from the 355th Fighter Group rendezvoused with twenty-four B-17s over the Channel. It was going to be a small bombing mission over the Netherlands. This was the same mission as scheduled a few days before, but this time the fog and clouds had lifted. This also meant that their flight came under the purview of the enemy. About sixty FW-190s were scrambled to intercept them. The Mustangs rushed in to head them off. Frank called over the radio for their flight to stick together. Scotty held tight formation with Frank and so did Paul. But, Ted's formation flying left a lot to be desired. It was loose and sloppy. Frank told him to close it up with Paul. He tried, but he was all over the place. Whenever his plane got close to Paul's plane he would abruptly jerk away from it. Rather than risk a mid-air collision, Frank told him to just stay close, but not too close.

As their flight was approaching four FW-190s slightly below them, Frank saw some tracer bullets arc by his left side. They were under fire from behind and below. They were being ambushed. So, he yelled for Paul and Ted to break right while he and Scotty broke left. In the process, both Scotty and Paul were hit. Scotty's engine was running rough and he was losing power. Frank told Scotty to head for home.

Paul was going down with glycol vapor trailing from his plane's radiator. His plane was being pummeled by two of the FW-190s as he jettisoned the canopy and jumped. Frank saw him land safely. Upon landing on the ground, Paul was captured and interred in a prisoner of war camp for the remainder of the war. Afternoon tea time with his wife would have to wait.

Then Frank began searching the sky for Ted. Not seeing Ted anywhere, Frank hollered over the radio for him to join up with him. But there was no answer. Frank had not seen him hit. There were no black holes in the sky where there would have been evidence of an exploding plane, nothing. Perhaps his radio was shot out. Frank continued to scan the sky looking for Ted and enemy planes. He was on his own. He was like the Lone Ranger without Tonto to act as cover.

Frank managed to shoot down a FW-190 and damage another. Yet, he did not know the fate of Ted. He had every reason to believe that Ted had become a statistic.

When he returned to Steeple Morden, he checked the hardstand to make sure that Scotty made it back safely. He had. However, what he saw next totally stunned him. It was Ted's plane parked on its hardstand. He climbed out of his plane and jogged over to Ted's plane. He walked around carefully looking for battle damage. The ground crew was already servicing the Mustang for its next mission. So, Frank asked the crew chief what damage it had suffered. The crew chief's response was, "None."

"Then, how about the radio? Was it knocked out of commission?"

"No, sir."

"Anything wrong?"

"No, sir?"

"Then, what happened?"

"Well, sir, when he returned, he was just sitting in the cockpit. He was trembling and weeping uncontrollably. We had to pry his hands off the control stick, drag him out of the cockpit, and haul him over to the infirmary."

"Was he wounded?"

"No, sir, not that I could see. I think it was those gremlins again."

Frank jumped into the back of a jeep and told the driver to rush him to the infirmary. There he talked to a nurse and inquired about Ted's condition. The answer was that he was suffering from battle fatigue, now known as Post-Traumatic Stress Disorder.

Frank thought to himself, *Battle fatigue? How the heck could it be battle fatigue? He hadn't really been in battle.*

Frank was enraged as never before. Ted had run at the first sign of adversity. He had left Frank, but more importantly, he had left the bombers. That was inexcusable. It would have been a different story to Frank if Ted had been in continued combat over a long period of time. Then Frank would have understood. But to turn tail and run before even firing a shot, without even trying to confront the enemy; that was dereliction of duty.

Ted recuperated in the infirmary for the next several days. Initially, he claimed that there were mechanical problems with his plane that forced him to return to base. Frank and Ted's mechanics knew differently, and so did everyone else. They knew him for what he was, a loud-mouthed, coward who could not be counted on when the chips were down. The men might have thought about him more fondly if he had tried to meet the enemy. But, the fact was, at the first sign of trouble he was out of there.

What minimal sympathy Frank and his fellow pilots had for Ted was tempered by the fact that when he was released he refused to fly combat again. Surprisingly, his pronouncement did not bother the pilots too much because no one wanted to fly with him anyway. They could not trust him.

His disdain for doing his duty was met with a swift court-marshal. During the proceedings, Ted lashed out at the presiding officers stating that Frank ought to be on trial for cowardice, too. After all, he had seen him trembling and vomiting. How was that any different than what happened to him? The officers were terse in their response. The two circumstances were as different as black and white. Yes, Frank admitted to being scared. But the key difference was the fact that he continued to do his duty and had received numerous citations for bravery.

It did not take long for the court-marshal panel to render its decision. The commanding officer could not wait to get Ted off his base as soon as possible. Following shipment back home in disgrace, Ted would be dishonorably discharged. One had to wonder about years later how he answered the question posed by his children or grandchildren as he sat them on his knee. "What did you do during the war?"

Chapter 14

Battle of the Bulge

With the failure of Operation Market Garden fading into the past, the Allies pushed on. There had also been a number of successes since the invasion of the Normandy beaches. Paris had been liberated and the U.S. Third Army continued its press toward the Rhineland. Having the most impact on Frank and other air crews was the complete dominance of the Allied Air Forces. American factories had produced about 100,000 fighters alone since the start of the war, with most being manufactured during these last two years of the war. The end appeared near for the Nazi war machine.

American bombers continued to make daylight bombing raids, flak still arced its way up to meet them. But enemy fighter response could not match its power just prior to D-Day.

Even with all the apparent successes in the air and on the ground, the Army suppressed news about what unexpectedly turned into a major campaign that was bogged down on the way to Germany. It was the battle for the Hürtgen Forest.

The Army took heavy losses that could have been avoided had it circumvented the dense woods and rugged terrain of the Forest. It was a protracted battle that did nothing to gain any sort of strategic advantage. It just happened. Two unsuspecting adversaries met in an area where neither one expected anything to happen because it was essentially unimportant and other routes were much more amenable for the movement of heavy equipment. About the only thing it accomplished was to wear out and deplete the American Army as a prelude to the next big event.

Then, once there was a breakout from the Hürtgen Forest, Adolf Hitler hit the Allies with his biggest surprise on December 16, 1944. He planned an attack through Allied lines via the Ardennes. It would be the biggest land battle of the war. It became known as the Battle of the Bulge. It was named for the bulge created by the wedge driven into the Allies' lines effectively splitting the front in two. This thrust would be followed by a drive northwest towards the North Sea to capture Antwerp, Belgium. Hitler believed his plan could possibly change the course of the war. Perhaps it would be a chance to negotiate for peace or reasonable surrender terms.

Hitler could not have picked a better time to attack. The Allies were still reeling from the long Hürtgen Forest campaign. The weather could not have been more miserable. It was the coldest winter in decades and visibility was non-existent. This meant that Frank, and the rest of Eighth Air Force, was grounded.

All Frank could do was to read newspaper accounts and listen to radio reports of the battle. The battle was going favorably—for the Germans. Allied commanders had been completely surprised by the breakout. If there was one flaw in the German plan, however, it was the routing of traffic through the crossroad town of Bastogne. Here they met strong resistance from the 101st Airborne Division along with the 9th and 10th Armored Divisions who had been rushed in to defend Bastogne by December 19th. German Panzer columns surrounded the town and cut off support from the Allies by December 21st.

Eighth Air Force awaited improvement in the weather in order to drop supplies to the beleaguered defenders. They were in short supply of food, medical supplies, ammunition, and most of all, warm clothing. The weather continued to prevent any meaningful missions to be flown. Frank felt helpless and so did everyone else. How much longer could the troops hold out in Bastogne? Elements of Patton's Third Army were racing north to relieve the besieged combat soldiers. But there was no guarantee they would make it in time or be able to repel the attack.

Then, there was good news on December 23rd. The weather was clearing over Belgium. Everything that could carry supplies did. Even bombers were loaded with lifesaving supplies. Thunderbolts and

Mustangs were loaded with two 500-pound bombs each. Although the Thunderbolts were the preferred tool for this type of operation, the Mustangs would help out, too.

Frank wanted to help make for a Merry Christmas for the boys who had suffered so much on the ground. Knowing he would return from each flight to a warm bed and decent food made him all the more adamant about helping these poor souls. He felt that the least he could do was to try to alleviate some of the suffering of his comrades on the ground.

Frank was ordered to lead his squadron to rendezvous with a flight of C-47s delivering supplies to Bastogne. Once the supplies were dropped, he was to linger in the area and cover against air or ground attack as needed. All the pilots were eager to do anything they could to help these comrades in arms.

Frank was flying high cover looking for enemy fighters as the C-47s made their run. They were coming in low and slow to make sure that the supplies landed where intended. Although some supplies were landing in German hands, many of them were hitting their mark. Frank could see the ground troops scurrying to collect the precious supplies. They were running low on all the necessities and this was like an early Christmas for them.

With his fuel getting low, it was time to return to base. The defenders of Bastogne had been re-supplied and could renew their effort to hinder the German's advance and to begin repelling it.

The next day, Frank returned with his squadron to the Ardennes. This time, he was escorting a flight of B-24 Liberators that were bombing rail yards behind enemy lines. Fuel supplies for Hitler's tanks were running low and the plan was to take out tank cars that might be supplying them with sorely needed diesel fuel.

The bombers appeared to be making direct hits in and all around the rail yard. But, there were no earth-shattering explosions as would be expected when fuel ignites. The tank cars were empty. So, Frank led his squadron on a strafing run to inflict as much additional damage as they could on Germany's railway system. In general, the day's results were disappointing.

At this stage, Germany's fuel supply was at a premium and its army was moving forward by using any means of transport it could, including trucks and horse carts. They would be the next targets of opportunity.

It was Christmas Day. You would think that the war would come to a standstill in honor of such a hallowed day. But war waits for no man, neither agnostic nor religious. While there were isolated instances of Christian civility, an unwary guy could still get himself killed out there, even on one of the holiest days of the year.

Back home on Christmas Day Dottie was helping her mother prepare for the festivities. The previous evening they had attended Christmas Eve services at their church—something done every year, but this year was not the same.

Now, the big cast iron stove, which served as additional heat during the winter months, was coming into its intended service—to cook the holiday meal. They had stockpiled their ration cards and accumulated nonperishable supplies in preparation for this big day. Dottie's mother, Ann, also had a green thumb. During the growing season she planted and harvested all sorts of fruits and vegetables that she bottled for use during the remainder of the year. So, there would be an adequate supply of potatoes, green beans, and butternut squash all from their very own victory garden. And for dessert, home-grown pumpkins for their pumpkin pie, and apples from their enormous apple tree for her mother's specialty, apple pie.

The radio piped Christmas music throughout the house. Every hour holiday fare was interrupted with war news. So, the family knew what was happening at the war front. Dottie would pause to listen intently to the reports and could not help but worry. In order to divert her attention, her mother gave her chores like setting the table in the dining room with elegant china and silverware. Aunts and uncles, along with their children, would be arriving for the celebration about noon. Nonetheless, as she sat at the kitchen preparing string beans, *White Christmas* began playing on the radio. A tear came to her eye as she thought about Frank and his situation.

Her mother was busy preparing the entrée, a beautifully decorated baked ham. By mid-morning, the aroma began to fill the whole house. Dottie's father kept checking out the oven as he monitored its progress. He got away with it a few times before Ann yelled at him,

"Eddie, it you don't stop doing that the ham won't be done in time for guests!"

Eddie got the message. He did not want anything to delay the sumptuous repast. However, a new aroma was filling the air. The pumpkin and apple pies had just come out of the oven and were cooling on the kitchen counter. It was almost too much for Eddie to bear. This was shear torture. He was salivating like a hungry dog.

As noon approached family began to arrive. Kicking the snow off their boots as they entered the foyer, the cacophony escalated to a higher pitch as everyone shared their holiday greetings and tried to relate stories. The children, obviously excited, ran into the living room to check for presents under the Christmas tree. The Christmas music almost became inaudible. Yet, it was a special time.

After all guests arrived, the adults were seated around the large dining room table. The children sat at a couple of small tables, one group at a small table in the dining room and the other in the breakfast nook in the kitchen. Everyone was ready to dive into the mountains of ham, mashed potatoes, butternut squash and, of course, the pies. But first, Eddie, who wanted to indulge himself more than anyone else, composed himself to say grace. He thanked God for the feast, for family, for health, and, finally, for the protection of the soldiers, sailors, marines, and airmen. Then he prayed by name for family and friends at the front. Amen.

Now it was time to eat; and, eat they did.

The Army Air Force was able to drop rations that included turkey and cranberry sauce, but it was nothing like your mother made. At least Frank had a chance to go to the mess hall and have a meal where he actually saw meat being sliced from a whole roasted turkey. What the combat soldier on the ground found himself eating could have quite literally come from several different turkeys. And there were questions circulating as to what parts were included in the mix. Nonetheless, they appreciated every single bite.

Before and after his meal, Frank was flying missions. The only breaks he received were during the time it took his ground crew to service and rearm his airplane. And those guys were working like demons. So, it did not take them long to get his airplane ready and he was off again.

On each and every flight, Frank kept a close look out for enemy fighters, but nothing was spotted. During those missions when he flew high cover for C-47s dropping supplies, he circled overhead to protect them. Once they were done, he would lead his squadron down to ensure that the ground troops were safely recovering the supply canisters.

As he did so, he noticed German Tiger tanks opening up on a group of American soldiers attempting to recover supplies from the canisters. They were being decimated, and they were trapped. Frank rolled his Mustang into a split-S and pulled out while firing at the tanks. He climbed and made a quick turn to the left to make a follow-up attack. Heavy fire was being directed at him from the two tanks' machine guns and from enemy infantry. He was also sure that he was picking up some crossfire from the American lines, too. He could hear the plinking sounds of bullets hitting his wings and fuselage.

As he swung in low he released his two bombs. One seemed to skid along the snow-covered ground between some pine trees and slammed into the side of one of the tanks, exploding on impact. Frank could see the turret fly off and other debris spray all around him. He was lucky that he wasn't hit. He looked over his shoulder as he made a climbing turn. The tank was aflame.

Immediately following Frank's attack Scotty dropped his two bombs, but just missed the second tank. He did cause considerable damage to a couple of armored support vehicles.

This time he made his attack from the rear. He hesitated in doing so because he was afraid his bullets might ricochet and cause some friendly fire damage to the Americans under siege. He remembered the friendly fire incident during the breakout from Saint Lo. He had heard that the fuel tank of German Tigers was the most vulnerable spot. So, that was his plan. He had no more bombs so he had to rely upon his .50-caliber armor-piercing incendiary bullets to do the job.

Frank came in low again. This time he was directly behind the second Tiger tank. The tank's machine gun was trained on him and he could see the tracers flying by his canopy. He kicked in a little rudder to slip out of the way of the direct line of fire. Then he opened up with machine gun fire himself. His bullets were hitting all over and around the tank, but nothing happened. His Mustang took some hits along his fuselage and horizontal stabilizer. Fortunately, his coolant temperature was okay. At least this meant that his coolant system had not been hit.

The infantry was still being hammered by the tank. Frank could not give up. He knew he was starting to run low on ammo and fuel. He had to make his attack successful this time or he would need to concede failure. So he whipped his Mustang around again, resolved to the fact that this would be the end for the tank or himself. The tank's machine gun swung around on him again. He started firing, ricocheting his bullets off the ground underneath the rear section of the tank. And then there was an enormous explosion as fuel and ammunition went skyward.

Frank pulled up sharply to the right in an attempt to avoid the flaming blast. He could hear debris plinking through his plane all around. Next, some shrapnel came whizzing right through the cockpit. He felt a burning sensation in his right calf. He had been hit. There wasn't anything more he could do to help the infantry, so he climbed back to altitude to reorganize his squadron. It was time to return to base. He just hoped he and his plane would make it.

Once back at cruising altitude Frank started to assess his situation. His Mustang seemed to be humming along. Actually, it whistled from all the holes in it. But its Merlin engine continued to purr. He, too, had a hole in himself. He was bleeding all over the inside of the cockpit. So, he pulled out his first aid kit and set about making a compression bandage for himself. The burning sensation had abated but the pain was intense. He wondered if he could overcome the pain in his right leg to control the rudder. You cannot land a Mustang without a lot of attention to the rudder pedals, especially the right rudder. They don't like to land sideways.

As he approached the field for landing, he fired his flare gun indicating that he was wounded. He managed to control the rudders enough to land safely and pull off to the side of the runway. He decided to let the ground crew tow his plane back to the hardstand because his leg was just too painful to continue to work the rudder and brakes to turn the airplane on the ground. His ground crew rushed to his aid in a jeep and on bicycles.

Frank rolled the canopy back as MSgt. Riley jumped up on the wing and helped him to unclasp his safety harness. MSgt. Riley could see that Frank was in pain as he helped him out of the cockpit and onto the ground. About then an ambulance pulled up to take Frank to surgery. His ground crew gathered around the Mustang. They could not believe their eyes. It looked like it had been used for target practice. There wasn't a square foot that had not been hit. Yet, key systems had been missed. It was a miracle. Surprisingly, Frank concentrated so hard to stave off the pain and fly the plane that he did not have time to dwell on his fear. This was the only time he returned from a flight where he did not exhibit his typical fear-driven symptoms.

The wound wasn't too bad. It hit muscle, didn't break bones, and it was relatively superficial. It just bled a lot. Frank would be as good as new in about two weeks. Then the chief surgeon decided that he only needed to be grounded for just the next five days. He could use the rest, both physically and emotionally.

The plane was written off as total loss. It was cannibalized for its engine and other components, but there was just too much sheet aluminum work to make repair worthwhile. As Frank recuperated, another Mustang fresh off North American's production line was delivered from the Air Maintenance Depot. Immediately upon delivery of the plane, MSgt. Riley and his crew jumped into action to verify that it was ready to fly its first mission. Moreover, they did something they knew Frank would appreciate. They repainted the cowling with Frank's favorite nose art, his screaming eagle "Freedom Fighter" design.

It was New Year's Eve 1945. The officers were gathered at the base officers' club for the standard partying that goes with the season. Liquor was flowing freely. Frank, being a teetotaler just sat back and observed. He was not being judgmental, but he wondered how such heavy drinking would translate for the next day's mission back into the Ardennes area. He thought to himself, *There's going to be a lot of these guys inhaling oxygen tomorrow trying to get rid of their hangover even with "eight hours between bottle and throttle." Boy, I sure would not want to fly, let alone go into combat, under those circumstances.*

Frank and Scotty sat at their table with a couple of other pilots and sipped eggnog and munched on some pastries and chocolate. In the background, music played on the radio. To the best of their knowledge, they were about to ring in another New Year—and another year of war. Frank and Scotty both decided that the New Year would arrive whether or not they stayed awake for it. So, they decided to hit the sack in order to be rested for the next day's missions.

With all the bad news being received back home about the Battle of the Bulge, hope for an early end to the war was fading fast. The Nazi surge in the Ardennes caused widespread depression in Frank's family and with Dottie, too. While Frank's and Dottie's families welcomed in the New Year together, they could not bring themselves to celebrate. After all, Frank and at least one of his brothers were still in harm's way.

The fighting in the Pacific was becoming more and more fierce with the worst yet to come. Presently though, all eyes were turned toward Europe and Hitler's last-ditch effort to prevent the Allies from crossing the Rhine onto German soil. They discussed that Frank's letters left much to the imagination about his missions although they were certain that he had to be involved somehow.

At any rate, the families enjoyed a nice dinner at the Johnson's as they listened to music on the radio interspersed with reports of the day's military actions. As the mantel clock chimed midnight they raised their glasses of apple cider as Frank's father offered a prayer for the coming year. It amounted to a simple, "Dear God, please allow us to be victorious over our enemies in this war and bring our boys home safely to us we humbly pray." This was followed by a hearty "Amen" from them all.

Just as Frank expected, most of the pilots awakened at less than peak form. Some were experiencing bed-spins. Others were nauseated. And still others had pounding headaches. None of them would feel very well in the rarified air at high altitude.

Before their briefing, Frank and Scotty stopped by the mess hall for breakfast. Attendance was pretty sparse. Few men had much of an appetite that morning, especially for scrambled eggs made from powdered eggs and powdered milk. In some ways it was nice for Frank and Scotty because there was no line waiting to be served and much of the raucous noise that was usually in the background was now missing. They had a chance for a rare relaxing meal before their mission.

In some ways, it would have been comical watching the gaggle of staggering pilots make their way to their airplanes and try to climb up on the wing. Yes, it would have been comical, if it was not such serious business.

This would be a seek-and-destroy mission. The bulk of the German offensive had been beaten back, although it would be another two weeks before the Germans withdrew totally.

When Frank's squadron arrived over their assigned position, they began scanning the sky for enemy aircraft while looking for targets on the ground. As he surveyed the battlefield, he saw burned out hulks of tanks, half-tracks, and any number of artillery pieces strewn all about the area. It looked like Armageddon had arrived.

As he circled the area, he heard excited chatter over the radio. A couple of the Allies' forward airfields were under attack. As he scanned the sky for signs of the enemy, he spotted tiny specks in the sky to the west. Frank led the squadron to confront the enemy. The two other squadrons in the Group heard the call, too, and were rushing to help. Meanwhile, American airplanes were attempting to take off from the airfields while under fire.

Frank could see that there was a small flight of German planes providing high cover. So, he called over the radio for the other supporting squadrons to strike the German planes directly involved in the attack while his squadron dealt with those at altitude.

The American squadrons tore into the Germans while they tried to avoid friendly fire. The Germans were taking a beating, from both American airplanes and ground fire. While they were still a dangerous foe, this was not the same Luftwaffe Frank had fought earlier in the war. Their combat techniques were not as well honed and they did not have the same aggressive nature about them. They flew more defensively. Regardless, Frank had no problem shooting them down, neither from a combat perspective nor from a moral one.

Frank could easily stay on the tail of a FW-190 and fire away with his foe taking only minimal evasive action. This was not very sporting, but it got the job done. Frank's second victory of the day was another FW-190. He caught the pilot totally unaware as he made a pass while firing his machine guns. The German pilot virtually flew right through the stream of bullets.

When the day was done, nearly 245 aircraft had been shot down, with more than 60 downed in air-to-air combat. Frank had two more victories to add to his tally.

When the air battle was done, Frank led his squadron back to their assigned patrol area and they continued to look for targets until their fuel quantity dictated their return to base. It had been a productive day. Frank went into it expecting a ground attack mission, but it turned into more exhilarating air-to-air combat.

As it turned out, the air combat had another benefit on the squadron. It was an excellent panacea for most of the pilots with hangovers. It gave them something else on which to concentrate. So much so, that they quickly forgot their headaches and nausea. Perhaps they would think differently before drinking so heavily the night before their next mission.

During the mission, several of the pilots had gotten so violently ill that they vomited in their cockpit. Upon their return to base, their crew chiefs were enraged. It would have been one thing to clean up an airplane if the pilot was genuinely sick. But, this was something totally within the pilots' control. They had taken their celebrating to excess. Frank confronted each of the pilots and ordered them to clean their own planes, and he told their respective crew chiefs to make sure they did a proper job of it. Frank earned a lot of respect among the ground crews that day.

The next several days were routine missions with sporadic encounters with the enemy. Elements of the German army appeared to be in general retreat. Most of what Frank and his squadron were doing was harassment attacks to keep them from rejoining the fight.

By the middle of January 1945, the Battle of the Bulge was officially over. It had lasted a month and was a massive ground war between the German army and Allies that had taken a horrible toll in casualties on both sides. The death knell had been sounded for the Nazis. Now, with the German army in full retreat, it looked like the end was in sight. Yet, there were still air battles to be fought and won.

Remaining air battles would involve some of the most technologically advanced aircraft of the war, while ground attacks would be reduced to attacks on horse- and human-powered carts hauling munitions. This was such a huge dichotomy in technology that it seemed surreal.

Chapter 15

Dangerous Ground Missions

Probably the least desirable missions were ground attacks. Airfields, factories, gun emplacements, refineries, and railroad yards were the optimal targets. Along with those optimal targets came the greatest risk. Attacking them meant flying a gauntlet of anti-aircraft defenses.

What made these missions doubly dangerous was the fact that once you were hit, there was little time to bail out. First, at speeds in excess of three hundred miles per hour, the rate of closure before a damaged aircraft hit the ground was measured in fractions of seconds. Second, there was no time to bail out. Even if a pilot could bail out, there was no time for the parachute to deploy fully. It was deadly business.

The best way to attack a ground target was to have up-to-date reconnaissance photographs. In this way ingress and egress could be planned to provide the most cover. That was a two-edged sword, however, because the more the aircraft remained hidden by cover, the less time the pilot had to sight on the target. Coming from altitude gave more time to align on the target, and an equal amount of time for enemy anti-aircraft gunners to line up on diving aircraft. Regardless of the technique, there were bound to be losses.

With the massive losses by the Luftwaffe and overwhelming domination in numbers of Allied aircraft, enemy aircraft were becoming less of a threat to the bombers. At this stage of the war, Allied fighters were being released from their escort duties once the bombers were safely on their way home. Most fighter pilots relished the idea that now they were free to roam and do some damage to the German infrastructure on their own.

If there was something moving it became a target for the free-wheeling fighters. Even horse carts became targets of opportunity because, as fuel and mechanized equipment became rarer, they were used to transport ammunition and other supplies. Still, the favorite targets among fighter pilots were railroad locomotives. They loved to see steam spewing from the boilers which signaled good hits. This meant the whole train was disabled and easy pickings as the fighters ranged up and down the box and tank cars. You had to be careful though. If the railroad cars happened to be loaded with explosives or high-octane fuel, the attacking plane could find itself incinerated along with it. It was dangerous but gratifying work because you kept the load from reaching enemy ground troops and gun emplacements.

Airfields were particularly dangerous places to attack. They had extensive open areas with plenty of protection. But the risks were worth it as it was far better to catch your prey on the ground than in the air. Generally, it was less risky for the first attackers because the defensive positions had not been fully alerted when they were attacked. As the next wave of aircraft attacked, the ground fortifications were ready and the tally of downed aircraft would invariably increase.

On this particular day, the 355th Fighter Group was assigned to attack an airfield just north of Hamburg. Intelligence officers examined several aerial reconnaissance photographs and concluded that the best way to attack was from the northeast. Frank disagreed. Enemy aircraft were lined up on both sides of the runway. They were spread out, but generally in a line.

Frank devised a plan which he set about selling to the intelligence people. He would split his forces with one wave coming from the northeast and the other concurrently from the southwest. To prevent shooting each other, the flight from the northeast would attack only those aircraft on the north side of the field and those attacking from the southwest would shoot only at those aircraft on the south side of the field. This would minimize their time over the target and, hopefully, confound the anti-aircraft gunners. The stubborn intelligence officers disagreed with his recommendation. So, Frank had no other alternative than to take his idea to the Group commander and elicit his approval of the mission.

The other detail that Frank worked into the equation was the timing of the attack. The Group would take off by 5:00 a.m. At a cruising speed of about 325 miles per hour that would put them over the target at 6:30 a.m. That was about sunrise. The flight attacking out of the northeast would start their attack a few seconds ahead of the one coming in from the southwest. This would put the sun in the eyes of the anti-aircraft gunners for the aircraft out of the northeast. Concurrently, it would put the sun in their eyes during the egress of the flight from the southwest. He also reasoned that the sun should not pose a problem for the flight attacking from the southwest because the pilots would be looking down at their targets while the gunners would be looking into the sun.

It all made sense, at least to Frank. Only time would tell if his tactic worked.

The next morning the pilots got to their planes at 4:30 a.m. and did a preflight. At 4:45 a.m. it was engine start. The first airplane, Frank's, pulled away from its hardstand and he began the lazy S-turns as he taxied toward the end of the runway. All the other Mustangs in the Group followed close behind each other. Their S-turns were the only way they could see around the Mustang's nose that was pointing upward like it was ready to grab for the sky. They looked like a large, slithering serpent as they taxied to the end of the runway.

Frank turned his Mustang into the wind and began his engine run up, propeller cycle, engine and instrument checks, and just getting himself organized in the cockpit. The other pilots followed suit. Frank contacted the control tower that he was ready to go. He and Scotty pulled onto the runway slightly offset from one another. They received their clearance from the control tower and Frank announced to Scotty, "Okay, Scotty, let's hit it."

They were off in unison. As soon as they started to roll down the runway, the next pair of planes pulled into position. They were all off the ground within a matter of minutes and linking up overhead for their formation.

The flight to Hamburg would be relatively fast. It was only 485 miles from their base. They were to maintain radio silence until the attack commenced. Frank would use hand signals or wave his wings when he wanted to get their attention.

With only the rumble of his Rolls Royce Merlin engine in the background he tried to divert his attention to something constructive. He was well-prepared for the mission. After all, he had planned it. He knew every detail and every checkpoint. So he tried to drown out his feelings of fear by concentrating on home. He wondered what his mother and father were doing.

He thought, *Let's see, it's Tuesday. Well, not quite. It's the middle of the night. They are all in bed.* That didn't help him.

Then he decided on a different train of thought. *I wonder what I ought to do when I get home. You know, it might be a good idea to make a career out of the military. Yet, I sure want a job where they won't be shooting at me anymore. I can probably use my experience and education to help design new military aircraft. Perhaps I can be a test pilot for the military or one of the big aircraft manufacturers. Or, I can go back to Eastern Air Lines if they'll have me.* Now that thought had run its course. Time to try another.

I'll have a pretty good nest egg set aside by the time I get home. Maybe I can put a down payment on a house and finally marry Dottie. I wonder where we'll live. I guess I'll have to wait to see where I get a job or, if I stay in the Army, where they decide to send me. Who should we invite to the wedding? Will we want kids? If so, how many? His mind was racing but, at least, he was focusing on something besides his fear. The time droned on as they neared the target.

Then Frank spotted the telltale signs of Hamburg. He looked to the north and saw the clearing that was the airfield. He signaled the second flight that it was time to split their forces. Frank made a slight turn to the north to adjust his course to fly north of the airfield. Once Frank's flight was about five miles northwest of the airfield he broke into a split-S and began diving for the ground. The flight entering from the southwest dived as well. Each force was attacking as two aircraft each in staggered formation. The wingman was to watch for anti-aircraft activity and deal with it. Frank's plane was screaming at treetop level doing about 400 miles per hour. The faster he went the shorter the time he would be in the gunners' sights. He would not be over the airfield very long, therefore he needed to be accurate. As soon as he broke into the clearing he was going to start firing his machine guns. He planned to hold the trigger down as long as he had targets in sight. This is exactly what he did.

As he fired, his six .50-caliber machine guns created a trail on the ground. He could see them streaking a patch running up to a transport airplane. A small fire erupted in the left wing and engine. The path of destruction continued along the ground as a line of three FW-190s was being sprayed. The armor piercing incendiary rounds were blasting holes in them and starting them afire. As he did this he could see the flight coming from the southwest. The timing was perfect.

The flights following Frank completely decimated all the aircraft on the ground and did considerable damage to the airfield's infrastructure. They destroyed fuel supplies, ground support vehicles, the control tower, the barracks, and a number of anti-aircraft gun emplacements. One of the "tail-end Charlies" had nothing left at which to shoot so, being a comedian, he blasted the latrine to bits. He was really going to make it uncomfortable for the Germans.

The plan worked with only some minor damage from anti-aircraft fire, ricochets from friendly aircraft, and collateral damage from exploding enemy aircraft. Frank was pleased and thankful for the positive outcome. He was only too happy that his plan resulted in success and not disaster.

It was March 17, 1945. An order came down from headquarters to attack railroad rolling stock in Frankfurt, Germany the next morning. Specifically, the mission was designed to prevent reinforcements from reaching troops amassing to meet General Patton's army which was approaching the Rhine. Pilots were instructed first to take out locomotives followed by attacking flat cars carrying tanks of other visible military equipment. Then, once that was accomplished, they were to strafe tank cars, box cars and troop cars.

Frank presented the general mission objectives at the 6:00 a.m. briefing while the intelligence officer provided detailed information via reconnaissance photos and maps. It looked like a prime, target-rich region. Planes would be armed with two five-hundred pound bombs and the normal complement of munitions.

Upon Frank's arrival at his Mustang, his crew chief, MSgt. Riley, was there and ready to strap him into the cockpit. Frank asked MSgt. Riley, "How does everything look?"

"Couldn't be better, sir. She runs like a Swiss watch."

"Thanks, Sgt. Riley. I couldn't ask for anything more."

"Give 'em blazes, major."

"I plan to do just that."

Frank hollered, "CLEAR," as he hit the starter. After six blades of the propeller passed by, the engine fired with a rumble and a puff of black, pungent smoke, and then it settled down to a purr. As he taxied for take off, the engine backfired as he retarded the throttle. This was normal.

Take off was uneventful as was the climb and link up with all aircraft in the formation. They were on their way. At a little over 400 miles each way, it would take about two hours to make the round tip plus time over the target.

Along the way, there was no opposition. It almost looked like this mission would be a milk run. It took about an hour-and-a-half to reach their destination. Frank expected things to heat up from ground fire as they made their attack runs. Sure enough, up came machine gun and anti-aircraft fire. Frank could also see soldiers shooting with small arms. They were desperate to try anything to take on the attacking marauders.

The flights broke up and concentrated their fire on locomotives. Frank thought it was thrilling whenever he hit a locomotive and saw steam spewing from bullet holes. The boys were really hitting them hard.

Frank came around again to drop his bombs. He wanted to take out sections of track and disable switches in order to prevent any movement. He located a nice, densely packed collection of switches. He reasoned that he could get more bang for his proverbial buck by taking out that section of track and switches.

He released his bombs and climbed to rejoin the attack. After the smoke cleared a little, he could see twisted track indicating a good bombing run. Now, it was time to use his machine guns to full effect. As he lined up his next target, he noticed a locomotive with about thirty box cars out of the corner of his eye trying to make its escape towards the west. It could have been operated by an engineer just trying to make his escape. Or, it could be a train operating under strict orders to get the cargo to the front no matter the cost. Frank could not take a chance. So, he decided to chase it down.

Frank approached abreast the locomotive, and then turned towards it. He started to rake it with machine gun fire. It was not long before the telltale signs of a ruptured boiler were evident. Now he could take his time and strafe the box cars.

Frank swung his Mustang in a tight turn and lined up to make a lengthwise attack on the line of box cars. He began to fire and could see his tracers smashing through the box cars, one after the other. Then, BLAM! He must have hit a box car full of munitions. Debris was flying everywhere and Frank was caught in the middle of a pillar of flames. He felt the heat penetrating the thin aluminum skin of his airplane.

Then something else was wrong. The engine felt like it was ready to shake itself loose from the engine mount. He tried to gain altitude as best he could in order to assess his damage and to be ready for a possible bail out. Once he leveled at 10,000 feet, he tried to figure what was wrong. He retarded his throttle and the shaking improved somewhat, but it was still pretty bad. Then he noticed that there was something different about the way his propeller spun in an arc. Finally he figured out what it was—half of one of the four propeller blades was blown away. He knew there was no way to get this wounded bird back home with all that vibration. If he tried, the Mustang would shake itself to pieces. He would have to bail out.

He called Scotty over the radio, "Scotty, I've been hit. My propeller has been shot away and it's about ready to shake the whole plane apart. I want to get out before there is a total structural failure. I'm going to head west and try to get as close to friendly territory as possible."

"Okay, Frank. I'll stay with you until you get down."

Frank continued to nurse the old bird as best he could, but it was a futile effort. As he jettisoned the canopy, there was an airplane-shaking bang, probably the crankshaft or bearing in the engine as it seized solid. It was time to get out. He was now over rolling farmlands just west of the city of Frankfurt.

He climbed out of the cockpit and onto the wing. This was frightening. He considered climbing back in and making a crash landing, but then he thought better of it, as he did not think his plane would hold together long enough to make it. So, he just closed his eyes and slid down the backside of the wing. Before he knew it, he was free falling and quickly pulled the D-ring on his parachute. There was a sharp jolt as the parachute's canopy opened. He thought, *Thank the good Lord for that! One less thing to worry about.*

As he wafted his way down, he looked up to see his Mustang plummeting to earth. It hit the ground in a ball of flames about two miles away. Then Frank looked down as the ground rushed up to meet him. He hit the ground with a thud. Frank felt his legs slam into his chest. Then he felt a sharp pain in his left foot. It had landed on a rock, badly bruising and spraining it. That would make the going painful and slow.

Scotty made a low pass and waggled his wings. Frank waved back to let Scotty know he was okay. He was down safe and sound. But he was trapped behind enemy lines.

Dottie awoke early that morning with an extraordinary sense of anguish. She had no rational reason for feeling that way. Somehow, she sensed something was wrong somewhere. When her parents arose from bed and came downstairs they found her just staring out the front window. When her mother asked her what was wrong, she snapped at her, and then she quickly apologized.

"Mom, I don't know why I reacted that way. I'm just really scared about something but I don't know what it is."

"Dottie, dear, we've all been jumpy, what with the goings on with the war and our loved ones overseas. I know that you especially worry about Frank."

"I know, Mom, he keeps telling me through his letters that he is safe and not seeing much action, but it is much more than that. I have a feeling deep within my being that I just can't explain. Something is very wrong."

"Why don't you spend the day shopping with your girlfriends? Go to Quincy and check out the new spring fashions. Do anything to take your mind off of whatever is bothering you."

"Perhaps I should."

"Yes, it would be good for you to get out of the house and enjoy yourself. You have been working so many hours at the hospital that you need to relax a little. You're probably just tired from working so much."

"That sounds like a good idea. I'll give the girls a call. Would you like to come along?"

"No, dear. You and the girls need some time to yourselves."

Could it be possible that she possessed a sixth sense when it came to Frank? Otherwise, why would she have such a premonition of gloom and doom on this day above all others?

Chapter 16

Evasive Action

Frank rushed to unhook his harness and bundle up his parachute. He needed to hide all evidence of his presence. He looked around for some place to stash it. There was a line of hedges. So, he jammed it in the middle and packed it down in them so that it would be out of sight.

Now, he needed to assess his situation. He had a little water, a small amount of food, a medical kit, a knife, a compass, and his .45-caliber semi-automatic with four clips of ammunition plus what was in the gun already. Before he bailed out, he had also grabbed his maps. They would be useful as he tried to make his way back to the Allied lines. After all, he had heard news that Patton's army was rapidly making its way towards the Rhine River headed for Oppenheim, Germany. Somehow he needed to make his way there. If only he could avoid capture until then.

He decided that he could not just sit around and wait. There was no way for him to know how long it would be before he could link up with the Allies, or where they would cross the Rhine. He would also need food, water, and shelter. In any event he had to start moving now because, surely, someone had seen his parachute. He knew that if he was captured that the Gestapo would want to get their hands on him as a major in command of a squadron with inside information about its operation. He could not let that happen.

So, he quickly checked the position of the sun and the map and aligned himself for a westward trek. If he kept the Main River on his left, he would eventually run into the Rhine River. The key now was to keep from being captured. Thus, he started to run as fast as he could, sprained foot and all. His foot was really throbbing, but he knew he needed to get as much distance between himself and his parachute, should someone find it. He felt like a criminal on the run.

As he moved westward he looked for ditches and depressions, rocks and bushes, anything that would provide cover. It was mid-day and the sun shone down on him. The day was temperate, but he knew he needed to find shelter for the night. The area was dotted with small farms. Perhaps he could find an abandoned barn and steal some sustenance along the way. For now, he had enough to get him through this first day. But beyond that, he would have to take some chances to meet his daily needs by scrounging the countryside and its farms.

As Frank was making his way west, he heard the muffled roar of an airplane engine in the distance. It was a lightly-built, German Fieseler FI-156C Storch observation plane looking for him. As fast as his sore foot would carry him he made a break for a row of hedges and dove into the center taking cover. The airplane was flying in ever-widening circles trying to locate him. He could see it through the leaves; however, he prayed that the pilot could not see him in turn. He remained motionless as the plane crossed overhead.

Forty-five minutes must have passed before the plane moved off. Perhaps headquarters called him back thinking that the parachute sighting had been a false alarm and that the pilot had gone down with his airplane. Consequently, Frank started to move again. He figured he had 25 miles to cover before he reached the Rhine, and it would be slow going.

It was approaching 5:00 p.m. and Frank needed to start thinking about what he wanted to do for the night. He decided to continue moving until he found what appeared to be a suitable shelter. It was nothing more than a six-by-six foot shack with missing siding but, at least, it would provide some cover from the elements.

It was a dark, cold night. Frank did not sleep well. Every little noise jolted him awake and he thought he would freeze. Although he had some matches, he did not dare start a fire because he was afraid the smoke would alert some farmer of his presence. So, he just suffered the night away as best he could.

His foot was swollen and he felt it throb with every heart beat. Although he would have gotten some relief by taking off his shoe, he worried about getting it back on his foot. So, he decided to bear the pain and hope that he would sleep through it.

Gazing at the stars and a crescent moon that looked like the Cheshire cat's smile, he pondered his fate. He was stuck behind enemy lines, injured, and alone. What would be the outcome? He could only do his best to elude the enemy and survive the elements.

Before sunrise on March 18th, he was awake and feeling hungry. He needed to scrounge for food and water. About a half a mile away, he could see a faint light in a farm house. He decided to take a risk and head for it. Staying low against the ground he moved towards the farm house. He could see movement in the backlit window. The farmer and his wife were up and preparing for their daily chores.

As the sun rose, he could see the silhouette of the farmer heading into the barn with a bucket in hand. It was time to milk the cows. Shortly thereafter, out came his wife with a basket—time to collect the eggs from the chicken coop. It was time for Frank to engage in some petty burglary. He did not believe in stealing, but this was a special circumstance and this was the enemy.

He stealthily crept up to the farm house, keeping the house between himself and the barn. As he neared the house, a dog came running around the corner and growled. So, Frank bent down and beckoned the dog to him. Fortunately, the dog was harmless and friendly. Frank petted it for a while in order to insure that it stayed quiet and then it was off to look for rabbits or to go back to sleep.

Frank carefully peeked through a window into the home. He could see that the kitchen was empty, but how about the rest of the house? He sneaked around the other side of the house and could see that the living area was also vacant. Perhaps there were children sleeping upstairs. Yet, he had to take the chance. He was getting hungry and thirsty.

There was a back door on the house and, luckily, it was unlocked. It squeaked a little as he opened it. Then, he gingerly closed it so that it would not slam shut. He was inside. He entered the kitchen and could see the barn and chicken coop clearly through the window. The farmer and his wife were still busy with their appointed chores. But he had to work fast. He checked the cupboard, the pantry, and the ice box.

He found a chunk of cured ham, half-dozen eggs, some cheese, and bread. He had hit pay dirt. He needed to be careful, though, because he did not want to take so much to let them notice that someone had been there and that they had been robbed. He also needed to stay away from the window as he did not want them to see him. The last thing he did was fill a couple of containers with water.

As he was preparing to leave, a thought ran through his mind. He grabbed some old newspapers and a small bar of soap. The newspapers would be useful as kindling for a fire, and for one of those necessary bodily functions. Frank gave a final glance out the window and saw the farmer's wife returning to the house. But just as he was leaving he found another item that would prove to be extremely useful, a walking stick standing in the corner by the doorway. Frank decided to requisition it in order to take some of the weight off his bad foot.

So, Frank slipped out the door and off he went in the opposite direction. He would find cover, have a bite to eat, and be on his way making a wide berth around the farm. Some remorseful thoughts ran through his mind because he regretted stealing, but that was the price of war.

After satisfying his hunger and thirst, Frank checked his progress on the map. He had only managed to cover about three miles the first day. He knew that he needed to do better on subsequent days.

Frank considered traveling during the night and sleeping during the day. However, this thought quickly dissolved when a short time later he was hiking along a creek and came around a corner face-to-face with—a cow. It startled the heck out of him. He grabbed for his semi-automatic before he realized what it was. He did not want this to happen at night when he had no way of knowing friend from foe or critter from man. It would be travel by day and sleep by night when possible. Besides, Frank had never been able to sleep very well during the daytime.

Frank made a little better time this second day of evasion—almost six miles. It would have been more except for the fact that he spotted a German check point along a road he needed to cross. He could see it as he hid at the top of a small, rounded hill. He also had a good panoramic view of the entire area for about five miles in each direction. There was the Main River right where it should be to his left. It wound its way like a snake towards the west, ultimately emptying into the Rhine.

Frank reconnoitered the area and determined his best approach to the road while avoiding the checkpoint. There was a row of barbed wire on each side of the road on either side of the checkpoint. He wondered how he would navigate that. He did not have any wire cutters.

Then night fell. It was pitch black as a thick cloud cover had moved into the area. There was not a star in sight. Frank waited until about 8:00 p.m. and made his move.

He hiked down the backside of the hill retracing his steps over familiar ground. Moving around the hill, he followed a creek, and he warily approached the barbed wire and the road. Just before he made his final approach to the barbed wire, he slathered some mud on his face to try to camouflage the pale whiteness and reflectivity of it. Now, he was crawling inch-by-inch, foot-by-foot. He tried to remain silent, but he could hear his heart beating loudly. This was unlike the games of capture he played with friends in the woods as a child. This was for real and for keeps. It was terrifying.

As he drew near the barbed wire, he opened his jacket and pulled out the bundle of newspapers. He rolled onto his back and used the paper to lift the barbed wire as he slipped under it little-by-little. It was working; he was making progress.

Then he heard the crumple of footsteps on gravel. It was two sentries making their rounds. They were about thirty yards distant. Frank, still under the barbed wire felt like a trapped rat. He could not move forwards or backwards without being seen. There was nothing he could do but stay perfectly still. For added insurance, he pulled out his semi-automatic, quietly pulled back the hammer and then pulled back the slide to chamber a cartridge. All he could do now was watch and wait. His heart raced all the more. He was certain that the sentries would hear its loud thumping. It was about ready to explode.

He drew a bead on one of the sentries preparing to fire if they raised their Mausers towards him. But they continued on past. Now, he raised the question to himself as to how far they would proceed down the roadway before they turned back. Fortunately, that question was answered forthright. They stopped for a moment and each lit a cigarette, took a few drags on them, and turned back. Frank breathed a sigh of relief.

As soon as he was sure the sentries were well clear of the area, Frank resumed his slow but steady move through the barbed wire. Once clear, he darted across the roadway. Now, he had to do it again for the barbed wire on the other side. Covering this short section of ground had taken over an hour and Frank was emotionally and physically exhausted. Upon finding the first available cover, Frank settled in for the night. He ate a little ham and cheese along with a bit of bread. He used the newspapers to provide some insulation by packing them into his jacket and pants. It had proven much more versatile than he originally thought possible.

On the morning of March 19th Frank was heartsick. The Main River was at his immediate left. That was fine and expected. However, there was a small garrison of Germans about a quarter mile to the north and it was all open ground to the west where he needed to go. Surely, they would spot movement if he tried to run and that would prompt them to investigate. All he could do at this point was to sit tight and stay out of sight until nightfall. His plan to travel only during the day fell apart on the second night in a row.

It seemed to Frank like it took forever for night to fall. He could see bright flashes of light in the distance. At first he thought is was lightning. But, then he realized that it was artillery fire. He could not tell if it was German or Allied. It seemed to encompass a wide area along the western front towards the Rhine.

It was time to move out. He remained as close to the ground as possible and looked towards the garrison to see if there was any activity signifying that he was noticed. Nothing. As soon as he was out of their line of sight he took off jogging as fast as he could while trying to make sure he did not slip, fall, or run into anything in the pitch blackness of night. He made reasonably good progress considering the adverse conditions and his painful foot. During the night, he covered about four miles.

It was now the morning of March 20th. Taking a rest for breakfast with adequate cover, he decided to scramble the eggs using some crumpled newspapers and some dry brush as kindling. The small mess kit that was part of his survival equipment was perfect for cooking. He made his meal as quickly as possible in order to minimize the time a fire was burning. As an added treat, Frank added some cheese to the eggs and created a good substitute for an omelet. That, with a little ham, produced a hearty meal and energy for the day's march.

Frank decided to cover as much ground as he could until noon and then take a nap for a couple of hours before heading on. After all, he had been awake the entire previous night.

Frank had earned a new appreciation for the hardships of the infantry. They had to do this day after day. He had been living like this for only three days and he was sick of it. How much longer would he have to endure this lifestyle?

Frank also had to consider the fact that he was on the wrong side of the river if he wanted to link up with Patton's army. He could not cross at a bridge because, in all likelihood, it would be guarded. So, the only alternative was to swim it, find a boat, wade through a shallow section if one existed, or raft his way across the Main River. The water would be frigid as the river water originated in the mountains. If he could make it straight across, it would be about a 125-yard transit. He was also going to have to make his move soon. He was coming up on the town of Flörsheim am Main and Raunheim was just on the other bank. There was no way he could just walk through the center of the towns either at night or in broad daylight.

Hugging the riverfront, he looked for any means to make it across without getting wet. As he neared Flörsheim am Main, he came across a small row boat lying upside down in the sedge. It looked like it had been there quite a while. The seals needed caulking and it looked like the planks had been ravaged by insects. But it was his best option. So what if it sank half way across. At least he would be halfway and he could swim the rest of the way. He had hoped to keep his provisions dry. Furthermore, it would be even better if he could keep himself dry because it was chilly.

Frank hid himself among the sedge and awaited nightfall. As dusk set upon the land, he ate a hearty meal. He opined that if his provisions were lost in the river, at least he would not go hungry or thirsty. He overturned the boat and slid it down to the river's edge. He had managed to find a flat board measuring about three feet long that he could use as an oar.

As soon as it was dark, he loaded his provisions and the board and pushed off. He paddled steadily but quietly. He did not want to create too much noise which might alert some nosy fisherman or, worst yet, sentry. As he paddled, he was transported downstream. So, he picked up his rate of paddling and started to make headway across the river. After about ten or twelve minutes, he reached the other side. He decided to set the boat adrift. That way, he surmised, if anyone found the boat missing, then they would have no idea where he crossed the river other than downstream of where he had found it.

Frank took a brief rest along the riverbank. He desperately wanted to circumvent the town of Raunheim under the cover of darkness and stay well east of Rüsselsheim. He moved quickly and quietly. The games he had played in the woods when he was a boy required stealth and wits. Those skills were coming in handy now.

By spending the night on the move, Frank managed to reach a fairly dense forest just southeast of Rüsselsheim. This would provide protection from the elements, give him some cover from ground forces, and make it difficult to be spotted from the air. Again, he heard the crashing thunder of artillery. It was getting closer. Was he approaching friend or foe?

It was now the morning of March 21st and time for a rest. During the longest of nights he had covered a little more than three miles and it was about an hour before sunrise.

Frank stopped to rest for about three hours after making himself a bed of pine needles and branches. The smell of pine filled his senses. It was fresh and aromatic and reminded him of home. At about 8:00 a.m. he arose and ate some of the last few bites of ham and cheese that remained. If it was much longer, he would have to make another raid on some unsuspecting farmer's kitchen. He did not really want to take the risk.

The dense forest also presented something of an added peril. He could not see much more than fifty feet ahead due to the dense stand of trees. Therefore, he did not know what lay around the next cluster of trees. As he walked, he kept his semi-automatic in hand with it cocked and ready to use at a moment's notice. This was some of his scariest time. But there was no easy way around the forest.

About mid-day, he reached the edge of the forest, opposite the town of Nauheim with Groß-Gerau just to the southeast. He decided to bisect them on a direct line to Oppenheim. He continued to make good progress during the rest of the afternoon as he was now in pastoral farmlands. If it was not for his current condition, he would have enjoyed taking in the countryside. But, he was focused on his objective to link up with Patton's army one way or another.

Frank did his best to follow irrigation ditches, creeks, or any other depressions. If he could have walked in a straight line, then he would have been in Oppenheim long ago. But three miles "as the crow flies" turned into five- or six-mile hikes following winding paths.

As he walked low along an irrigation ditch, he spotted several children playing further along the ditch. It looked like they were floating sticks in it and pitching stones at them. They had not spotted him, yet. He did not want to harm them, but he could not afford for them to tell their parents or the authorities of his presence. What could he do?

Then he heard an adult male voice close by. Hesitantly, he poked his head above the bank of the ditch and saw a farmer leading a small heard of cows back to the family barn. Evidently, he was calling to the children to come along. It was time to go home for supper. Frank thought about his supper, too. This would be the end of the ham and cheese tonight, and he needed more water, too.

He did not want to raid the kitchen of a farm where he knew there were children present. So, he moved on looking for another favorable candidate.

He was hoping for the same scenario as he had at the first farmhouse where he had relieved them of some provisions. He found a likely target. It was a small farmhouse with good cover surrounding it in the form of a windbreak about a tenth of a mile away. He nestled in among the bushes and watched. He saw a strongly built farmer working on some of his harvesting equipment and his wife collecting laundry off the clothesline. Better yet, there were no children or dogs in sight. This could be the one.

Then Frank saw a boy about twelve years old approaching the farmhouse. It was their son. He was returning with a few cows that had been feeding in the pasture. This presented an additional complication. Now there was another person who needed to be out of the house before Frank could enter.

Throughout the day, and now as it approached dusk, Frank could hear the rising pitch of artillery fire. It was moving ever closer. He also saw the farmer and his family standing on their porch and pointing towards the west. They also seemed concerned for the heightened crescendo, probably for a different reason than Frank.

Still, Frank needed to re-supply his recently depleted provisions. He kept watch until their lights went out. Then he crept closer to the house just to get a better idea of the lay of the land. He planned to make his move in the early morning hours after the house was vacated. While he conducted his reconnoiter mission, he decided to check out the barn. Why not grab a few eggs? No problem, there were enough to last him a few days. There was also a bucket of fresh water in the barn, so, he refilled his containers. Better yet, next to the barn was the smokehouse. He would not need to wait to enter their home. He had everything he needed right here.

When he opened the smokehouse door, it creaked as most rustic doors do, but this one sounded like a loud screech. Frank ducked for cover and waited in the shadows. Ten minutes, twenty minutes passed and no response. So, he sneaked inside and lit a match momentarily so that he was sure to get a properly cured ham. Rather than take a whole ham, he sliced a large piece off the backside so no one would notice. He could tell it was tender by the way his knife cut through it. He was hungry and could not wait to eat; so, he shoved a slice into his mouth.

When he finished, he was hesitant about closing the door for fear it would let out another shrill shriek. As a precaution, he spit on the hinges hoping it would lubricate them and keep them from awakening the farmer and his family. It worked. His raid was successful and he was off on his adventure with the family none the wiser.

He took his prizes to a secluded spot where he could dine in peace. The ham was savory and delicious and melted in his mouth, and he built a small fire to cook a couple of the eggs. If it had not been for his current condition, the meal would have rivaled the best of restaurants.

Frank managed to have a fairly restful night. He was getting used to the routine although he was awakened from time to time with the crack of artillery fire. In fact, he slept so soundly that he did not rise until nearly 9:00 a.m. the next morning. He needed to hit the trail again.

It was March 22nd. Regardless of his good night's sleep, Frank was still feeling fatigued and weak. The constant threat of discovery was causing him great anxiety and concern. He was only about four miles from Oppenheim. Although he was eager to move on, he remained cautious about being too eager.

As he was walking, he spotted someone in the distance, probably a farmer, and the farmer spotted him, too. So, Frank did all he could—he waved to him. And the farmer waved back and kept going on his way. That was such dumb luck. Frank thought to himself, *Sometimes it pays to be brazen.*

Frank continued to weave in, around, and through the countryside, following the terrain to his best advantage. As he did, he noticed a strange sound and feeling. The ground was rumbling, literally rumbling. It felt like an earth tremor. But it wasn't a tremor. It was a mechanized army comprised of heavy equipment. He could see a stand of trees ahead that lined the bank of the Rhine River. He was almost to his destination and the noise seemed like it was really close. In fact, it was just on the other side of the river.

He was still about a mile and a half outside Oppenheim. He certainly was not about to walk into town. He was still subject to capture. So, he waited to positively identify the source of all the commotion. Besides, it was getting dark. He would have to wait until morning to find out what was happening. Whatever it was, it sounded like a lot of activity and associated small arms fire.

Early on the morning of March 23rd, Frank arose to small arms fire. About a hundred yards off he spotted something. It was a Sherman tank and a squad of American infantry. It was a scouting party from Patton's Third Army. They had crossed the Rhine the day before and were pressing hard into the heart of Germany.

Frank did not want to jump up and startle one of the GIs before he had a chance to identify himself. So, he decided to holler to them from a distance and indicated by throwing up his arms that he was "surrendering" to them. The soldiers pointed their weapons at him as he called out that he was a downed American pilot trying to make his way back to the American lines. They directed him to approach them slowly with his hands raised. All the while, they kept their fingers on the trigger of their M-1 Garand rifles. They were not going to take any chances. Their lines had been infiltrated by enemy posing as Americans in the past. It was not going to happen again.

A lieutenant came forward and Frank showed his dog tags to him. Still unconvinced of Frank's truthfulness, they disarmed him and due to his injured foot called for a jeep to take him towards the rear. Frank made it very clear to the lieutenant that he understood his caution, but that he wanted his personal semi-automatic returned to him once everything was cleared up. The lieutenant told the private escorting Frank to return the pistol if what he said was true.

When Frank arrived at the rear lines, he was taken to a temporary command post. There he was put under the charge of a captain who seemed to have better things to do than help Frank. So, Frank decided to take the tact of giving him an order. He told him, as his superior officer, to make contact anyway possible with his air base in England to get confirmation of his identity. The captain shot back that he did not know who Frank was and would not take his orders. Frank told him in no uncertain terms that he was Major Frank Johnson with the 355th Fighter Group, 354th Squadron, and if he did not do as ordered he would bring him up on charges for disobeying a direct order.

That seemed to make the captain a little nervous. If Frank was telling him the truth, then that could be big trouble. If he wasn't, then there was no harm really done other than finding out he was an infiltrator. The captain ordered the message to be sent. After about an hour of relaying messages, they had their response. Frank was legitimate. The captain apologized profusely, but Frank shrugged it off saying he was a little testy from his ordeal. He shook the captain's hand and asked where he could wash up and shave. Under the circumstances, the captain let him use his tent.

Meanwhile, the captain called for a medic to take care of Frank's battered foot. The medic had to unlace his shoe before he could remove the foot from it. His foot looked a mess. It was still swollen and black and blue. About all he could do was clean it and wrap it with a bandage. There was no way his shoe was going back onto his foot. The medic told him it did not look like it was broken but there was no way to be certain unless it was x-rayed.

Now, arrangements needed to be made to get Frank back to his air base in Steeple Morden, England. In a couple of days, a C-47 arrived to return him to England along with some of Patton's wounded soldiers. Frank was itching to get back into the air. He had spent long enough caught up in his mini-ground war. It would be a matter of only a few hours before he was back at his home base.

Upon his return, he was rushed to the infirmary for a medical examination and x-rays. Except for a bit of exposure and exhaustion, he was in excellent condition. No bones were broken. After a brief recovery period, he was back with his Squadron. They were all elated, as was Frank. In the interim, Scotty had been assigned as temporary squadron commander. But with Frank's return, he was reinstated as commander, and Scotty was all too happy to have him back there.

Earlier in the war, pilots shot down over German-occupied land were not returned to action because there was fear that they would give up information about resistance units who had helped them escape, if they were shot down again and captured. However, this was not the case for Frank because he had gone down in Germany and had no information that would harm the resistance movement. Therefore, after a short recovery period and intelligence debrief, he would be back in action.

Chapter 17

Turmoil on the Home Front

Although war had not reached the United States mainland, there had been, of course action in the U.S. territories of Hawaii, the Aleutian Islands, Midway, the Solomon Islands, Wake, and Guam. As a result, it remained firmly entrenched in everyone's mind that the Axis powers could, and would attack.

Perhaps it would be a long-range attack from some theoretical bomber on the German's drawing board. Or, it would be a Japanese bomb-dropping balloon with a timing mechanism set to drop a bomb over a U.S. city? Or, could it be an attack that came from within, like sabotage or subterfuge? The latter two could and did happen. The former never materialized. In any event, America remained on alert. It was not limited to coastal areas either. Even cities in middle America practiced blackouts and air raid drills. However, as the war progressed, many of these precautions were relaxed or eliminated.

Of course it is common knowledge that there was also rationing of gasoline, sugar, and meat. Non-essential travel was curtailed. There were widespread metal and rubber drives to provide the necessary resources for the war effort. Laboratories around the country were searching for ways to increase production for those essentials, like rubber, that could not be produced for lack of raw materials. The lack of raw materials resulted from shipping interruptions due to u-boats operating off the U.S. coast, or because geographical areas that produced them had been captured by the Axis powers. Fortunately, scientists were successful in developing a synthetic rubber produced from polymers.

The efforts of the workforce, and those who entered the workforce during the war, are legendary. The construction of ships, tanks, and planes far surpassed anyone's wildest imagination. Production was so great that war matériel were supplied to the Allies via Lend Lease. Being untouched by bombs allowed U.S. factories to convert from producing everyday goods into factories producing anything and everything needed for the war effort without interruption.

The greatest sacrifice of the common family was the donation of the father, son, brother, uncle, nephew, and cousin to the fight. In many cases there were multiple family members serving in the military. This does not diminish the contribution of women on the battle front, too. Many sacrificed their lives while serving as nurses at forward areas. Each and every day while they were away from home family members lived in torment. Due to communications blackouts, they never knew where their loved ones were, if they were safe, or on a battle front. All they could do was wait for a letter from their loved one or, worse yet, from the War Department.

At best, a telegram from the War Department meant that their loved one had been wounded and was on the way home. Hopefully, it would not be a debilitating wound. Too often they were. They could be anything from a flesh wound which, in many cases, could put the wounded soldier back in action quite quickly or they could be crippling in both body and mind.

If the family was notified that their loved one was captured, all they could pray for was that they would be treated respectfully. While German prisoner of war camps were not known for their five-star accommodations, the Japanese were notorious for their cruelty. Starvation, beatings, and murders were more the rule than the exception. The Japanese looked down on any soldier who surrendered or allowed himself to be captured. Their ideology demanded full sacrifice by dying in battle or committing ritual suicide if capture was imminent.

Then there was the possibility of hope if the soldier was listed as missing in action. He could be separated from his unit, on the run in enemy territory, or captured and not reported as such. Or he could be dead—blown to oblivion or lost at sea. In those cases, family members could be tormented for years to come because they just didn't know what became of their loved one. There could be no solace in not knowing.

Finally, it was the devastating news of the loved one's death. Often, the War Department's telegrams were terse, providing only the most basic information. What more can be said about this greatest of sacrifices? It was not just the soldier's ultimate sacrifice. It was the family's sacrifice, as well. That soldier and his family would not have the joy of reuniting after the war. The soldier had no future; no career, no relationships, no marriage, no children, no grandchildren, no vacations, no retirement, nothing. For him, life was over.

Driving across America up and down any street, boulevard, avenue, and country road all one had to do was look at the front window to see how each family sacrificed for the war effort. There was proudly hung the "Blue Star Service Banner." Each star represented a family member serving in the armed forces. Then, should there be the supreme sacrifice, the blue star was supplanted with a gold one. Your heart could not help but ache for their loss. Often, their sacrifice would be in the form of multiple gold stars. How could families deal with such losses without having the knowledge that their loved one had done so for a noble cause?

Frank's family was no different. In their case, their torment was multiplied by three for each one of their sons, Frank, Danny, and Billy.

Billy, who spent most of the war in the Aleutians, was not really placed in harm's way. Although the Japanese had invaded the island of Attu, they had summarily been defeated during one of their classic bonsai charges. After that, a Japanese presence in the Aleutians was a non-issue.

Of course, they still missed him and worried about him. After all, he was the baby of the family. Furthermore, he was thousands of miles from home in a naturally hostile environment. He was, in fact, closer to the island of Japan than he was to the continental United States. So, there continued to be reason for concern throughout the war.

Being on Attu after the defeat of the Japanese there, Billy had to service aircraft patrolling the Bering Sea looking for Japanese ships. It was also the jumping off point on the westerly route for aircraft being delivered to Russia under Lend Lease. Billy had to work under conditions that were appalling. Even during the summer, the winds coming off the Bering Sea were frigid and biting. During the winter, conditions were absolutely intolerable. The days were short and the nights long. Planes had to be serviced in all kinds of weather at all times of day or night. Mechanics could work only so long before they needed to take a break to get warmed up. And aircraft oil became so viscous and fuel became so cold that it was almost impossible to get the engine to ignite and run. Batteries lost energy quickly. So, it was imperative to preheat aircraft before attempting to start them. This really slowed down the process of getting them airborne again even if they had been sitting for only a short time. There were not enough hangars to put them under cover. So, they were left to the elements.

Most of Billy's letters back home related his hardships dealing with the cold, merciless weather. Although he had reasonable winter gear, he was always cold. He truly felt isolated, and he was.

On the other hand, Danny was definitely in harm's way as the U.S. Pacific Fleet maneuvered its way in the island hopping of the Pacific campaign. As a gunnery officer aboard a front-line destroyer, he was prone to see plenty of action. Fortunately, he was mostly on the giving end. Constantly on the look out for enemy aircraft, surface ships, and submarines, anything not positively identified as friendly became a target for his guns. Danny's ship provided cover for the invasions of Tarawa, Iwo Jima, and Okinawa.

During the kamikaze attacks off Okinawa towards the end of the war, it was primarily the main line ships that came under attack with the premier targets being the aircraft carriers, followed by the battleships and cruisers. However, every ship of the line did its part to fend off the relentless and desperate attacks from the kamikazes.

Danny was credited with personally directing fire that shot down two Japanese Kates. During the battle for Okinawa, he took over an adjacent gunnery position after its crew had been knocked out of commission during a strafing run by a Japanese Zero. While manning that position, he received a minor wound to his left arm. It was not debilitating and he continued to man the position until he was relieved. He was cited for bravery during that engagement and awarded the Silver Star and Purple Heart.

Danny had a more gregarious and outgoing personality than Frank. It was not that Frank was not personable; he was just more reserved and private about his affairs. Thus, Danny was more prone to tell his family like it really was; that is, when his message could make its way past the censors. Danny was a bit of a complainer. As an officer he never complained to his superiors or to his men. He just complained to his family about the food, the long sea duty, and the constant concerns about Japanese submarines and aircraft. He was also very open about his two airplane kills. So, the family back home was keenly aware of his medal and his wound. They were extremely proud of him.

Contrary to his brother's open and brash personality, Frank kept everything related to his missions and action to himself. There were two reasons for him to do this. He did not want to upset his family or Dottie, and he was not a good self-promoter. He was fighting this war to protect his family and his country. He was not fighting for the purpose of grandstanding. Frank did as much as he could to suppress any news about himself and, for the most part, he was successful. He refused to grant interviews to combat reporters, and he generally tried to give the credit to the men in his Group. In fact, he even insisted that the ground crews be afforded some publicity for their monumental effort to keep the air fleet in service.

His family learned of his exploits only from the information gleaned from newspaper reports published in mid-April 1945. Then there was no way he could suppress the news. Had they been aware of Frank's frequent missions, his forays with enemy aircraft, the harrowing ground support missions, his being shot down and evading the enemy, and his continuous brushes with death, they surely would have been panic-stricken. However, Frank always painted a picture that he was just flying routine missions and enjoying tours of the English cities and countryside. His letters home could not have been further from the truth. But his "truth embellishments" were for their own good and it wasn't hurting anyone.

Dottie always worried about Frank. From the time he decided to enlist, she always prayed for him before she went to bed. She prayed for him in church. Often, during the course of the day she felt compelled to pray for him. It was almost as though she sensed that more was happening than he would let on in his letters to her.

She scanned the newspapers every day for news about Frank, the 355th Fighter Group, or about the Eighth Air Force. She knew that the bombers of the "Mighty Eighth" were taking a beating until about mid-way into the United States' involvement in the European air war. Then she heard the news about extended fighter escorts. She had to know that Frank was involved.

Worrying about family members serving overseas was not unwarranted. Too many had been lost. These losses also extended to friends and neighbors. Their next door neighbor lost two sons, one in Italy during the Anzio campaign, and the other earlier in North Africa during a running tank battle.

The family on the other side of their home was worrying about the ultimate fate of their nineteen year-old son. He was a tail gunner on a B-25 Mitchell bomber. He was severely wounded during strafing runs on Japanese positions on Vela Cava. He had spent the last fourteen months recuperating in a veteran's hospital outside Boston. It was not known how he would recover from the loss of both legs.

The family across the street was still awaiting word about their son. He was a waist gunner of a B-24 that was shot down during a raid on the Ploesti, Romania oil fields. He bailed out, but was captured and interred in a prisoner of war camp. At least, according to information received from the International Red Cross, he was alive and safe.

The family living to their right was an elderly couple whose daughter had married and moved away years before and their grandchildren were too young to serve. At least, there would be no heartbreak in their lives.

The family living to the other side of the house across the street was fortunate, too. Their eldest son was considered essential to the war effort at home. He was a shipfitter working for Bethlehem Steel at the Quincy Shipyard. He participated in the building of key ships of the fleet including the aircraft carriers "U.S.S. Wasp," "U.S.S. Bunker Hill," and "U.S.S. Lexington." He also worked on the battleship "U.S.S. Massachusetts." Additionally, he helped build the cruiser "U.S.S. Quincy." So, no one can say that he did not do his part to support the war by staying stateside.

Their second eldest child, a daughter, trained initially as a nurse cadet in Washington, D.C. Then, she was assigned to duty at Pearl Harbor on Oahu in Hawaii providing subsequent care for the wounded returning from the Pacific Theater. Their third child, a son, was given a deferment because he had asthma. As far as they were concerned, his breathing condition was a cross to bear, that is, until the coming of the war. In the end, it was his condition that kept him safe at home. Their youngest son was still in high school and too young to serve.

Finally, there was the family who lived in the house directly behind Frank's home. They had two sons and a daughter. Their daughter, who was the eldest, was married, but volunteered at Weymouth Hospital. She also devoted her time helping at the local USO canteen by serving coffee and donuts to soldiers and sailors heading off to training or overseas.

Their middle child, a son, flew C-47 cargo planes over the Himalayan hump and helped supply Allied forces fighting in China and Burma. These were dangerous missions over unforgiving terrain. But he came through the war unscathed.

Then there was their youngest son. He was the same age as Frank's brother Danny. He was always wild and adventurous. His demeanor reminded Frank of his close friend David Billings. It was only natural that he would enlist in the Marines. He was physically strong even before he joined. But, the Marines would toughen him to a much higher level and turn him into a fearless fighting machine. He was not old enough to join until mid-1944. By the time his unit caught up with the Pacific war, it was time to invade Iwo Jima.

As men were being slaughtered around him on the beach, he charged an enemy machine gun and took it out with a grenade. As he tried to circle behind a second machine gun nest, he was cut down by enemy crossfire. The bullets had raked him across the backside. Still, he managed to toss another grenade into the second machine gun nest, destroying it. Two Marines following him dispensed with the final machine gun nest. He could go no further. He had been hit seven times by machine gun fire. A corpsman administered medical treatment in the field. Then, he was transferred back to the beach for the boat ride back to the hospital ship. He had been hit in the left forearm, left side, once in the left thigh, twice in the right thigh, in the right hip, and in the right arm. In the process, nothing vital was hit, but the bullets still tore him up pretty badly, and it did not diminish his bravery. For this overt act of courage he was awarded the Navy Cross along with the Purple Heart. His family was justifiably proud of him.

These were just the homes adjacent to Frank's home. Before America became so mobile, neighborhoods had a chance to mature with the same families living there for at least a generation. They became as one. They talked to each other in their front and back yards, over the fence, and on the sidewalk. You came to know the most intimate details about each other's families. And you knew everyone by name.

These were difficult times. Too many of Frank's friends and schoolmates had made the supreme sacrifice. The war had taken a horrible toll on so many young, promising lives. A number of returning vets not only suffered battle fatigue, but also suffered from survivor's remorse. They could not understand how they had the luck or even the right to survive when others, who may have seemed more worthy, did not.

One thing can be said about Frank's community. The churches never had better attendance. Even during the middle of the week, members of the community could be found praying at all times, day or night. The churches never locked their doors. And people who had not been in a church in the years before the war were now becoming devoted, if not to a specific religion, at least to prayer, especially if they had a loved one serving overseas.

Some families, like Frank's, kept a detailed record of their families' involvement in the war. For example, Frank's mother kept a separate scrap book for each of her sons. It included letters and cards from them, newspaper clippings about the various campaigns of the war, and articles directly related to each of her sons' exploits. And she kept a separate scrap book with news about their friends, neighbors, and other relations. Surprisingly, she had the least information about Frank. It was all by his design.

These simple scrap books became a veritable history of the family during World War II. They would become invaluable as recollections faded during subsequent years. The letters alone gave an interesting perspective of the time and they were written by the hands that lived during those historically significant events.

Although Frank was protective of the information his family received about him during the war, he did, in fact, keep a personal journal. It contained intimate details that he never intended to share. It was meant to be his personal recollections of each day's events merely to help him get some of his fearful thoughts out of his head and onto paper instead.

The journal included his entire military service history, from the time he began his train trip to Biloxi, Mississippi right through the entire war. It was a treasure trove of his innermost thoughts and feelings. It also provided insights into what he was thinking during combat and presented a detailed picture of his fear leading up to combat, during the stress of combat, and on his introspective flights back to base. This was more about the man than any newspaper or magazine article could ever capture.

Chapter 18

Combating New Technology

When everything seemed to be going the Allies' way, out of nowhere came a new menace. It was the innovative German jets, Messerschmitt Me-262s. These new machines were capable of 540 miles per hour in level flight. They were at the pinnacle of aircraft development during the war.

If they came at you head on, the rate of closure was nearly a thousand miles an hour. There was not much time to react, let alone shoot. If you didn't have excellent eyesight, they would be on you before you knew it, and you'd be nothing more than a puff of black smoke in the sky.

Dealing with their attacks on the bombers would present the fighter pilots with a whole new learning curve. The jets would make diving attacks and only be within range of the bombers' guns for a few seconds, hardly enough time to draw a bead on them with the .50-caliber machine guns.

Even as fast as the Mustang was, it could not outrun or chase down a Me-262. So, Frank and his fellow pilots had to devise opportunities for an advantage; new tactics were needed to combat them. After a couple of encounters with Me-262s and reports from other Groups' encounters, they learned an important fact. Me-262s were notorious for their high rate of fuel consumption. They did not and could not stay airborne very long. After American pilots learned of that weakness they waited for Me-262s to break off their attack. The Mustangs would follow them down as they made their approach for landing. At this point they were the most vulnerable because they were flying slowly with their gear and flaps extended and had limited maneuverability. So, they could not make quick evasive moves in that configuration. Consequently, they made easy targets.

Another technique that Frank used proved a bit more innovative and exciting. He was leading a flight of four Mustangs in their normal four-finger formation just ahead of the bomber formation. Frank had just taken delivery of a new P-51D Mustang, his new "Freedom Fighter," with a streamlined bubble canopy. Now he had a clear 360-degree view. No one could sneak up on him now. Not only that, the panoramic view of Europe was great.

They were about three hours into the mission on April 5, 1945. Using his keen vision, Frank spotted some small specks moving ahead and to the left. He also noticed the outline of two engines, one on each wing, but no propellers. It was them, the Me-262s. They were about to begin their assault.

Frank used hand signals to communicate with his flight mates to put their plan into action. He and Scotty, who was now a Captain, started to grab some altitude while the other two Mustangs swept in to head off one of the Me-262s. Other aircraft saw what was happening and started to initiate the same tactic. Each flight took a different target, and with so many Mustangs some doubled up on single targets.

Now began a serious game of cat and mouse. As the Me-262 turned right, the two Mustangs protecting the bomber turned left to prevent the Me-262 from getting a clear shot at a bomber. When the Me-262 climbed, they climbed as best they could while continually preventing the enemy from aligning on his target. Even though the Mustang could not climb as fast as the Me-262, it could still stay between the jet and the bomber. You could tell the German pilot was getting frustrated. This went on and on. The German pilot was persistent. Eventually, the Me-262 pilot became so preoccupied with this game that he forgot about the two Mustangs that had climbed to altitude. This would prove to be a deadly mistake.

Frank intensely watched the action unfolding below him. He circled to line his plane up just right. He was ready. He signaled Scotty that it was time. At this point, the two Mustangs at altitude began a high speed dive at full throttle approaching their never exceed speed of 505 miles per hour. The engine was roaring and Frank could hear the supercharger whining and propeller screaming. The air raced by his streamlined canopy. Speed built up rapidly. The controls were getting stiff.

Frank carefully planned his attack. He did not want to miss. He led his target slightly using the blip on his K-14A gunsight. Then he pulled the trigger. Rounds of .50-caliber armor piercing incendiary (API) projectiles being fired by his Mustang with six machine guns began peppering the German jet. Jet fuel readily explodes when hit by the incendiary slugs. Often the Me-262 pilot never knew what hit him. Such was the case this time.

Even if the Me-262 pilot was alert enough as to what was happening, the Mustangs still had enough momentum to get more aim time at the jet. Even with all their excess speed, it was difficult for the jet to outrun or out maneuver a couple of Mustangs working in concert with one another in a situation such as this while another pair worked to head him off. If the jet pilot chose to try to break right or left, or up or down, there was a Mustang waiting there for him. It became a game of numbers. There were so many Mustangs and so few jets.

Still, the Allies were fortunate that Hitler did not recognize the potential of the Me-262 and originally relegated it to bomber service as opposed to deploy its full value as a fighter. But he had other tricks up his sleeve, like the Me-163 Comet, a tiny rocket powered aircraft. They were really fast. Yet, they were not overly effective as they had only about two minutes of highly volatile rocket fuel at their disposal. If they were hit, they would explode like a Roman candle.

But there was no time to dwell on other thoughts. There were still Me-262s creating havoc with the bomber formation. Frank noticed one trying to break away from the formation. Perhaps his fuel was running low or he was out of ammunition. In any case, he was alone and a reasonable target and he was not going very fast.

Frank and Scotty picked up on the opportunity and closed for the kill. Frank lined up his gun sight and prepared to fire. Then, suddenly, the Me-262 started to accelerate and climb away and loop over the top. Frank realized he had been baited and the talented German pilot intended to come back on their tail. He boosted his Merlin engine into war emergency power at 67 inches of manifold pressure. As he did, he formulated in his mind his options. If he did not react quickly, then the German would have his way with them. So, Frank yelled over the radio for Scotty to break off in the opposite direction in order to give the German someone else to worry about. As Frank pulled back hard on his stick under full power, he dropped in a notch of flaps. He was trying to tighten his turn while reducing the chances of an accelerated stall. He also felt that by doing so that he could effect a tighter turn than his faster German counterpart.

It must be remembered that the Germans flying the jets were the remaining cream of the crop of the Luftwaffe. They were the best of the best. There was no way they would trust a novice with such an advanced piece of technology. Such was the case here. This pilot had seen action in Africa, Italy, France, Belgium, and homeland Germany. He was certainly no novice and he had amassed the kills to show for it, in excess of 80. He had been shot down four times and rescued each time to fly again. So, he was not invincible. But Frank did not know that, nor did it matter to him.

Frank was pulling so hard on the stick that his plane started to shudder. He had no more power remaining in his engine so he dropped another notch of flaps. Yes, it would cause some more drag, but it would also lower his stall speed yet allowed him to continue the tight turn.

As he came over the top of the loop and started on the way down, the bubble canopy came into its own. He could look straight overhead and see the Me-262 just above his head about a quarter mile away. At that point he rolled his Mustang upright. It was slow to turn at the relatively low airspeed. But it came around. The Me-262 also righted itself. It was just above the nose of Frank's plane. He pulled his machine gun trigger, but the tracers showed that he was firing below his target.

He did not want to go through this again and he was afraid that the Me-262 would pull away and escape. So, he firmly yanked the control stick back and continued to fire. The nose of his plane whipped up as the tracers sparked off the right wing and engine of the Me-262.

BANG! Off came the wing and the jet started to spin uncontrollably to earth. Off popped the canopy and out came the German pilot, narrowly missing Frank's right wing. But, Frank was not out of trouble. His quick maneuver to pull up the nose had thrown his Mustang into an accelerated stall and the torque of his propeller subsequently tossed him into a spin. This would not have been a big deal except for the fact that he was less than six thousand feed above the ground.

He quickly closed the throttle and shoved in opposite rudder and forward stick. As the spin stopped, he pulled back on the stick and began applying increasing back pressure to it. The Mustang was recovering, but the ground was approaching fast, real fast. He left his flaps deployed. He hoped the additional lift created by the flaps would help him pull out. The plane started to level. Then there was a horrible racket. He did not know what it was. Was it ground fire? Was it an attacking airplane? He did not see anything. He started to climb for altitude, and as he regained his airspeed he began to retract the flaps. But his plane was acting sluggish. Had he been hit?

About that time, Scotty pulled up to rejoin him. The action had happened so quickly that Scotty never had time to help out. Frank was still having trouble with his plane's performance so he looked around the cockpit. His manifold pressure and tachometer showed that he was making adequate power. His oil pressure and temperature were fine. His fuel flow was okay.

Then he looked outside. Oops! He had forgotten to retract the flaps. Or had he? He thought he had. He reached down to the flap control and, sure enough, it was in the retract position. He checked his hydraulic pressure. It, too, was okay.

Frank asked Scotty to check out his plane to see if he saw any problems with his flaps because they were not retracting completely. Scotty was flying on Frank's right wing and noticed nothing wrong. He maneuvered to his left wing, and there it was. A clump of tree branches was crammed in a hole punched in the flaps which jammed the mechanism. The ungodly noise Frank heard had been a tree. He realized now just how close to buying the farm he had been—literally. It would be a long, slow flight home. But his buddy and wingman, Scotty, would stay with him all the way.

By the time they returned to their base, the ground crew had almost given up hope. Their flight was slow and they were all alone as all other aircraft had gone on well ahead of them. Then, about ten miles out Frank called the control tower over the radio announcing their approach. Word filtered down to the ground crew that the squadron commander was on his way in with some damage. A cheer went up.

At this point, Frank did not know if he could lower the flaps. He definitely could not raise them, but could he lower them for landing? If he could not lower them, then he knew he would use a lot of the runway due to a much higher landing speed to stay above a stall.

Frank and Scotty made a high speed, low pass over the field and pulled up to break for the landing. Frank did a quick downwind leg, then an abbreviated base, and then a turn to final. He hit the flap lever to lower full flaps. Good! They were coming down. The landing was uneventful. As he taxied his plane back to the hardstand his ground crew ran up with MSgt. Riley in the lead.

Riley could see the hole in the flap clearly. He also noticed the branch sticking through the hole. He walked around the plane looking for other damage, but there was none.

"No disrespect, sir. But these planes are meant for flying not for trimmin' hedges," he quipped while shaking his head.

With that Frank said, "Yeah, you don't need to tell me that, Sergeant. That's the last time I plan to fly that low except for landing. How long will it take you to fix her?"

"We'll get right on it, sir. We'll work through the night and have her ready for morning."

"Oh, Sergeant, you'd better check the engine. I had to run war emergency power for a while."

"By the way, did you get anything for all this trouble and work you're making for me and my crew?"

Frank held up two fingers as he went to be debriefed.

MSgt. Riley turned to his crew and said, "Well, I guess that's a reasonable trade, a little damage and a burned engine for two Nazi aircraft. Let's get to work on this old bird, boys."

There was nothing better than a responsible, talented, hard-working ground crew led by an equally gifted crew chief. Frank's ground crew was just that and he knew it. He owed much of his success to their efforts. They did work through the night and his plane was ready the next morning as promised.

During debrief by intelligence, Frank told them of his technique. The entire Group also watched his developed gun camera film of the combat sequence. Now everyone could keep a watchful eye for attempts by the enemy to sucker them into a lopsided fight. From that point on, the two-plane high and two-plane low method became the standard way to defang the Me-262s superior speed.

A review of Frank's actions by his superiors led to their decision to award him his second Distinguished Service Cross (DSC) and another Distinguished Flying Cross (DFC). The DSC was awarded for his overall leadership through the handling and tactics of the air battle against a technologically-advanced foe. Additionally, the DFC was awarded for his victory over the last Me-262. Yet, even with all these accolades and acknowledgements of his courage, he could not put his deep feelings of fear behind him. They continued to gnaw at him and grow. The more he flew combat missions he had to wonder if his number was coming up. He had been too lucky or fortunate to have survived this long.

Although most of the pilots in the 355th Fighter Group knew of his emotional battle, they never openly talked about it. They just observed his behavior, his shaking and his bouts of vomiting. He couldn't bring himself to talk about it with anyone lest it might cause those who reported to him to question his leadership or, worse yet, his courage or sanity. He couldn't write about it to his family or Dottie because he did not want to worry them. So, he continued to struggle with it alone. He did not know how much longer he could go on. But, he knew he must go on no matter how he felt inside. He just prayed that the war would end before he cracked.

Chapter 19

Honors

As it turned out, air engagements became isolated and few and far between. For the most part, Frank's combat in the skies over Europe had come to an end. Without ever intending it, Frank had earned fame throughout the Eighth Air Force. If anyone served with an altruistic intent, it was Frank. He had not flown combat for personal glory. There was a certain element of flying for revenge after Major Corcoran was killed. Mainly he had done it solely for the purpose of beating back a determined and dastardly foe. He wanted to protect his friends and family from National Socialism and Fascism. If it became necessary, he would go on to defend them against Imperial Japan as well.

Unlike some other pilots around him, while he was an aggressive combat pilot in the air, he was extremely bashful and reserved on the ground. He never bragged. In fact, getting him to talk about his missions outside of the briefing hut was next to impossible.

The local and national newspapers had accounts of his aerial exploits, but he had never openly cooperated with them about the story. They were always looking for a positive slant on the war. There was even a brief newsreel highlighting Frank's big day. It was all restaged for the cameras after the fact. Frank really did not want to do it, but his superiors and those in public relations told him that it would do a lot to boost morale back home. So, he quietly submitted to do it.

Frank understood the need to provide positive images to the people on the home front. But he was caught in a dilemma. If the papers, magazines, and newsreels reported on his actions, then his family and Dottie would certainly discover that his letters about staying safe and avoiding the fray would be less than truthful. Well, there was not much he could do. Perhaps they would not run the articles in the local newspaper and they would never see any of this. Maybe his secret would remain his secret.

Nevertheless, photographers and reporters swept onto the base with fervor to get his story. They wanted to sell this ace, who was making the Nazis run for cover, to the folks back home. During the filming of the newsreel, the director wanted him to "act." He was uncomfortable with this game of pretending. Perhaps it was okay for John Wayne or Humphrey Bogart, but not for him.

He was supposed to taxi his Mustang up to the hardstand, roll back his canopy and, in a very cocky way, grin and hold up three fingers. This was to indicate that he had just finished off three Nazi airplanes. He never felt that way in real life and he did not feel good about doing it now. Frank could see that the public relations people were trying to paint a picture for the American population that he was some sort of super hero, like Superman or the Green Hornet. All he wanted to do was to get the message back to the American people that they still needed to produce modern fighters at a breakneck pace. He certainly did not want to be a media icon. So, as an alternative, he told them he would just give a thumbs up sign. That would have to appease them.

The honors did not stop there. After further review of the events of February 22, 1944, General Eaker had forwarded the complete file of Frank's military record stateside. After further examination, the United States Congress came to the unanimous conclusion to award Frank the Congressional Medal of Honor for his selfless exploits of that day.

Army public relations personnel saw this is a great coup. They wanted Frank shipped home to travel the U.S. on a war bond tour and to visit aircraft manufacturing factories to help build the inventory of modern aircraft.

Frank felt uncomfortable and embarrassed by all this attention. After all, so many others in the Eighth Air Force and elsewhere had made the ultimate sacrifice. He did not want to abandon his fellow pilots for the safety of a stateside tour of duty while being wined and dined.

On April 9, 1945 Frank was ordered to General Jimmy Doolittle's headquarters. He was not sure what was happening. When he arrived, he noticed that there was a large gathering of personnel on the parade grounds adjacent to the runway. Upon his arrival at headquarters, he was immediately admitted to General Doolittle's office. He saluted the General smartly. Then General Doolittle rose from behind his desk and quickly ushered Frank out the front door to a waiting car. From there they drove to the same parade grounds he passed on the way in. He could see what appeared to be the full base turned out for review. As soon as General Doolittle and Frank exited the car, the band started to play the *Army Air Corps Hymn*. What was happening? Nothing seemed to register in Frank's mind. Had he forgotten something?

With the band playing, General Doolittle told Frank to just walk over there in front of the reviewing stand and wait at attention. Frank did exactly as ordered. Was this going to be a firing squad for some infraction of military rules to which he was totally unaccustomed?

As soon as the band finished playing the *Army Air Corps Hymn*, there was a drum roll. This was followed with the *Star-Spangled Banner*. Then, as the band played *American Patrol*, General Doolittle and several other General Officers marched up to Frank. Doolittle saluted and the other officers followed suit. Frank threw back the salute and continued to stand at attention. Then General Doolittle began to read … "For service over and above the call of duty … "

With full military honors, Frank was presented his Congressional Medal of Honor by General Doolittle along with a congratulatory letter from President Roosevelt. Little did anyone know that President Roosevelt would be dead only three days later from a massive cerebral hemorrhage.

Being totally flabbergasted, Frank tried to retain his composure. General Doolittle motioned to Frank to join him on the reviewing stand while the units from Frank's surrounding air bases marched in review. Frank never felt more special, while feeling embarrassed from all the attention.

Following the ceremony, there was a reception, at which time Frank was told that he would be reporting back to the states for a public relations tour. But, General Doolittle made a minor mistake. He asked Frank if there was anything special he wanted. To that he replied, "Yes, sir. I respectfully request to stay here. I feel that I can do more to support the war effort by shooting down more of the enemy. This is my duty to my fellow fighter pilots and the bomber crews we protect."

General Doolittle looked him in the eye and said, "I understand, my boy. Let me see what I can do."

Over the next couple of weeks Frank suffered great anxiety. In order to protect him, he was grounded by General Doolittle while he awaited a decision from the Pentagon. The boys back home did not want anything to happen to their hero in the mean time.

Then, General Doolittle called, "Okay, it's all been worked out. I'll take care of the PR people. I'm sure they can use your future combat exploits to give them something to promote back home. Just make sure you don't get yourself killed in the process. That would not make good press."

He went on, "However, you have a new assignment. You're being transferred to Bodney to take command of the 352nd Fighter Group. You know those boys have quite a reputation and I think you'll be a great addition. By the way, you are hereby promoted and, by virtue of your Medal of Honor, jumped by Lieutenant Colonel to full Colonel."

The 352nd Fighter Group had already established itself as a respected and feared air armada. Frank had a tall order to maintain that reputation. He had no plans to let them down. Besides, his own reputation would precede him. No one at the 352nd Fighter Group could possibly question his leadership skills, flying ability, or combat experience.

With his arrival at Bodney, Colonel Frank Johnson knew he had his work cut out for himself. He would be replacing a commander who had already established himself as one of the best. He was such a good leader, in fact, that he was promoted to the General staff and transferred to headquarters. Frank had a lot to live up to. But he had the credentials and ability to do it. He decided to bring his good friend, Scotty, along with him. Scotty was promoted to Major and given a squadron command of his own. He had certainly earned it. And Frank wanted to reward Scotty for his stalwart devotion and friendship.

Frank was all business. Here he was in his mid-twenties and a Group commander. He was determined not to let his men down. Right from the start, he instituted orders to ensure that his Group would maintain their keen fighting edge. Days between missions would be used to hone their tactics and flying skills. Even a few days off in an advanced fighter plane could cause one to get rusty. Frank wanted his pilots to make it through the war safe and sound. One of the drawbacks of his new position was the fact that he was responsible for writing letters to family of missing, captured, wounded, or killed pilots. He did not relish having to write letters to families back home about the needless loss of a husband or son.

At this point, Allied forces had already crossed the Rhine and were on their way to Berlin. The Luftwaffe was able to put up only token resistance. Much of the aerial support was in the form of ground support.

In an effort to reduce his pilots' exposure to ground fire, Frank developed a plan to minimize their time over the target. To do this, he used reconnaissance photos to pinpoint target and defense locations as well as local topography and obstructions. Then he instituted a demanding training program where his pilots practiced ultra-low level flying.

During his briefings, he combined all the elements to make a carefully choreographed attack just above the terrain, hit the target in short bursts, circle to come in from another predefined direction, and then attack again. This tactic worked well. The enemy did not know they were coming, from what direction, or how many aircraft were attacking. It also minimized his pilots' time over the target while inflicting the most damage. This strategy worked well regardless of the target, whether it was an airfield, rail yard, or factory. They just had to be careful of towers, guy wires, or other obstructions that could tear through an airplane and the pilot.

Still there were mishaps. Sometimes inattention caused his pilots to lose control and impact the ground, or have a mid-air collision, or impact an obstruction they did not see. But these were few. It was widely believed that Frank's tactics proved invaluable at getting the job done with minimal loss.

Frank continued to lead the 352nd Fighter Group into battle. Occasionally, there would be a run-in with enemy fighters, but Frank could see that these pilots were not the well trained pilots he faced earlier in the war. It was relatively easy to out maneuver them and shoot them down. In just the space of one week, he managed to shoot down three more enemy aircraft. Even with the anger he felt against the enemy, he was remorseful because he felt that his foes just did not have a chance. He was not doing it for sport; nor was he looking to give the enemy an advantage; he just had a hard time shooting down someone who seemed so helpless and ill-equipped to face him. But he still had a job to do and he worried that this helpless foe could shoot down an American bomber if he did not do something to stop him.

Chapter 20

The End at Last

Then came May 7, 1945. The war in Europe was finally over. Hitler died about a week earlier. Frank had survived the war in some of the biggest air battles. He had honored his country, his Fighter Groups, his family, and himself. Yet, he knew there was more to be done. There was still a murderous war being fought in the Pacific. The Allies were still fighting their way toward Japan with the belief that it would go on for another year-and-a-half, if not longer. There was still the possibility of a pending invasion of the main island of Japan in the Fall of 1946. Frank wrote to General Doolittle asking for a transfer to the Pacific. Although he continued to be nagged by fear, he refused to let it get the better of him.

This time, however, the answer was different. The General called him and told him that, while the offer of his services was greatly appreciated, the Allies had gained overwhelming air superiority over the Japanese. Besides, Frank had done enough. Frank would be going home, like it or not. But not right away. In the meantime, there was still work to be done in Europe. In the depths of his mind, he thanked God he did not have to fight again.

Frank's aeronautical engineering experience would be useful for evaluating captured German technology, like the Me-262. As a result, he was assigned to Germany. He had seen it from the air and a small portion of the terrain after he crashed behind enemy lines. Now he had an opportunity to see it from the ground up. The treasure trove of captured advanced aircraft was phenomenal. Interrogation of captured Me-262 pilots provided insight into the operation of these futuristic marvels. Pilot operating handbooks were translated into English and the instrument panels and controls renamed using English as well.

It would be Frank's job to lead a select group of pilots to put the Me-262s through their paces prior to shipping them back to the United States. He designed a test schedule that would examine every phase of operation and determine the aircraft's operational limitations.

One thing Frank noticed about the Me-262 right away was the time it took for the jet engine to spool up to take off power and, more importantly, how quickly it drank fuel. Once the engine got up to speed, it felt like a kick in the rear end. The acceleration was extraordinary. Frank and his fellow pilots ran a very regimented series of test flights. They determined maximum speed in level flight, maximum climb rate, and maximum ceiling. They also compared published values for stall speed in various flight configurations. And they pushed the aircraft to near structural failure. Frank was determined to provide the Army Air Force with the best data that he could. This information would be useful as the United States continued to develop its own jet program and considered possible developments of similar technology by future enemies.

Frank enjoyed this type of flying. He did not need to look over his shoulder continuously. No one was trying to shoot at him. Yet, this program was not without its inherent dangers. Although the aircraft Frank was testing had seen service during the war, the technology was largely new to American pilots. It took some getting used to the flight characteristics of the jet aircraft. Furthermore, jet engines of the period were unreliable. Frank found that out one day.

As he was flying at 20,000 feet he decided to test the cycling of the throttles and the aircraft's ability to speed up or slow down in response to the throttle setting. So, he would shove the throttles forward and after a short delay the aircraft would accelerate smartly. Then he pulled the throttles back to idle and the aircraft seemed to take forever to slow down. He cycled the throttles at various rates and found a point at which smooth application or reduction of power led to a fairly equal response in overall aircraft performance. Then he decided to close the throttles followed by quickly opening them in order to simulate an aborted landing and a go around.

No sooner had he jammed the throttles to full power than there was a horrible explosion. The right engine had blown itself to pieces. Shards of metal were flying everywhere. Flames were shooting out the engine and spreading to the wing. Debris from the engine must have sliced through the aileron control cables as the jet was out of control.

Frank needed to get out. The Me-262 was becoming a blazing inferno. The flames began to spread to the fuselage as the aircraft began to spin. Frank struggled to release the canopy and disconnect his safety harness. The g-forces were building and it made it difficult to move. He could see the altimeter spinning wildly as his plane plummeted toward the ground. The canopy flew off, but because the force was so great on his body Frank could not push himself away from the seat and the cockpit that would soon become his coffin. He was running out of time. His mind raced back to the day when he did his first split-S at low altitude in the P-47. He never wanted to repeat that experience, but here it was happening again.

Time seemed irrelevant. The altimeter was everything and it was winding down in a blur. Then, he thought of a solution to his dilemma. He gave a quick and firm shove forward on the control column. The next thing he knew he was flung out of the cockpit. His legs slammed against the instrument panel on the way out and he narrowly missed being hit by the tail. As soon as he cleared the aircraft, he pulled the ripcord on his parachute.

Imagine the serenity he felt as he saw the parachute's canopy open above him. But all was not well. He felt excruciating pain. His knees had been ripped open and he was bleeding profusely. His next thought was how it would feel when he hit the ground. This would not be fun. He was right. The pain was unbearable and he passed out. The next thing he knew, he was in the back of a horse cart. His legs had been tightly bandaged and he was being taken to a little nearby town by an elderly German couple. As he passed out, he thought, *Am I alive?*

Although Frank's wounds were painful, most were superficial. No bones were broken. Thanks to the skilled hands of the base's chief surgeon, Major George Putman, M.D., his wounds were cleansed, disinfected, sutured, and packed with ice off and on for the next 24 hours to keep down the swelling.

Amazingly, it was Dr. Putman who had also removed the shrapnel from Frank's leg when he was wounded on a mission during the Battle of the Bulge. It was Frank's good fortune that the doctor had since been transferred to the 352nd Fighter Group. The doctor was even nice enough to save the piece of shrapnel as a memento for Frank. The good doctor told him that he had to stay off his feet for about ten days if he wanted to recuperate more quickly. And the way his legs felt, Frank was not in any hurry to walk right away. They throbbed and ached for the next three days. When he needed to be on his feet, the best he could do was shuffle. Fortunately, Frank's staff officers were available to assist with his needs.

While he was laid up, he used the time to catch up on his correspondence. He reread old letters, as he could never bring himself to throw away any of them. Then he set about filling his parents in on the great time he was having. Of course he never mentioned a word about his misfortune and that he was lying in bed with his legs elevated. Then he wrote a letter to Dottie about his joy of flying without the additional hazards of combat. Neither his parents nor Dottie were ever aware of his hazardous existence while he was stationed overseas. They would not learn of his wounds or achievements until he returned home.

Following ten days of recuperation, Frank had difficulty walking for about a month. After that experience, Frank led the Me-262 flight evaluation program from a desk. His legs just could not handle the stresses associated with the rudder pedals.

As Frank recuperated he had a chance to reflect on what had happened. Had not the German couple tended to his wounds, he could have bled to death. There was no compelling reason for this couple to help. Surely, they had to hate him for taking part in the destruction of their country and its populace.

Then Frank came to the realization that he unfairly misjudged some Germans and lumped them into the category of Nazi. Just as he had to deal with bad people in his own ranks, like Ted Holenski, Germans had their good and bad, too. He had been too hasty in his assignment of blame and now he began to feel an inner peace overcome him as he began to reconcile his years of hatred and anger towards them. He now felt compassion for those he formerly considered his enemies.

After Frank had a chance to recover he decided to look up the German couple to thank them for helping him. He requisitioned a jeep and had his aide drive him to their little farm on the outskirts of the village. When Frank arrived at their quaint little home he got out of the jeep and hobbled up to the door. The little old man opened the door and had a look of fear on his face. Who was this American colonel and what kind of trouble was he in?

Frank asked, "May I come in? I am the pilot you helped about a month ago."

He was not sure if the couple understood him. But the elderly man enthusiastically responded with, "Ja, ja!"

They could speak only broken English. What was most amazing was the fact that they had learned it from American and British airmen. It seems that they hated Hitler and the Nazis. They kept themselves as far from the war as possible. Not only did they despise everything for which the Nazis stood, but they did their best to help downed Allied airmen. Had they been discovered by the Nazis, they surely would have been executed. Frank had more of a reason to like these people besides what they had done for him. They had really put their lives on the line to save Allied airmen.

Frank told them that he was there to thank them personally for helping him. However, after hearing their story he wanted to do more. He knew that the German Reichmarks had been devalued and were essentially worthless. So, he decided that the best way he could reward them was to give them some American dollars. They resisted, but Frank insisted. It was then that he realized that he did not hate all Germans. There were still some shining lights out there who worked behind the scenes to disrupt the Nazis.

When Frank returned to the base, he wanted to do even more for them. So, he sat down and wrote a letter for the elderly German couple. It stated that they were friends of the Allies, that they had aided downed airmen, and that they were to be accorded every possible courtesy. They could use that letter anytime they felt they were being accosted, persecuted, or needed help from the occupying forces. It was worth its weight in gold.

As the testing program neared its end, most of the Me-262s had been shipped to the United States and Britain for further evaluation. Frank continued to regain his strength and was eventually able to return to flight status. He was sore, but he could fly.

While in Germany, Frank got a chance to see some of the countryside. He thought it was so serene and beautiful. This part of Germany had not been touched by the bombing campaigns. However, when he visited Bremen, Hamburg, and Hannover, they were a different story. It was total and complete devastation. Nothing was left untouched, except for a few buildings. And he thought it amazing that the buildings left standing were cathedrals. All that could run through his mind was a single philosophical question, *Was the Allied bombing that accurate or was it the will of God to leave those particular buildings—places of worship—still standing?*

Here were once great and old cities with a rich history that were now turned into rubble because of some misguided despotic ideal. The German people were rummaging through the ruins looking for anything salvageable. Dead horses and mules were converted into open air meat markets. The children were dirty and destitute. He felt sickened by what he saw and smelled and he could not do anything to help. He could not wait to return to the open skies and green countryside far away from these broken cities and the equally broken inhabitants. Such was the legacy of war and tyranny.

Then came some exciting, longed-for news. The Pacific war was over. An atomic bomb dropped on Hiroshima on August 6, 1945 followed by another on Nagasaki August 9, 1945 drove the Empire of Japan to sue for an abrupt surrender. The final surrender was signed aboard the *U.S.S. Missouri* in Tokyo Bay on September 2, 1945, six years and one day after the start of the Second World War. Peace was restored to a war-torn world, and free people celebrated as never before in their history.

Chapter 21

The Homecoming

Finally, on Tuesday, October 9, 1945, Frank received orders to return to the states. He was elated and fully recovered from his wounds. The war was over. His inner war of hatred was finally over. He was going home. Yet, he still questioned why he could not shake his feelings of fear for the duration of the war.

Nearly all of the air crews were headed home, too. Yet, many of the aircraft that had served so valiantly throughout the war would suffer an unkind fate. There was such a glut of excess aircraft that a large number of them would be bulldozed into little pieces and buried on the spot. Many of those lucky enough to make it back to the states were sent to the desert to be cut up and recycled into new automobiles. Relatively few would continue in service.

The Mustang still showed potential as it was at the pinnacle of piston engine development. Frank's orders directed him to lead a flight of three squadrons of P-51s to Andrews Field, formerly Camp Springs Army Air Base, outside Washington, D.C. by way of Greenland and New Brunswick, Nova Scotia for refueling stops. Their aircraft would be fitted with 110-gallon drop tanks for the long legs of the flight. They would be led on this long journey by a flight of B-24 Liberators that would provide navigational assistance. It would be slow going because they could not outrun the lumbering bombers. It would take them twice as long to make the crossing as a result of their slower escort speed.

Frank took off from Bodney with his flight on Thursday morning, October 11th. They rendezvoused with the B-24s a short time later. Then they set out on their long trek to southern Greenland. It would be a long, cold flight. But he felt warmed by the thoughts of going home and seeing his family and especially Dottie.

Upon arriving in Greenland almost ten hours later, Frank climbed out of his plane ready for a hot meal and a night's rest in the barracks. Being a bird colonel, Frank rated reasonably good accommodations. So, he managed to get a good meal and a solid night's rest before starting on the next leg early in the morning.

Then, they were off. The sun was just rising as they departed. They were close to the Arctic Circle so daylight hours would be relatively short. But they wanted to get an early start so that they would make New Brunswick before dark.

It was another long leg. This time it took about eight hours as they ran into some strong head winds and steady turbulence. The crews were cold, tired, and stiff. The turbulent air took a heavy toll on their physical stamina and by the time they reached New Brunswick they were all feeling pretty beat up and exhausted. All were ready to hit the sack as soon as they ate and had a hot cup of coffee.

Early the next morning they were off again, non-stop to Andrews. Frank's plane just droned along. The flight path took him over some familiar territory. While soaring along the Maine Coast tears welled up in his eyes as he came to the stark realization that he was finally over American soil again. He was back in the greatest land on earth.

As he passed over the rocky coast, he did a little sightseeing. He marveled at the scenic beauty. So much of it looked pristine. Arcadia National Park was breathtaking. The rocks jutting into the Atlantic in Kennebunkport were being slammed by the surf while they attempted to beat it back. As he passed over Kittery, he thought, *Gee, I remember stopping for lobster right on the ocean with dad, mom, and my brothers when I was about fourteen.*

Then some time later he flew over Ipswich. *Imagine,* he thought to himself, *we used to get some great fried clam dinners down there.* Frank loved his seafood and he missed it so much that he started to obsess about getting some. Yes, he could get the British fish and chips, but it just wasn't the same as a good old New England seafood dinner.

He could not wait to get a steaming bowl of rich homemade New England clam chowder.

Next, they were turning almost directly over Boston. He looked down to see cars and buses moving between the great canyons created by the buildings. It was really something to see when you didn't have to worry about someone coming up on your six o'clock. The shooting was over; now it was time to enjoy the sights.

Probably the most notable thing about his view of Boston was how much it differed from the cities in Europe. Here was Boston unscathed by war and its population was living life just as they did before the war. In contrast, few major European cities escaped the destructive forces of war. Buildings were rubble. Large segments of the population were dislocated or dead. And those that remained were starving and dependent upon the conquerors for their daily sustenance. At least the British and American occupying forces were magnanimous and largely noble in their victory.

Then, to his amazement, the flight was passing almost directly over his house. He was only about a mile away from home, yet, he was so far. It would be so easy to bail out and be there in a couple of minutes, but that was foolishness. When you spend three years fighting a war, sometimes you just need to think foolish thoughts to keep yourself sane.

As he looked down, he could see children running down the street and a couple of dogs playing in a neighbor's back yard. The children stopped playing for a moment to gaze skyward at the massive formation of aircraft flying overhead. They were too far away for Frank to recognize any faces. Besides, he had been overseas for more than three years; so, he probably did not know any of those youngsters anyway. Well, he would have to wait to land before he could wend his way home.

Shortly after his flight landed two hours later, Frank was approached by a Captain who escorted him to a waiting car. Frank didn't know what was going on. Waiting in the car was the base commander, General Harwell. He briefed Frank on what was to come. He was to return with the General to his quarters where he would clean up and dress for a reception in his honor at the home of General of the Army Air Force, Henry "Hap" Arnold. Frank was flabbergasted.

He quickly shaved and showered. While he was getting ready, the General's aide brushed and pressed his dress uniform. It was neatly laid out for him. It was the first time Frank had seen it or would wear it since he had earned all his commendations. It looked impressive, and Frank looked equally impressive when he put it on.

General Arnold sent his staff car and driver to pick up Frank and took him to the General's home. It was a Who's Who in attendance. There were senators, congressmen, cabinet members, military brass, and other dignitaries present. Frank felt overwhelmed by the attention he was getting from them. He was greeted by his host, General Arnold, who introduced him to the other guests. Frank felt honored and he really enjoyed the socialization although he felt a little out of place. He was tired, too. The food was fabulous, but Frank felt a bit nervous and could not eat too much. Besides, he was continually questioned about his exploits. He answered the questions as best he could while maintaining a reserved and somewhat bashful demeanor. He was not cocky or boisterous and this endeared him to everyone there. By the time the night was over, he was ready to hit the sack.

General Arnold's driver returned Frank to Andrews close to midnight. He was exhausted. No sooner had his head hit the pillow and he was asleep.

Seven a.m. arrived early. He had to get ready quickly to catch the 8:30 a.m. train from Union Station to New York City's Central Station followed by the express to Boston's South Station. The train was packed with other service men trying to make their way home. Just as with his first train ride when he headed off to war, there were those who were braggarts. But there were far fewer, as many of those who bragged before seeing action came to the realization that war was not all fun and games and bravado. They had come to the sickening realization that war was not all glory.

Frank did his best to sleep the rest of the way, and sleep he did. Before he knew it the rocking of the train and clacking of the tracks lulled him to sleep. Then the call of the conductor startled him awake as the train was pulling into Central Station.

It was time to change trains for Boston. Everyone was rushing to catch it before it left the station. There were so many soldiers trying to get home that the railroad was running extra trains, and their schedules were a lot tighter to accommodate them. Frank managed to grab a seat next to a young Marine corporal with a patch over his left eye. They struck up a conversation. It seems the Marine had been wounded by a grenade during the final days of the war. He had seen action on both Iwo Jima and Okinawa. Now that he had recovered from more serious wounds, he was on his way to a Boston hospital for specialized treatment to remove some tiny metal splinters from his eye. He had not lost his vision, but there was a danger of infection.

When the corporal finally saw Frank head on, which he had not done as his peripheral vision was blocked on his left side, he noticed Frank's impressive display of ribbons. But self-deprecating Frank discounted his own action while expressing his admiration for the Marine surviving the Pacific War. He had read newspaper accounts and heard radio reports about the absolutely vicious battles of the island-hopping campaign. It was amazing that more Americans did not die. And they would have if the atomic bomb had not been dropped, twice.

Then Frank excused himself. With the long flight from the previous two days before and the events of the preceding evening, he had no trouble falling asleep again. There was also the difference in time to which he had to adjust. The train was just outside Boston when he awoke. He started to get himself and his things together.

Although he had slept, it still seemed like the train was taking forever to cover the two hundred miles between New York and Boston. Frank was used to whipping along at 350 miles per hour. This slow going was so tedious. He wanted to get home.

He began growing anxious as the train pulled into South Station. No sooner had it stopped then he jumped off and ran out front to hail a taxi cab. It was mid-afternoon and he wanted to be home for one of his mother's home cooked meals. It was about three years since his last one.

As Frank ran towards the taxi cab he hailed, two middle-aged business men tried to jump in ahead of him. One, a veteran of the First World War, saw Frank's impressive display of combat ribbons including the one for the Medal of Honor. So, he grabbed his colleague by the elbow and pulled him back. He said, "Let the colonel take the cab; he's earned it."

Frank tipped his hat as he climbed into the back seat and closed the suicide door of the cab. Fortunately, the traffic was not too bad even though gas rationing was over. Not much had changed to Frank's eyes as he began approaching the familiar territory of his youth, although he seemed so much older to himself now.

He had witnessed some of the great air battles over Europe and he had seen comrades die. But he was not going to let his absence for the last three years stand in his way of going on with a normal life. He had plans for Dottie and himself.

As he left Boston, he passed through Dorchester, then into Quincy along Wollaston Beach. From there, he passed over the Fore River Bridge and into North Weymouth. As he crossed the bridge he saw bustling signs of recent shipbuilding activities at the Fore River Shipyard and, across the river, he could see the Edison plant belching thick black smoke as it converted energy stored in coal into electricity. The Quincy shipyard to his right appeared to have several ships still awaiting launch.

As the cab transported him closer and closer to home, he started to have clear visions of the way the town looked before he left for war. He was entering his old stomping grounds. He remembered how he would ride his bicycle or walk to Columbian Square. Just down that way was David Billings home. He wondered how David was doing. One positive result of David's lost arm was the fact that he did not have to go to war. At least he could be thankful for that if nothing else.

Frank debated within himself to see his family first, or to go to see Dottie. He finally rationalized that he wanted to make himself more presentable for his girl. He wanted to make a good impression on her after all these years. He would go home first and get cleaned up a little.

Frank told the cab driver to turn right down the next street. There was his elementary school and the playground where he had played so much tackle football and baseball. Now another right turn, and he was on his street.

The taxi cab drove slowly up his street. Frank tried to take in all the sights. Not much had changed in the old neighborhood. Lawns were well manicured and the houses seemed to be in pretty good repair. There were colorful chrysanthemums still blooming in the gardens, and it was like the whole neighborhood had been preserved in a time capsule.

Frank directed the driver to the neatly-kept, white Cape Cod house with the black shutters and white picket fence. The driver stopped in front of his house.

"That'll be $5.65, soldier."

"That's kind of expensive, isn't it?"

"It's the war. Everything costs more now."

After paying the cab driver, he slid out the back seat dragging his gear. He looked around at the old neighborhood. The leaves were changing color. He had come from the dingy gray of war into a world full of hopeful colors. He was back in the land of red, white, and blue. And he was surrounded by brilliant shades of gold, orange, yellow, and scarlet, too. It was the peak of autumn and the leaves were changing color with the shortening days and cold, crisp nights.

As he sauntered to the front steps he thought to himself, *Should I knock on the door or just walk in?* He really didn't know. He had been gone for so long that he did not know if this was still really home. He felt a little out of place. As he opened the rickety screen door, he heard a voice call out, "Who's there?"

It was his father.

"Oh, it's just me dad, I'm home."

His astonished father rushed to embrace him as he tried to hold back the tears of joy. His father cried out, "Nettie, your son is home!"

Something crashed in the kitchen as Nettie rushed though the swinging door that separated the kitchen from the dining room. She was hysterical.

"My baby boy! Oh, my baby boy is home! "Why didn't you let us know you were coming?"

"I didn't want you to be waiting on me. I didn't know exactly when I'd get here."

She could not contain her elation as she grabbed him in a bear hug. Then there was a stampede down the stairs as Danny and Billy ran down them to greet their big brother. They had been mustered out of the military nearly a month earlier. Their home was filled with more joy than it had seen in the last three years. Frank was home. He was safe and sound. And life would go on as God intended it.

"Mom, Dad, it's so great to be home. Danny … Billy … I'm so glad that you two were kept safe. I'm just so thankful our family is back together again."

"And it's great to have you home, son," said his dad as he proudly looked at his straight and tall son who had grown from a boy to a man.

The family sauntered into the parlor. It was time to catch up on the last four years and take a moment to relax. Frank was still pretty tired from his long flight and train ride.

"Gee, son you never wrote us about all those medals. Although we knew something was up when we read all those articles in the newspaper and *Life* magazine. In fact, we saw you in a newsreel at the Cameo Theater. We wrote you about it."

"Well, dad, not all my mail has caught up with me because the Army was moving me around a little bit after the close of the European war, and I was kept pretty busy. Besides, there was no sense worrying you and mom."

Billy chimed in, "You must have seen a lot of combat?"

"I saw my fair share, and I would say it was enough for me to last a lifetime. Just count yourself lucky if you didn't have to deal with it. I was terrified the whole time."

His dad jumped in, "Only an insane person would not be afraid under the circumstances. I'd have some serious concerns if you said you were not afraid."

As Frank sat there, he finally realized that he was home. There would be no more combat and he could live the American dream of life, liberty, and the pursuit of happiness.

Furthermore, his family's response to his combat action validated the fact that he was not a coward. A light went on in his head. He came to understand that his attempt to shield his family from his combat action may not have served him well. Now that he was at home and he was hearing their supportive words, he knew he should have made them aware of what he was dealing with earlier. Their moral support at that time was just what he needed in order to deal with his fears. All this time he had been trying to do it on his own. Yet, the psychological distress was more than he could handle himself. It took the support of family and he felt a surge of that support now.

His mother interrupted, "Are you okay? You must be hungry."

"Mom, you bet I am. This is something I have been waiting for since I left home."

Frank was not responding to the question about being hungry. He really was okay emotionally. He had finally resolved the feelings he felt not only for the duration of the war but also since the David Billing's tragedy. It was good to feel normal again. Surprisingly, he felt like he had an instantaneous and miraculous healing.

"Harry, please set the table and I'll finish putting dinner together."

As they sat down to dinner, Frank said, "Gee, it looks like you were expecting me because they're all my favorites."

There were roasted chicken, mashed potatoes, green beans, stuffing, and cranberry sauce. It was like a mini-Thanksgiving dinner.

As the family sat together for a meal for the first time in four years his father offered the grace with a hear-felt prayer of thanks for bringing the family back together again after so many long years apart. As he ate he inquired about Dottie and said that he would drive to her house after dinner. He wanted to see her so much. He was pining for her.

But first things first—he savored every bite of his mother's home cooking. For a moment Frank thought he was going to have to pull rank on his brothers to get a thigh, but they acquiesced to his desire and let him have his pick. The chicken was juicy and luscious. It wasn't bland and dry like the usual military fare. And the stuffing—the Army cooks could not make it like his mother. He often wondered if the Army made theirs from processed cardboard because he imagined that it had the same texture and taste as a shredded cereal box. And finally, he had a tall, cold glass of milk that had really come from a cow. Not powdered milk, which was supposed to have originated from a cow, though he questioned, what part? It just did not taste the same or have the same consistency.

Frank ate and ate. He had not eaten so well for a long time. It was the absolute best. There was nothing like home-cooking.

"I need to get cleaned up and changed so I can run over and see Dottie."

"She won't be home for a while. She normally works the 9:00 a.m. to 6:00 p.m. shift at the hospital. Then she has to catch a bus home. So, just relax and enjoy some dessert."

Frank's mother suggested that he should call Dottie first so that he would not shock the poor girl. But a little bit of Frank's impish behavior shined through. He wanted to sneak up and surprise her. And he wanted to hold her and know that she was real.

After dinner, he sat back in an overstuffed chair and just let out an extended sigh of relief. Then they all retired to the living room to catch up on family news while enjoying the biggest slice of chocolate cake he had ever seen in his life along with a large cup of coffee. He was certain that his mother must have had a premonition that he was on his way home. Frank was such a chocoholic that he had two huge slices of cake. Then he felt as though he was going to be sick from overeating. Yet, it was heaven.

Then he ran upstairs to his old bedroom to get cleaned up. He did it in record time. Luckily, he didn't slit his throat with his razor as he hacked away at his face to remove the stubble. He showered and threw on a fresh shirt and his uniform and off he went. He wanted to look his best.

Luckily, his father used his car periodically for local errands. So, it started right up and it had some gas in it. It probably needed a wash, but it was not too bad. After all, it was now getting dark; so, who would notice anyway?

As he drove he surveyed the old neighborhoods as he passed through them. Children were playing in the street as the sun sank in the sky. They were different children than he remembered, but still they were children. They had been fortunate to be separated by the distance from war elsewhere on the globe. Frank had done his part to see to that. They were safe and they could continue to behave like children. They were so unlike the ones he had seen in London and Germany. Those unfortunate children had had to grow up far too soon. They had experienced horrors that no children should have to endure. Their childhoods were lost forever never to be regained or remembered.

The colors of the autumn leaves were changing with the onset of the gloaming. They seemed to be even more brilliant than they appeared during mid-afternoon. The houses took on a different aura, too. They seemed to glow in pastel earth tones. The scene was awe inspiring. He had forgotten just how beautiful the neighborhood looked. He considered that it took some time away from all this in order for him to fully appreciate what he left behind.

He was now turning onto Dottie's street. Then he thought to himself, *I wonder if she is home, yet? Well, he was there now. It would not make any sense not to pop in to say hello to her folks.*

Frank was now better prepared to reunite with Dottie. His heart and mind were in a better place than they had been in years. His newfound inner peace would translate into years of loving and nurturing for his future wife and family. God had somehow dealt with Frank in his own heavenly time and that timing was perfect.

He stopped in front of the house and turned off the engine. He climbed out of the car, closed the door, and walked around the back of the car. Then to his surprise, open flew the front door, and out scurried Dottie nearly missing all of the steps down her front porch. She had been sitting in their parlor reading a magazine when she just happened to look up and see him through the front window getting out of his car.

She was yelling and screaming and cheering, "Frank! Frank! Frank! You're home! I just knew it! I just knew it was you!"

She threw her arms around him and he threw his around her. It was an embrace that would not be broken—ever.

He spoke softly into her ear, "I missed you. I love you. Now, marry me."

Finally, he was really home.

Chapter 22

A Quiet Hero

Before Frank or anybody else knew it, three hours had passed. Everyone had gathered in silent awe to hear Frank's story, including Brandon's brother and cousins who had been playing on the beach. No one uttered a sound for fear they would break the flow of the epic tale or miss some of the key details. By the time he was done Frank had sweat rolling off his forehead, just as he had following the heat of battle. Frank had just relived those past events like they were happening at that very moment.

It was not so much the great airmanship that made Frank great. It was the fact that he accomplished it through all the fear. Shortly after returning to the states, Frank came to the realization that all sane people—soldiers readying for an attack on the ground, firemen preparing to enter a blazing building—struggle with fear. He probably always knew that was true, yet it was difficult for him to rationalize his own deep-seated feelings in the face of the constant and intense circumstances he faced so often. But it is what a person does with that fear that determines how they will be seen by others and, more importantly, by themselves.

Frank had set an example for others to follow. It was not so much that you have fear; everyone has a fear of something or other at some time in their life. It is what you do with it that counts. Frank had done the honorable thing; he confronted it and fought through it head on and won.

"Frank … Frank!" Dottie called out to him.

Frank snapped out of an almost trance-like state.

"Show Brandon this box," she said as she handed him a highly polished walnut box.

"I gave this box to Frank as a gift many years ago," she told the gathering.

"What is it Grandma?" Brandon inquired.

"Well, open it and see," she said.

Brandon carefully lifted the lid. It had not been opened for more than fifty years. It held a treasure trove of artifacts.

"Wow! What's all this?" he screamed, barely able to contain his excitement. Neatly laid out was a display of all of Frank's service medals and awards. In the drawer at the base of the box was a collection of official-looking papers.

"Frank, why don't you tell him about each of these items?" Dottie pleaded.

Somewhat embarrassed by the attention, Frank reluctantly began, "Let's see, this first one is a Bronze Star." The written citation stated that it had been awarded for meritorious service for shooting down the Bf-109 during his first mission.

"This fancy one with the profile of President Washington is a Purple Heart. I got it for a minor wound I received during the Battle of the Bulge."

"You got shot, Grandpa?"

"Not exactly, Brandon. Remember, this was from the piece of shrapnel from a tank that blew up in front of me. I just didn't get out of the way fast enough. It was my own fault."

There, just under the Purple Heart, was a jagged piece of steel.

"This is the piece of Tiger tank the Army surgeon pulled out of my leg. This one is a bronze star that I got after I shot down my first plane after it was on my tail. These two are Silver Stars for shooting down a few planes."

He continued, "Here is the Distinguished (Presidential) Unit Citation. It was given to our entire Fighter Group for action during Big Week. We really did a job on the Luftwaffe that week. We lost some good pilots, but the Nazis lost a lot more. What happened during that week did a lot to ensure the success of D-Day because the Germans didn't have any aircraft to hassle the troops landing on the beaches in Normandy. I felt like we really accomplished something to support the invasion."

"These three that look like propellers are Distinguished Flying Crosses. I got some of them in combination with other medals. So, it was like a two for one sale. I don't know if I deserved them."

"These two shaped like crosses are Distinguished Service Crosses. The first one was awarded for taking out a couple of tanks that were bearing down on one of our infantry units during the Battle of the Bulge. I took a lot of hits from ground fire during that one, and I'm not so sure it all came from the enemy. The second one was awarded for shooting down two Me-262 jets that were raising havoc in the bomber formation. I was lucky the second one didn't get me. You know, those jets were really something, and if the Germans had had more of them, well, I'm not so sure of the outcome of the war or that I'd be here to talk about it."

"How about these other medals, Grandpa?"

"Oh, yes. I'm honored to have these, too. This is a Good Conduct Medal. I got it because I behaved myself. The one next to it is the European-African-Middle East Medal because that is the theater where I served, and this last one is the Victory Medal. I got it because we won the war."

"Grandpa, you've told us about all these other medals, but what about this one with the long ribbon?"

"This is one that I don't think I deserved at all. I lived through the war and so many of the men who served during the war made the ultimate sacrifice. They're the ones who deserved this more than me."

To everyone's amazement, located right at the top center of the display case, there it was, the Congressional Medal of Honor. It was awarded for conspicuous bravery above and beyond the call of duty for action on that day when he dispatched a total of nine aircraft including the FW-190 he downed with empty machine guns to save Scotty. The citation as read by General Doolittle during its presentation to Frank was among the documents. The government of the United States recognized not only his spectacular exhibition of flying skill, but also his extraordinary valor in doing so. He was willing to sacrifice everything for a friend and fellow pilot.

During and after the war, many pilots claimed to be fighter pilots. Yet, they never saw an enemy airplane, never engaged in any combat, nor even made it into a theater of war. In such cases, they were pilots who flew fighters. Frank was a true fighter pilot. He had met the enemy and placed himself in harm's way.

Frank's family surrounded him aghast at his story. How could this have been kept a secret from the family for so long? In Frank's own mind he was not trying to keep it a secret. It was just something that happened in the past and life had to go on with a look to the future. It was just the way the Greatest Generation handled events of its time, like the Great Depression and the Second World War. It was all done with a special sense of duty and quiet patriotism. In their minds they didn't do anything special; it was what they expected of themselves for the protection of their nation and their family.

While Frank explained to Brandon about the medals, Dottie sneaked upstairs. She came down a couple of minutes later with a garment bag.

"Oh, Dottie, you didn't need to bring that old thing down here."

It was Frank's dress uniform.

"Just hush, dear. The kids'll get a kick out of it. Brandon, would you please help me hang it up over here?"

Brandon jumped up to help his grandmother.

"Now, Brandon, please remove your Grandpa's uniform from the garment bag and place it over here on the couch."

"Wow! Look at all the colorful ribbons!" exclaimed Brandon.

There were his pilot's wings and ribbon upon ribbon stacked above them. Plus, there were his colonel's eagles on each epaulet. This was an amazing treasure that none of them had seen before this time. They all stood around the uniform staring at it.

Then, Brandon blurted out, "Put it on, Grandpa!"

"No, no, that's not necessary," Frank stated demurely.

His daughter gently nudged, "Dad, please try it on. We'd love to see you wearing it."

"It probably doesn't even fit anymore."

"Try it anyway."

Reluctantly he responded, "Oh, okay."

So, Frank lifted himself out of his chair and excused himself to go upstairs and put it on. He had not worn it since the war ended. A few minutes elapsed. Then he came down stairs with a bit of a spry step.

Meanwhile, his daughter ran to get her purse and the camera in it.

"I've got to get a picture of this."

He looked fantastic. It was a little looser than when he wore it sixty years earlier, but he still looked dashing and debonair. Dottie blushed with pride in her husband.

She ran to get her camera, too. She had her children and the grandchildren take turns posing with Frank. He felt uneasy at all the attention, but everyone else was having a grand time. They were standing in the presence of greatness and he just liked having family around him.

Later in the day it was time for one of Grandma's famous roast chicken dinners. Brandon's and the family's questions continued throughout dinner and into the early evening. Everyone had a new appreciation for the elderly gentleman who always sat quietly reading or doing a crossword puzzle or gazing across Cape Cod Bay. This time, however, he had said plenty.

Brandon's mom finally blurted out, "How could I have been so blind? I can't believe that I never knew any of this."

Grandma confided, "Well, dear, you were busy with your own little play activities with your friends and the war was not a subject that dads would talk about with their daughters. It would have been different if you had been a boy. You know, boys are into that kind of stuff. Besides, he did not want you to know that he had killed people."

"I guess—but it still would have been nice to know. What he did was war. But maybe you're right. I don't know how I would have taken the news as a child that he killed. I am certainly happy that I know it now. I really think that dad ought to have his memorabilia displayed in the house for all his family and friends to see."

"You know your father, dear. He was never one to boast."

"Well, perhaps his family would like to boast for him! We're so proud of him."

That is how the whole family felt. It took Brandon's mom to articulate all their feelings. There was a sense of history sitting there with them at the dinner table.

After a little dessert and relaxation it was time for everyone to go home. Frank was ready for bed; he was as exhausted as if he had just completed a long escort mission. He would really sleep tonight.

During the drive home Brandon pondered the events of the day. He went there not expecting much. Little did he know that this would essentially be a life-changing event for him. As his brother slept next to him in the back seat of the car, he sat in the darkness and visions ran through his mind as he put himself in his grandfather's place. He could not conceive of what adventures his grandfather had endured. It was the most astonishing story he had ever heard. Now he wanted to prepare his presentation in such a way as to make the story as exciting for his classmates as it was for him.

Upon his return home at about 9:00 p.m., Brandon realized that his homework assignment had taken on new meaning. It was no longer a meaningless chore. He was going to do his best to honor his grandfather's legacy. In fact, he was so excited that he began compiling the details into an organized presentation and worked late into the night. It was well after midnight before his head hit the pillow finding it difficult to sleep as he recalled his grandfather's story. But, finally, he nodded off to sleep and to dream.

Brandon spent the next two weeks preparing and honing his presentation. He wanted to do justice to his grandfather's amazing story. He quickly completed all the homework assignments for all his other classes during study periods at school so that he could concentrate solely on his history project when he got home. Brandon was so engaged with his project that he disregarded his chance to play baseball with his friends, even on the weekend. He was serious about doing the best job he possibly could to honor his grandfather. Yet, he was continually tormented by the prospect of making an oral presentation.

He prepared note cards. His grandmother had provided him with photographs of his grandfather that were taken during the war with some famous personalities of the period, like Doolittle, Eaker, Arnold, and Eisenhower, while they honored Frank for his accomplishments. It was a World War II compendium of "Who's Who." There were also photographs of Frank with his airplanes, and some others of the pilots in his squadron, like his trusty wingman, Scotty.

Brandon carefully mounted the photographs on a poster board and neatly wrote a caption for each photo. He placed a title in bold letters at the top that simply stated "Col. Frank Johnson, 352nd and 355th Fighter Groups, 8th Air Force." And his grandmother also loaned him something else very special, the walnut box.

When the day of class presentations arrived, Brandon felt an air of excitement the like of which he had never experienced. Upon arriving in his history class, he looked around and saw other students with various visual aids at the ready. He felt a little nervous, while concurrently exuding confidence. He controlled his breathing in an attempt to calm down. He wanted to display the proper decorum to honor his grandfather's achievements.

When Mr. Evans entered the classroom he reminded the students of the day's schedule. Each student would make a ten- to fifteen-minute presentation. Their topic involved a book report, a research topic, or an interview. All presentations had to relate to World War II.

Normally, Brandon never volunteered for anything in class, let alone an oral presentation. In Brandon's mind giving an oral presentation was almost as bad as death itself. But as his nerves started to get the better of him, he harkened back to his grandfather's saga.

Then he came to the realization that if his grandfather could deal with fear on such a magnificent scale on a regular basis, then how could he possibly let something as trite as an oral presentation frazzle his nerves. The legacy of his grandfather's courage was already paying dividends by helping Brandon overcome his nervousness. Besides, unlike his past oral presentations, this time would be different. He was well-prepared and this time he had something profound to say. When Mr. Evans asked for someone to volunteer to go first Brandon's hand shot up so fast that he almost fell out of his chair.

"Well, Brandon, this is a novelty! Since you appear to be so eager, you evidently have a burning desire to go first. Okay, go for it."

Brandon hurriedly arose from his chair, strutted to the front of the class with a special feeling of pride in his heart, paused for a moment, then began ...

"Let me tell you about my Grandpa. I learned some interesting things about his World War II service that only my grandfather and grandmother knew until now. I know you are going to find this story hard to believe, but it is true."

With that, he produced the polished walnut case that his grandmother had given Frank so many years earlier. He reverently opened it and carefully caressed the first of many visual aids.

As his classmates and teacher sat enrapt with his introduction, he cleared the tremor in his throat and began.

"I'm going to tell you about my Grandpa, a quiet man, a kind man, a man who our family thought we knew. Yet, we all discovered that he is the bravest man we know and I want you to know about him, too."

Brandon's newfound inner strength had now prepared him for this moment. He knew that his grandfather went into every battle with fear and trepidation. Yet he still faced them with courage. It was the fact that he faced those fears head-on that made him courageous. He truly possessed valor beyond measure.

End